Clubbed to Death

Clubbed to Death

A DEAD-END JOB MYSTERY

Elaine Viets

AN OBSIDIAN MYSTERY

Obsidian
Published by New American Library, a division of
Penguin Group (USA) Inc., 375 Hudson Street,
New York, New York 10014, USA
Penguin Group (Canada), 90 Eglinton Avenue East, Suite 700, Toronto,
Ontario M4P 2Y3, Canada (a division of Pearson Penguin Canada Inc.)
Penguin Books Ltd., 80 Strand, London WC2R 0RL, England
Penguin Ireland, 25 St. Stephen's Green, Dublin 2,
Ireland (a division of Penguin Books Ltd.)
Penguin Group (Australia), 250 Camberwell Road, Camberwell, Victoria 3124,
Australia (a division of Pearson Australia Group Pty. Ltd.)
Penguin Books India Pvt. Ltd., 11 Community Centre, Panchsheel Park,
New Delhi - 110 017, India
Penguin Group (NZ), 67 Apollo Drive, Rosedale, North Shore 0632,
New Zealand (a division of Pearson New Zealand Ltd.)
Penguin Books (South Africa) (Pty.) Ltd., 24 Sturdee Avenue,
Rosebank, Johannesburg 2196, South Africa

Penguin Books Ltd., Registered Offices:
80 Strand, London WC2R 0RL, England

First published by Obsidian, an imprint of New American Library, a division of Penguin Group (USA) Inc.

First Printing, May 2008
1   3   5   7   9   10   8   6   4   2

OBSIDIAN and logo are trademarks of Penguin Group (USA) Inc.

LIBRARY OF CONGRESS CATALOGING-IN-PUBLICATION DATA
Viets, Elaine, 1950—.
Clubbed to death : a dead-end job mystery / Elaine Viets.
p. cm.
ISBN: 978-0-451-22394-4
1. Hawthorne, Helen (Fictitious character)—Fiction.   2. Women detectives—Florida—
Fiction.   3. Country clubs—Fiction.   4. Divorced women—Fiction.   5. Florida—Fiction.   I. Title.
PS3572.I325C57 2008
813'.54—dc22   2007050086

Set in Bembo
Designed by Ginger Legato

Printed in the United States of America

To my club colleagues—

you know who you are, and I know who you are.

ACKNOWLEDGMENTS

The Superior Club does not exist. No successful country club could survive with the staff that I created, including Helen. Especially Helen. Golden Palms and its police are also mythical.

Many people helped me with this book, including Synae White, Detective R. C. White, Fort Lauderdale police department (retired), and Rick McMahan, ATF Special Agent.

Special thanks to Susan Carlson, Valerie Cannata, Colby Cox, Jinny Gender, Karen Grace, Kay Gordy, Jack Klobnak, Bob Levine and Janet Smith. Many others helped, but I cannot publically acknowledge them. I appreciate their help all the same.

Thanks also to Carole Wantz, who could sell dogs at a cat show.

Thanks again to the librarians at the St. Louis Public Library and the Broward County Library, who tracked down the time the sun sets in Fort Lauderdale in mid-January. Anyone who believes we don't need libraries because we can get the information from the Internet has never needed a serious search.

Thanks to my editor, Kara Cesare, and to the staff at the Penguin Group. I am lucky in my editor, who sends thoughtful, detailed critiques.

Thanks also to my sister bloggers on the Lipstick Chronicles for their good advice and encouragement—Nancy Martin, Michele Martinez, Harley Jane Kozak, Sarah Strohmeyer and Rebecca the Bookseller. You can read us at thelipstickchronicles.typepad.com.

I'm also grateful to the many booksellers who hand-sell my work and encourage me. I couldn't make it without you.

It would take another book to thank all the members of the mystery community who helped me when I was sick. Thank you all. You proved my theory—mystery writers may kill for a living, but they are secret softies.

Is the six-toed Thumbs a real cat? He belongs to librarian Anne Watts. That's his portrait on the cover of this book. Or you can check out his photo at www.elaineviets.com.

CHAPTER 1

"Do you know who I am?" The woman's high-pitched whine sliced through Helen Hawthorne's phone like a power saw cutting metal.

Yes, ma'am, Helen thought. You are another rude rich person.

"I am Olivia Reginald. I am a Superior Club member. I spend thousands at this country club."

Everyone spends money here, Helen thought. That's how they get in. "How may I help you, Mrs. Reginald?" she said.

The power-saw whine went up a notch. "I'm sitting by the pool waiting for you to call. I left a message at eleven o'clock. It took you half an hour to call back."

"I'm sorry, Mrs. Reginald, but we've had a busy morning."

"My husband is *in* the pool but I can't go *in* until I arrange a guest pass for my sister. Laura is staying at our home while we're on vacation. How can I enjoy myself when I have to wait by the phone?"

I'm sitting in a stuffy office on a fabulous January day in South Florida, Helen thought. How can I enjoy myself when I have to deal with you?

"I'll fax the paperwork right now," Helen said.

"I am on vacation. I am not sitting by a fax machine. Just give Laura the guest pass. I said it was OK."

"I can't," Helen said. "I need your written approval. It's for your protection. When you give someone a guest pass, she can charge thousands of dollars to your account. It will take two minutes to fax the paperwork to your hotel."

"Well, hurry up. I'm wasting my vacation on the phone."

Helen fought the urge to say something straight out of high school: "My heart bleeds purple peanut butter."

Instead, she summoned heroic willpower and the memory of her new credit-card bill and said, "Yes, ma'am."

"Do you know who I am?" should be the Superior Club's new motto, she thought. In the old days, the members would have never asked that question. Everyone knew the Prince of Wales, the queen of Romania, and Scott and Zelda Fitzgerald. For the club's gently bred socialites, the question would have been unthinkable. A lady didn't want to be known outside her circle. The painted mistresses of the robber barons were politely infamous, but always discreet.

The new members were a different breed. They'd invaded the historic Superior Club like a swarm of termites, and they were just as destructive. Helen prayed the balky fax-copier machine was working, or she'd have to listen to Mrs. Reginald's power whine again.

Helen never made it to the copy machine. She was stopped by another club member before she got down the hall. This one looked like he'd escaped from the Early Man display at the natural history museum and hijacked a suit. His forehead was so low it seemed to collapse on his thick eyebrows. Make that eyebrow. The man only had one, and it was fat and furry. Helen was sure his back and chest were covered with a thick pelt.

The surprise was his hands, which he must have swiped from a higher primate. They were long and slender and only slightly hairy around the knuckles.

The creature spoke with an educated accent.

"I'm a doctor," the caveman said. "This is an emergency. I need to speak to the department supervisor."

"I'm sorry, she's out to lunch," Helen said. In more ways than one, she thought. "Solange will be back in about two hours. How may I assist you?"

"You can't." His eyes narrowed to feral slits. Helen wondered if he had a stone ax up his sleeve. "I need someone important and I need him now."

The doctor's simian face was hard, but not from exercise or responsibility. This hardness came from too much cocaine, too much money or both. It stripped the softness from the personality, leaving only the nasty "gimme" part. Helen had seen many versions of the doctor at the Superior Club, although none quite so hairy.

He was right. She couldn't help him. She was only a clerk in customer care—a polite name for the country club's complaint department. The other staffers didn't even look up when the doctor screamed at Helen. They'd heard these tantrums before.

"How much longer are you going to keep me waiting?" The doctor's soft, smooth fingers drummed the marble countertop. His brownish hair bristled with rage. "Didn't you hear me? I said this was an emergency."

Maybe someone really was dying, Helen thought. He was a doctor, after all. "Let me find Kitty, our manager. May I have your member number, please?"

"What's that got to do with anything?" the doctor said.

"I can assist you faster, sir."

"I'm a doctor," he corrected her, as if he expected her to bow down and worship him.

Helen dropped Mrs. Reginald's paperwork on her desk and sat at her computer. She looked expectantly at the caveman, her hands hovering over the keys. He capitulated. "My Superior Club number is eight-eight-six-two."

Helen typed in the number and saw the confidential profile.

Doctor Rodelle "Roddy" Dell, breast augmentation specialist, married to Irene "Demi"

Dell. Status: Paid in full. See comments on behavior.

A boob doctor. So what was the big hurry: Someone needed an emergency C cup? Of course, there was that young woman at the fitness center who'd picked up too heavy a weight and busted the stitches on her new implants. She had to go to the emergency room. Imagine the embarrassment when you bust your boobs, Helen thought.

"Are you going to stare at the computer all day?" the doctor demanded.

Helen picked up the phone and called Kitty. "Dr. Rodelle Dell is here, and he has an emergency. His member number is eight-eight-six-two."

Helen heard the clack of Kitty's keyboard as she looked up the account. "Oh, no. Roddy the Rod. Is he foaming at the mouth?"

"That would be correct," Helen said. "He says it's an emergency."

"He's too important to have anything else," Kitty said. "Bring him to my office, please. And stay. I need a witness with Dr. Dell."

"This way, doctor," Helen said. She noticed little hairs trapped in the gold-and-steel links of his TAG Heuer watch. He looked like a well-dressed Cro-Magnon.

And what do *I* look like, in my navy uniform with the gold Superior Club crest on the chest? Helen thought. A nobody. An eleven-fifty-an-hour clerk. The sad part is, this is more money than I've made in years.

Helen knocked on the door to Kitty's comfortably cluttered office. She could hardly see her Kewpie-doll boss over the vase of yellow roses, the piles of paper and framed photos of her children. A teddy bear in pearls and a pink dress slouched next to her computer. The only empty space was where the photo of her almost ex-husband once stood.

"Please sit down, doctor." Kitty indicated a leather wing chair that shrieked "country club." Usually, Kitty's soft voice and big brown eyes disarmed the angriest club member.

The doctor paced in front of her desk, too agitated to sit. Helen stayed in the office doorway, but he didn't notice her.

"I have an emergency," he said. "I need my bill."

"The monthly statements will be mailed this afternoon," Kitty said. She checked the computer. "Yours will go to your home in Golden Palms."

"That's the emergency, dammit. I can't have my wife see that bill."

"Is there a problem, sir?" Kitty said.

He was too upset to correct her about his proper title. "I treated a friend—a young woman—to a day at the Superior Club. She's one of my office staff. Strictly business. It helps her perform better."

Doing what? Helen wondered.

"She needed to relax," the doctor babbled. "Job stress. We had breakfast in the Superior Room before I went to the office. Then she used the pool, the fitness club, had some lunch and bought a few things in the gift shop. The total came to three thousand dollars. I let her put the charges on my club account. My wife, Demi, will completely mis-understand the situation when she sees those charges."

The doctor was sweating, though it wasn't warm in the office. Helen was sure Demi would understand perfectly. That philandering cheapskate. As a club member, the doctor got a 15 percent discount on meals, goods and services if he used his club card. That could be the most expensive four hundred and fifty dollars the doctor ever saved.

"What would you like me to do?" Kitty's dark hair curled inno-cently around her smooth forehead. Her lips were soft and pink. Only her determined chin gave a clue to her real strength.

"I'd like you to give me the damned bill right now so Demi doesn't see it," the doctor said.

"I'm sorry," Kitty said. "I can't do that. Your wife is a member of this club. I cannot deny her access to her own account, which she shares with you. Club rules require me to send the statement to your billing address. But I can give you a copy now if you wish."

The doctor's fist crashed down on Kitty's desk. The teddy bear jumped and the children's pictures rattled. "I don't want a copy. I want the bill. I'm entitled. I make all the money."

"But it's also her account as long as you two are married," Kitty said.

"That's just it," the doctor said. "She'll give the bill to her lawyer."

"If I were you, doctor, I'd be home tomorrow when your mail arrives. Then I'd explain those charges to your wife. Have a nice day. Helen, please show the doctor out."

Helen had no idea how Kitty managed to defeat him with her soft words, but the doctor realized he was dismissed. He pushed past Helen and slouched out of the office.

The two women waited until he slammed the mahogany door to customer care. "He is a brilliant boob doctor," Kitty said. "But rumor has it the only way he can cop a good feel is through his specialty. Otherwise, he has to give the ladies lavish gifts."

"But why bring his mistress to the club?" Helen asked. "He knew he was going to get caught."

"That's part of the thrill," Kitty said. "You've only been here a week, sweetpea. You'll see a lot more emergencies like this one. Some idiot brings his bimbo to the club and then tries to cover up his mistake. Do these guys really think their wives won't find out? Demi plays golf and tennis here. One of her friends is bound to spot her husband with another woman."

"If I knew the name of his wife's lawyer, I'd fax the bill to him," Helen said.

"I know Demi," Kitty said. "She's no fool. She won't divorce the doctor during his peak earning years. Besides, he still cares enough to try to cover up. My guess is she'll get another little gift from Harry Winston. When she's finally had enough, Demi will cash in her diamonds for a good divorce lawyer."

Helen saw Kitty staring at the empty spot where her almost-ex-husband's photo used to be. She still loved him. Helen had no idea what caused the split. A single tear slid down Kitty's cheek.

Helen silently shut the door to the office and went back to her desk to unearth Mrs. Reginald's guest pass paperwork. The woman was still languishing by the pool. She'd call back any minute and assault Helen's ears with that power-saw whine.

Jessica, at the next desk, was on the phone with a club member, making placating noises without making promises. It was an art form Helen had yet to master.

"Yes," Jessica said in her hypnotic voice. "Yes, I do understand."

It's her acting training, Helen thought. Jessica sounded so sincere.

She had remarkably pale skin for someone who lived year-round in South Florida, and long straight blond hair that was either natural or a first-rate dye job. Helen really envied Jessica her bones. She had razor-sharp cheekbones, a strong chin and a thin elegant nose.

Jessica's aristocratic face had earned her small, choice parts in the New York theater, but she made her real money selling champagne and pricey chocolates in TV ads. Four years ago, Jessica and her husband, Allan, moved to Florida. Their luck ran out about the same time as her acting career went on hiatus, and she took a job at the club. Fifty was a tough age for an actress. Jessica liked to say, "My greatest role is pretending to like the members at the Superior Club."

Helen heard her finish another bravura phone performance. "Oh, I'm so glad you're feeling better," Jessica said, and hung up.

Helen wanted to applaud.

"I saw the doctor slam out of here," Jessica said. "What was that all about? Was it really life and death?"

"Yes. His death. The doctor's wife will kill him when she gets this month's statement," Helen said. "He's been fooling around with some bimbo at the club."

"They can't even come up with an original sin," Jessica said.

"You actresses," Helen said. "Always complaining about the script."

Jessica laughed. "I'm not much of an actress these days."

"You're resting," Helen said. "Isn't that the phrase?"

"If I get any more rested, I'll be dead."

"If I don't get Mrs. Reginald her guest pass, I'm dead," Helen said.

The Superior Club was like a stage set, Helen thought. The imposing pink stucco buildings were designed by Elliott Endicott, Addison Mizner's greatest rival, in 1925. Critics called Endicott's semi-Spanish architecture derivative. Helen thought it looked like it came from a Gloria Swanson movie. But that was OK. Gloria was once a club member, too. She must have felt right at home with the lobby's thronelike chairs, massive wrought-iron chandeliers and twisted candelabra.

Behind this imposing front was a warren of battered storage rooms and dark passages that reminded Helen of backstage at the theater. They were used by the staff. But it was the club members who provided the drama. Too bad Jessica was right. The stories were old and trite, and it was easy to guess the endings.

Helen picked her way down the narrow, scruffy back hall of the customer care office to where the fax-copier machine growled and groaned in a former coat closet. The noises reassured her. The beast was working. Mrs. Reginald could receive her forms, sign them, fax them back and then go soak her head.

Helen's office was part of the stage set. She sat at one of five original desks designed by Elliott Endicott, coffin-sized mahogany affairs carved with parrots and egrets. Endicott loved parrots and used to have them fly freely around the indoor garden in the lobby, until members complained the ill-mannered birds ruined their clothes and hair.

The drawers stuck on her antique desk and one leg tilted inward. The matching chair, with its original parrot-print fabric, was fabulously uncomfortable. But the view from Helen's window made up for it. She could see the yacht club basin and the seagoing mansions. Today, the place looked like a boat show. Yachts the size of cruise ships were docking. Hunky young crew members in tight white uniforms were scrubbing decks and reaching for ropes.

"What's going on?" Helen said. "Where'd all the yachts come from?"

"It's the party tonight," Jessica said, as if that should explain everything. "Oh, I forgot. You're new. Every year Cordelia van Rebarr, of the Boston van Rebarrs, has a yacht party. She invites some amazing entertainer to perform at a private party for one hundred of her closest—and richest—friends. This year it's Eric Clapton."

"The real Eric Clapton? Not an impersonator? How can she afford him? The man sells out stadiums."

"The man himself," Jessica said. "Some people have money. Cordy is rich. She hires the major names for her parties the way you'd get a DJ."

"Ohmigod. Imagine listening to Eric Clapton at a private party."

"You won't have to," Jessica said. "Customer care helps out at the party. That's why you're working late tonight. We all work on party night. We'll get to hear Clapton. It makes up for what we have to listen to during the day.

"It's the social event of the season. Cordy's guests arrive by private plane or helicopter. About twenty come by yacht. That's twenty yachts at fifty dollars per foot per day. And none of the guests stay on their boats. They all take rooms at the yacht club for another thousand a day."

Jessica broke off and said, "Look at that one. It's huge, even for this crowd. Must be over a hundred feet long."

The flashy white yacht's dark windows gave it a sinister look, like a drug dealer in a white suit and sunglasses. A very successful dealer, Helen thought. The yacht had a helicopter and a swimming pool.

Then she saw its name.

"The *Brandy Alexander*," Helen said. She didn't even realize she'd said the name out loud.

"Now there's a real-life mystery," Jessica said. "Anyone who says there are no good roles for older women doesn't know this story. That yacht is owned by a merry widow somewhere south of sixty. She's had five—or is it six?—husbands die on her. Her first one, the rich old one, died of a heart attack in his eighties. His death may have been natural. After that, she married one young stud after another. Rumor says they played around on her, and shortly after she found out, they died. Sometimes it was a boating accident, or a problem with a dive tank, or a fatal case of food poisoning. She's never been charged with murder, but she's notorious. I can't remember her name, but she's a club member."

"Her name is Marcella," Helen said. "The Black Widow."

"You know about her?" Jessica said. "She's married again. I wonder how long this one has to live."

"His name is Rob," Helen said. Her voice seemed to come from far away. "I tried to stop the wedding, but he wouldn't listen."

"Really. How do you know him?"

"He's my ex-husband," Helen said.

CHAPTER 2

"I can't work the Clapton party tonight," Helen said.

She stared out her office window, as if it were the portal to another dimension. She watched the Black Widow's sinister white yacht slide into its slip like a ghost ship. There was no sign of its shady owner—or Helen's sleazy ex-husband.

"But you said yes a week ago," Jessica said. "We need all the customer care staffers at that party."

"Nobody told me what I'd be doing," Helen said. "Kitty just asked me to work late."

Nobody told me Rob would be there, she thought. He was supposed to be cruising the Caribbean with his killer bride. He doesn't know I'm working at the club. He can't find me here. Helen realized she was gripping her antique desk with the frolicking parrots and egrets hard enough to leave nail marks in the wood.

"Helen, all you have to do is check the guests' names off the list, make sure they find the food and drink, and then you can hear Clapton live. Tonight will rock. You know what I'm stuck with? Gate duty." Jessica sounded like she'd been sentenced to a chain gang.

"I'll trade you," Helen said. "I'll take the gate." The main gate would be safe, she thought. No chance of running into Rob. Only guests who came by car used the main gate.

"No!" Jessica said. "Gate duty is the worst. You'll have to check member cards. We get lots of crashers on party night. They can turn mean."

"I want it," Helen said.

She couldn't run into her ex. She was still a wanted woman. Wanted by the court, unwanted by her ex. She'd rather go to jail than face Rob tonight. He'd be squiring his diamond-drenched wife to the social event of the season—and Helen would be passing out name tags with obsequious "sirs" and "ma'ams."

I should have killed the son of a bitch when I had the chance, she thought. I would have only served eight years for murder. Divorce is forever.

I've been on the run for so long, trying to avoid him. I gave up my career in St. Louis. I lost my old life. This is the best job I can expect now. Rob wouldn't get out of his wife's bed for my salary. And what do I get?

"Roses for my ladies."

Helen stared at the man in the office doorway. He was a preppie prince with spun-gold hair and dazzling tennis whites. He carried an armload of long-stemmed roses. Not rubbery hothouse flowers, but lush garden roses in hot tangerine, sunshine yellow, lipstick red and baby pink. Some were tight buds. Others were full-blown. All had a ravishing perfume.

"Mr. Giles." Kitty held out her arms. "You never forget us."

"How could I forget the ladies who love my roses almost as much as I do?" He filled Kitty's arms with the flowers. She breathed in their scent, radiant as a Miss America contestant.

"Helen," she said, "meet our favorite club member. Mr. Giles always brings us roses from his garden."

"Lovely to meet you, Helen," he said. "My court awaits, ladies. Off to tennis. TTFN."

Ta-ta for now? "Who was that?" Helen said.

"A gentleman of the old school." Kitty rummaged in a cabinet for vases.

"What's he do?" Helen said.

"Mr. Giles plays tennis and grows roses." Kitty filled six vases with water and cut the flower stems at an angle.

"Does he have a crush on you?" Helen said.

"Me?" Kitty looked surprised. "No, sweetpea. The roses are for all of us. He's just generous." She arranged the roses and set the vases on the customer care desks. Helen's were vibrant orange with a spicy perfume.

"This is heaven," Jessica said, and inhaled the perfume of her soft yellow roses. Helen thought the actress looked like she was auditioning for a florist commercial.

The clerk next to her reacted as if Kitty had handed him a vial of Ebola virus. "Not on my desk," Cameron said, waving away the blood-red blooms. "Roses are bad for my allergies."

Xaviera, who sat in front of him, laughed. "Give them to Helen," she said. "She's new. She needs more reminders that club members can be nice."

Jackie, the fourth clerk, took her pink roses and said, "Giles has grown into such a thoughtful young man. His mother would be pleased."

Helen's phone rang. "I need to speak to Solange," said a woman with a little-girl voice. "This is Roz Cornelia."

The heiress? Helen wondered, and quickly checked her computer. That was her. Roz was no child. Her age matched her millions—a healthy fifty.

"I acted up at lunch." Now Roz sounded like a little girl who had to see the principal.

Helen thought she was joking. "Just what did you do?"

"I called a waitress at the Superior Room a stupid bitch. Then I threw my dessert at her. She knows I hate chocolate chip cookies."

Helen hesitated, unsure what to say. The Superior Room waitresses were grandmotherly women who wore starched white pinafores.

"I have to talk to Solange," Roz said. "She'll be so disappointed."

"Why don't I take a message? She'll be back soon," Helen said.

"Thank you," Roz said, meekly.

Helen hung up the phone.

"Wish you could see your face," Jessica said. "That call must have been a doozy."

"Roz Cornelia cursed a Superior Room waitress and threw her cookies," Helen said.

"Tossing her cookies again," Jessica said. "Her rehab is unraveling."

"What will happen to her?" Helen said.

"Nothing much. Solange will write another letter of reprimand," Jessica said.

"The club puts up with that behavior?"

Xaviera looked up from her computer. "Check out Roz's account." She typed in some numbers, carefully arranging her long, red nails around the keys.

Helen stared at Xaviera's screen. "Jeez. She shells out twenty thousand a month for club restaurants and services."

"That doesn't count her dues," Xaviera said. "As long as you spend money here, you can do what you want."

"But what about the other members?" Helen said. "Do they want to associate with her? People are banned from redneck bars on the Dixie Highway for less."

"The Superior Club used to have the cream of the Social Register," Xaviera said. "Now our membership looks like the FBI's Most Wanted list. We have convicted felons, disbarred lawyers, wife beaters, cokeheads, and members of the Russian, Italian and Asian mobs."

And at least one murderer, Helen thought. This was probably the only club that would let in the Black Widow.

Xaviera glanced at the clock. "It's noon. The new rules say two customer care staffers must go to lunch now. Come on, Helen. I'll explain the facts of club life."

"I want to go first," Cameron whined. "I didn't have breakfast. I have low blood sugar."

"Then learn to eat right," Xaviera said. "You're almost thirty. You went first yesterday."

Cam pouted. Xaviera tossed her long, curly brown hair and ignored him.

"He's such a baby," she said, as they clocked out.

Cam did look like a giant rubber baby doll. He was six feet tall and pudgy, with tight dark ringlets and a red cupid's bow mouth. His hands were small and feminine. Helen thought hard ambition lurked under Cam's soft surface. He'd worked his way up from valet to customer care too quickly.

"You want to take the back way?" Helen asked.

"Of course." Xaviera pushed the EMPLOYEES ONLY door to the scuffed passage that ran behind the elegant club rooms. Her high heels clicked on the worn green linoleum. Her curvy figure swayed with the rhythm.

"I'm not wasting my lunch time on the rich idiots at the club." Xaviera gave her long hair another toss. "The last time I went through the lobby a new member wanted to know where the Endicott Room was, and I spent ten minutes taking her there. I barely had time to eat."

"That's another unfair rule," Helen said. "If a club member needs directions, why should we have to escort the person to the place, even on our lunch hour? Any moron can find the Endicott Room. It's straight down the main hall, with a big brass sign."

"I'm lucky she didn't want to go to the beach," Xaviera said. "I wouldn't have been able to eat at all. Besides, it hurts to go through the lobby after that hotshot decorator destroyed it."

"He's a big deal in New York," Helen said.

"Just because you're from New York doesn't mean you're good. He threw out a fifty-thousand-dollar wrought-iron chandelier designed by Elliott Endicott himself, tore out the tropical gardens, and replaced the lobby orchids with silk because artificial flowers have more 'durability.' Silk flowers at the Superior Club. No class."

"I never saw the old chandelier," Helen said. "The new one looks like it's from Pier 1."

"That's not the worst," Xaviera said. "The decorator painted the original cypress paneling white because it was 'too dark.' The old club members were up in arms."

The staff lunchroom was painted hospital cafeteria green. Two wide-screen TVs blared E-SPAN.

"Football game reruns," Xaviera said. "We can't escape them. We have to eat here. Staffers are not allowed to eat on the grounds, at their desks, or heaven forbid, in any club restaurant."

"We wouldn't want to spoil the lower orders," Helen said.

A cheer went up for a touchdown made last Sunday. "At least no one can hear us over the football fans." Helen slid her tray past the gooey chocolate cake and took a crisp apple. She felt so virtuous, she laced her coffee with cream and sugar.

"No hot coffee for me," Xaviera said. "I need a big cold cock."

Helen nearly dropped her tray until she realized Xaviera had slightly mangled her English.

"It's Coke," Helen said. "Be very careful that you say Coke."

"What did I say?" Xaviera said.

"You asked for a big cold penis," Helen said.

Xaviera giggled. "I think I'd want that hot. My English is so bad."

"Your English is excellent," Helen said. "You speak better than most club members."

"I learned English in school in Peru. It's different when you speak it every day."

They set down their trays at a table behind a pillar. Xaviera began her club history lesson.

"The old country club had Social Register types, rich social climbers, and executives who did business on the golf course. It was an easygoing place.

"The old management respected us and understood what the members wanted. They didn't have all these stupid rules. Then the club was sold to Mr. Ironton's group. He's determined to make it profitable. He says the Old Guard don't spend enough. He's bringing in expensive trash—South Beach cokeheads, high-priced hookers and mobsters. He wants big, splashy spenders."

"But they'll drive away the old members," Helen said.

"That's fine with him. Mr. Ironton wants rid of what he calls the 'fifteen-dollar hamburger' crowd. He doesn't realize they pay their bills."

"Or that fifteen dollars is nearly three times what most people pay for a burger," Helen said.

"The flashy new members throw money around, but they're living on the edge," Xaviera said. "They'll go bankrupt, wind up in jail or in rehab. Roz is a good example. She's busy snorting her inheritance. She came in the office once and I thought she'd had a powdered sugar doughnut. Instead, she had a fortune in coke on her black sweater.

"You must remember one thing. Never trust any member, old or new."

"Not even Mr. Giles?" Helen said.

"Very few people—rich or poor—are as nice as Mr. Giles. The new club members are vicious and crazy. The Old Guard are mean and cheap. They'll get you fired to save themselves fifteen dollars.

"Normal people would be ashamed to be so cheap. The old rich will order a glass of water and ten lemon slices and make their own lemonade, using the sugar on the table. They'll steal shampoo from the locker rooms. Their thousand-dollar Prada purses are stuffed with five bucks' worth of cookies stolen off the tea trays."

"My Aunt Marie did that," Helen said. "She took the bread and sugar off tables in restaurants."

"Your Aunt Marie didn't have a hundred-foot yacht."

"No, she lived on Social Security and was afraid she'd go broke," Helen said.

"These people are afraid, too," Xaviera said. "Afraid they'll lose their money and have to work. That's why they hang on to every dime. Old rich or new, document everything they do in your files. That will be your salvation."

"How do you stand working here?" Helen asked.

"I love to fight. I love to say, 'You signed the documents, sir, and you must abide by them.' I love to make people who think they are above the rules follow them. I get paid to do it. We have a good crew in customer care. Jessica is a delight. Cam is spoiled, but he's not a bad person."

Helen kept her opinion of Cam to herself. She'd seen too many Cams in other corporations.

"Jackie is too beaten down to bother anyone," Xaviera said. "She used to be a member here."

"What happened?" Helen said.

"She divorced badly. Her husband got a shark lawyer and stripped her of her share of their money."

Helen felt a pang of sympathy for a sister sufferer.

"Jackie never worked a day before her divorce. Her friends got her this job at the club where she used to be a queen. They take every opportunity to make the poor thing feel bad. When they don't, Brenda does. You've probably figured out Brenda is a witch."

"In about two seconds," Helen said. "Is she working tonight?"

"Of course. Right now she's golfing with that nasty Blythe St. Ives."

"I thought staffers couldn't associate with club members," Helen said.

"They can't. But Blythe got an exception because she's another big spender. None of the members want to play with her. She cheats. Brenda lets her win. Brenda can golf with Blythe, but she can't have a club locker. She has to change in her office.

"Brenda is after Kitty's job. She does everything she can to make Kitty and the rest of us look bad. Kitty tries to defend us, but she's too sweet to be a good fighter. Don't expect that ditz Solange to protect you. She'll do anything to save her job. With the old regime, she'd wiggle her boobs and bottom. But the only bottom Mr. Ironton is interested in is the bottom line." Xaviera checked her watch. "We'd better run. If we don't clock in on time, we'll be docked. More new rules."

Helen tagged the time clock, slid into her antique desk and snagged her panty hose on an ancient splinter. A fat ladder ran down to her toes.

"Shit," she said.

"That word is not part of the Superior vocabulary," Jessica said. She began a mocking version of the Superior Club ad: "Superior Service. Superior Surroundings. Superior People."

The entire staff chanted the final line: "You deserve a Superior life at the Superior Club."

"What is the meaning of this?"

Brenda was back. The spindly brunette was red with rage. Her furious face matched the ruby-and-diamond bumblebee on her pink golf visor. She seemed made of geometric shapes: cones for breasts, a triangle for her face, a trapezoid for her dark sharp hair. The hard angles clashed with her baby pink golf outfit.

"Doesn't Brenda know anger causes wrinkles?" Helen whispered to Jessica.

Cameron tried to turn his laugh into a cough and managed a barnyard snort.

Jackie kept her head down. She never laughed.

"Can you wear a tennis bracelet with a golf outfit?" Jessica whispered back.

"I always wondered who wore those ugly jeweled bugs from Tiffany's," Helen said. "I didn't realize lady golfers stuck them on their visors. If a real bumblebee buzzed her, she'd scream bloody murder."

Brenda's recently done eyes bulged with anger. Her lips bulged with collagen. "Silence!" she said. "I'm your supervisor. Show some respect."

Helen bit her tongue until she could taste the blood. If only she didn't owe another nine hundred dollars for her stupid car repairs. If only she hadn't bought all those new shoes and clothes when she got this job. If only she wasn't in debt, she could answer back.

"I leave this office for a short time and come back to this high school performance. What if Mr. Ironton came in?"

"He'd be pleased we can recite the Superior Club slogan," Xaviera said. She stood up and crossed her arms, five feet of curvy, curly-haired insolence. "If you want to call him, I'll tell him."

"You'll sit down and work," Brenda said. "It's twelve thirty-five. Cameron, have you gone to lunch yet?"

"No, I—"

"I didn't ask for excuses. Go. You're five minutes late. Deduct the time from your lunch. Jackie, you go with him." Jackie scooted soundlessly out of the room, shoulders hunched to make herself invisible. Jackie had a flat chest and wide bottom, a shape that was not fashionable among the white-bread rich. But her face was classically beautiful, far prettier than Brenda, her tormentor. Next to Jackie's beauty, Brenda looked old and haggard. Jackie was an excellent office mate, except for one bad habit. She gnawed her nails.

"I hope your behavior will be more professional this evening," Brenda said. "If not, I'll send you home before the concert starts." She slammed the door to her office.

"Her heart is as hard as her fake boobs," Xaviera said.

"You met Dr. Dell this morning," Jessica said. "He did Brenda's man-made mammaries."

"She can afford Dr. Dell on an assistant manager's salary?" Helen asked.

"Rumor says he took it out in trade," Jessica said.

Helen shivered at the thought.

Seven o'clock found Helen standing at the main gate, swallowing insults and car exhaust. Her high heels pinched. Her jacket itched. She didn't notice the fabulous avenue of towering palms and shimmering fountains. The pink stucco Superior Club, decorated with lacy wrought iron, was a rich man's dream. Helen was in a poor worker's nightmare: She'd been checking IDs and confiscating outdated member cards for two hours.

"Do you know who I am?" said an irate woman with hair like crows' wings. She'd presented a 2005 member card.

"Yes, ma'am," Helen said. "You're someone with a seriously outdated card."

She rather liked the young man in the red Ferrari who offered her a hundred-dollar bribe along with his old card.

"Sorry," she said, as she gave the bill back.

He shrugged. "Can't blame me for trying."

A thin dowager in blue lace insisted, "I'm on the list. Look again, you silly girl. Cordelia always invites me."

"I'm sorry, ma'am, your name isn't here."

The dowager swatted Helen with her purse, and it fell open. Fortunately, her evening bag was only big enough for a lace handkerchief and a lipstick. Helen picked them off the ground when the purse popped open. A run opened in the second pair of panty hose that day.

As she crawled along the asphalt, Helen heard crazed cheers from the club theater. Clapton rocked, as Jessica predicted. Even outside, three buildings away, she could feel the energy storm the star created, building like approaching thunder.

I'm missing a magical evening because I'm afraid to face my ex—and my past, Helen thought. I am a fool. But she already knew that.

At midnight, she walked to the employee lot, alone and angry: at Rob, at herself. The winter moon was hidden by scudding clouds that matched her stormy mood. The wind blew spray from the marble fountains onto her uniform. Soon, it would be rain spotting her jacket. The sky was black enough for a downpour.

Her car was parked in the back under a massive ficus tree. She watched the wind-shifting shadows and wished she'd parked under a light.

A gust sent a soda can skittering across the pavement. Helen started at the sound, then felt foolish. She was tired and jumpy. There was only one good thing about this day: She'd managed to avoid Rob.

As she unlocked her door, a man stepped out of the dark.

It was her ex-husband.

CHAPTER 3

"How did you find me?" Helen asked.

She could hardly see Rob in the dimly lit parking lot. Wasn't that ironic? She'd loved him for seventeen years. Then she'd hated him. She'd wished him dead a thousand times and tried to save him once. But had she ever seen the real man?

The wind shifted and she caught his scent—that late-night Rob smell, a blend of spicy aftershave and booze she'd once found intoxicating. Now she didn't find his drinking quite so attractive. But it no longer led to wild after-hours sex. Not with her, anyway.

"I always knew where you were." She heard the fine edge of contempt in her ex-husband's voice. "I knew you were at Margery's. She didn't fool me with that story that you'd moved. But it was time to let go of the past."

"It was time to grab yourself a rich wife," Helen said. "Why go after my pitiful bucks when you could score Marcella's billions? Did you know your wife was called the Black Widow?"

Rob shrugged and moved slightly closer. Now she had a clear view of him.

"Obviously, you're still alive," Helen said. She added grudgingly, "Marcella must be good for you."

Even to Helen's jaundiced eye, her ex looked good. He was wearing a beige Tommy Bahama shirt and pants. The club gift shop sold the same outfit for a thousand dollars. His Gucci loafers cost even more. His watch glittered with gold and diamonds.

But it was more than the expensive clothes. Rob had the burnished glow of the very rich. He was as carefully clipped, waxed, and manicured as a show dog. His skin seemed steam-cleaned. He was perfectly tanned and leaner than the last time she saw him.

"You've lost weight. Trainer?" Helen said.

"Plus a personal chef to keep me on a low-carb diet. She doesn't like fat men. I've lost thirty pounds."

"Good hairpiece," Helen said. Rob's bald spot was gone. "Your hair looks natural."

"It is," he said. "I'm using Rogaine. She can afford it."

She. Rob didn't call his wife Marcella.

After working with the superrich, Helen was an expert at spotting nip-and-tuck work. Rob's eyes had been done, his forehead Botoxed, and his double chin liposuctioned. The chin was still a little weak. She wondered if an implant was next.

She saw him studying her face and knew what he saw: a tired forty-something woman in a rumpled uniform.

He looks better than I do, Helen thought. My ex is younger, fitter and more rested. Why did I waste my time trying to save his worthless hide?

Once again, Helen saw herself running across the Seventeenth Street Causeway, wild-haired and sweaty, screaming Rob's name. She'd tried to stop his marriage to the Black Widow. She felt her guilt and despair as Rob sailed away with a serial husband killer. She was certain he would die. Each morning, she'd checked the paper for stories about Americans killed in the Caribbean.

All that time, he'd been living large. Meanwhile, Helen's life had shrunk to sore feet, a plastic name tag and a polyblend uniform. I'm Cinderella in reverse, she thought. I went from a fairy-tale marriage to a pile of ashes.

Once upon a time, Helen lived with her prince in a castle in a splendid St. Louis suburb. She'd had a husband she'd loved, a successful career and a six-figure income. Then she came home early from work and found her prince had turned into a troll.

Get real, princess, she thought. Your husband was a mooch who pretended to look for a job while you worked your tail off. You came home early one day and found him having mad-dog sex with the bleached-blond witch next door. He and Sandy were humping so hard your Ralph Lauren chaise was leaping across your back deck like a wild animal.

That's when Helen picked up a crowbar and starting swinging.

Too bad she didn't beat Rob. Instead, she reduced his SUV to rubble. He cowered, naked as a plucked chicken, inside the vehicle she'd bought him.

Armed with her outrage, Helen filed for divorce—and was wronged by another man. The divorce judge gave Helen's unfaithful husband half of her future income. Her lawyer sat there like a department store dummy, so Helen swore on a Bible (OK, the *Missouri Revised Statutes*, but she thought it was the Good Book) that Rob would never see a nickel.

Then she hurled her wedding ring in the Mississippi and took off on a zigzag journey across the country, determined to make sure he never found her. Her car died in South Florida and Helen wound up working dead-end jobs for cash under the table, keeping out of the computers and away from Rob.

Until her ex tracked her down in Lauderdale. Rumor said Rob was desperate for money. Instead of claiming Helen's paltry cash, he'd sailed away with a billionaire wife. Now he was back, rich and gloating.

Years of seething anger boiled up inside her. Her hands twitched. Helen wished the tire iron wasn't locked in the car trunk. She wanted to pound her worthless ex into a pulp.

Who am I really angry at, she wondered: Rob or myself? Maybe I should use that tire iron on me. Or maybe it's time I stop beating myself up. I want this man out of my life. Now. I've earned that right.

"Helen Hawthorne," Rob said. "That's the name you're using, isn't it? I hear you have a boyfriend. Phil somebody." His sneer was painful as a paper cut.

"What do you want?" Helen asked.

"I need your help," Rob said.

"Mine? What can I do for you? You're married to one of the richest women in the world. You're her problem now. I don't care what happens to you."

"Yes, you do," Rob said. "The dock master told me you tried to stop my wedding. He said you were shrieking your lungs out, trying to keep me from marrying a billionaire. Very sweet." He laughed.

Helen felt an angry blush flash up her neck and face. She didn't know anyone had witnessed her pointless rescue attempt.

"Now someone is really trying to kill me," Rob said. "I don't know who. It could be my wife. It could be some man who wants to be her next husband. It could be someone else."

All the artful work on Rob's face hadn't altered his guilty look. Helen still recognized it. Her ex had been up to something illegal or immoral. Maybe both.

"What have you done?" Helen asked. "Did you cheat on your wife?"

His silence was answer enough.

"You idiot," she said.

"You don't know what it's like," he said. "She watches me all the time."

"She should, with your track record."

"It's like being in prison," he said.

"Some prison," Helen said. "You're on a yacht with a personal chef, a pool and the largest collection of Impressionists outside a museum. I feel for you. Especially tonight, when you were forced to go to a private Clapton concert. Cruel and unusual punishment, Rob."

"It's not a big deal," he said. "Not like it would be for you."

Helen hated his condescension.

"I've already heard Eric twice," Rob said. "Along with Billy Joel, Elton John and Pavarotti—who was past his prime, by the way. The

entertainment changes, but nothing else does. It's the same people saying the same things."

"Yeah, well, at least they don't say, 'Do you know who I am?' You
don't have to take their abuse."

"I'm nothing but her gofer and whipping boy."

"A very well-paid gofer. As for whipping boy, I don't see any
bruises," Helen said.

Rob ripped open his Tommy Bahama shirt. His chest was splotched
with hideous purple, green and yellow patches. A scabbed wound
slashed his chest.

Helen winced. "She did that?"

"She plays rough," Rob said.

Helen looked at his face. This time, she didn't think he was lying.
"You're afraid she'll kill you accidentally?"

"I'm afraid she'll kill me on purpose."

"What did you do?" Helen asked again. "You never answered my
question."

"I needed a little money. Pocket change by her standards, but
enough so I could leave her. I may have stepped on some toes."

May. His face was earnest and sweaty. He tried to look sincere, but
only succeeded in seeming shiftier. Rob had done something seriously
crooked.

"There have been two attempts on my life," he said. "Both were
made to look like accidents. The first time, someone tried to push
me down four flights of marble steps. It was in a crowded theater,
and I never saw who did it. But I felt the push. It was no accident. I
grabbed a stair rail and saved myself. The second time, a huge
terra-cotta flowerpot fell off a rooftop and landed at my feet. You
can't accidentally knock over something that heavy. It missed me by
inches."

"Third time's a charm," Helen said.

"It's not funny." He tried to frown, but the Botox wouldn't let him.
"Somebody wants me dead."

"Good," Helen said.

"You don't mean that," Rob said.

"Try me," she said. "I don't care what happens to you. I hope you die slowly and painfully. We're divorced, remember? You chased me around the country, trying to get my last dime, but I managed to escape."

"Escape?" he said. "Excuse me, but isn't the court still looking for you? You owe me, lady, until I say so. I could turn you in tomorrow. I bet you're using fake ID."

"Go ahead. You never got my money," Helen said, "and you never will. I quit my job in St. Louis to keep you from sharing my six-figure salary. I'll live in a cardboard box before I see you get a cent. You've married again. You're another woman's problem now. You cheated on me, just like you're cheating on Marcella. Or have you forgotten why I dumped you?"

Helen realized that she was screaming. Rob was smiling. No, smirking. An irritating, self-satisfied smirk. She wanted to rip it off his face.

"Helen, I know how you feel," he said, his voice softly smug. "I'm sorry."

"You don't know how I feel. You couldn't. Just answer me one thing: Why? Why Sandy? You told me you didn't like her."

"I didn't," he said. "But she gave good head."

Helen's hand seemed to move by itself. It clenched into a fist, then struck Rob in the mouth. She felt his teeth graze her knuckles and saw the blood well out of the tiny cuts.

"Ow!" he shrieked. "What was that for?"

"For me," she said. "I should have done it years ago, instead of beating up your innocent SUV."

"You hurt me," he whined. "Look what you've done."

She'd split his lip. It was bleeding. She watched two red splotches drip on his Tommy Bahama shirt. She wondered how he'd explain that to his watchful wife.

"Is anything wrong?"

Brenda, the skinny assistant manager, had materialized in the parking lot. Even at midnight, her club uniform was crisp and every black hair was perfect. She must have varnished it to keep it in place in this wind. Jessica was beside her, eyes big with shock, long hair flapping like a distress flag. A drop of rain plopped on the ground. The sky was going to open up any minute.

"We're fine," Helen said.

"Are you sure?" Jessica said. "Did he hurt you? Do you want me to call security?"

"Hey, I'm the one with the busted lip." Rob tried a crooked smile, then turned on the charm full force. "I'm Helen's ex-husband, Rob." He put out his hand to shake Jessica's. She took it reluctantly, as if it were unclean. Brenda was more eager to shake his hand. She seemed reassured by the rich gleam of Rob's Rolex.

"This is my fault," Rob said. "I surprised Helen. I shouldn't have done that in a dark parking lot. She hit me. She has good reflexes."

Another fat raindrop. This one hit Helen on her nose.

"We should report this to security," Brenda said.

Helen could hear the glee under her officious words and see the malice glowing in her angular eyes. Helen had hit a wealthy club member. There would be hell to pay.

"Any fight on club property should be reported. If an employee is caught fighting, it's a firing offense," Brenda said.

"Please, I'm fine," Rob said. He waved his hands as if wiping away the incident. There was a splash of blood on one finger. "It wasn't a fight. It was an accident. I scared Helen when I stepped out of the shadows. My wife, Marcella, is a member. Her yacht is the *Brandy Alexander*—the one with the helicopter. I'm asking you to forget this incident. If there are any problems, your superiors can contact myself or Marcella. We're staying at the yacht club."

We're rich and important and you'd better do what I say, was the subtext. Brenda could read it as well as anyone.

"Well, as long as you say it's OK." Brenda was still unwilling to let Helen go.

"I insist," Rob said.

"I have to leave. It's late," Helen said. "Good night, Brenda. Good night, Jessica." She didn't say anything to Rob. She was still shaking from anger and adrenaline. The raindrops were coming faster now.

She peeled out of the lot in her boxy green junker, tires squealing.

Her hand throbbed, but it was a good hurt. She'd ached to hit Rob for years.

Now, at last, she had that satisfaction. Maybe it had been a good day after all.

CHAPTER 4

The storm broke just as Helen's green junker lumbered onto I-95 for the long drive back to Fort Lauderdale. Wild gray slashes of rain cut her visibility to a few feet.

She'd named her heap the Toad, because of its faded green-brown color. This Toad was no amphibian. It slid on the rain-slick road when she went fast and threatened to die when she slowed. More confident drivers blew past her, spewing fountains of oily water that overwhelmed her squeaky wiper blades.

Cold water dripped in her right shoe. The Toad had a mysterious leak no mechanic could find.

The windshield fogged over. Helen turned on the defroster, and the fog thickened. She fished a tissue from her purse and wiped at the glass. Red brake lights suddenly popped out of the night. Helen slammed on her brakes and the Toad fishtailed. She steered into the slide, and prayed the junker hit something cheap. It stopped three inches from a BMW.

The driver flipped her off, swung into the breakdown lane, and roared away. The Toad died to the blare of impatient horns. Helen ground the starter, pumped the gas pedal, and cursed the car. It hic-cupped like a drunk, shuddered, and suddenly leaped forward, farting clouds of black smoke.

I can't believe I traded my elegant silver Lexus for this hunk of junk, Helen thought. She did a lot of stupid things when she was run-ning from Rob. She'd picked up the Toad in Kansas from a used car dealer who swore it was driven by a little old man only on Sundays.

The guy wasn't lying, exactly. The car worked about one day a week.

If I ever get back to Kansas, that car dealer will think a tornado hit him. He gave me this rattletrap and a thousand dollars cash in trade for my beautiful driving machine. Her hands itched for the crowbar. Her scraped knuckles throbbed at the memory of meeting Rob's mouth.

Damn, punching her ex had felt good. If she'd slugged him sooner, would she have had a different life?

I hope not, Helen thought. I like where I live—and who I love. That's why I can't be too angry at the Toad. It died here in Lauderdale and brought me my new life.

Helen had kept the dead Toad in her apartment parking lot, where it leaked oil and odd fluids, including something oily and pink. She didn't need the car—or have the money to fix it—until she got her lat-est job. The Toad had already swallowed her first paycheck, and she knew it would eat at least four more. It still needed more work, and it guzzled gas with an alcoholic's abandon. She was surprised they even let the Toad in the Village of Golden Palms.

The Village of Golden Palms was a chunk of beachfront carved out of Miami-Dade County. A small, pricey slice with houses starting at three million dollars, the Superior Country Club, and a few apart-ments near the railroad tracks for those who tended the Golden Palms' gilded homes.

There were no services in Golden Palms. If you needed a dry cleaner, a doctor or a loaf of bread, you had to go to Miami or some other low-rent place. Golden Palms had two main moneymakers: the country club and a speed trap on U.S. 1. Helen could have cut ten min-utes off her trip home if she'd taken U.S. 1, but she swung way west on

I-95 to avoid the notorious trap. Golden Palms claimed it had "zero tolerance" for speeders. She'd seen people get tickets for going four miles over the speed limit—nonresidents, that is. Cars with Golden Palms stickers seemed to breeze through untouched.

Golden Palms residents liked to say they were Miami "before." If you were clueless enough to ask, "Before what?" they'd delicately say, "Back when everyone spoke English." They meant before the Cubans, Brazilians, Haitians, Jamaicans and God knows who else poured into South Florida. Golden Palms did not believe in the melting pot.

In the good old days, when the privileged could say what they pleased without fear of a lawsuit, Golden Palms residents put out NO IRISH NEED APPLY signs and stayed at hotels that promised "always a view, never a Jew." Sometimes, Helen thought the people there looked sideways at her because she was a brunette. About 95 percent of the residents of Golden Palms had golden hair. She couldn't guess how many were natural blonds. Helen knew they winced or sniffed the air when the Toad belched down their pristine streets toward the employee entrance of the Superior Club. She'd seen them.

The rain was slackening by the time she got to Hallendale Beach. Her forty-minute drive home had taken more than an hour in the rain-crazed traffic. When Helen turned off the highway ten minutes later, a silver-white moon was shining. She was home. Helen liked Fort Lauderdale. It wasn't as clean or perfectly groomed as Golden Palms, but it was alive.

The night was filled with sounds of slow jazz from a club on Las Olas and salsa music from a restaurant. Tourists drifted by in laughing clusters, intoxicated by margaritas and the warm winter weather. Locals smiled at them indulgently. It was fun to live where other people wanted to be. Nobody ever said, "I hate to leave" when they visited Helen in St. Louis. They couldn't wait to get out of town.

She dodged a speeding bicyclist and pulled the Toad into her parking space. The car shuddered and died before she could shut it off. Home at last.

The Coronado Tropic Apartments looked best by moonlight. Its ice-white walls glowed with a surreal beauty in the silvery light. Its lush

S-curves were softened by blue shadows. Storm-tossed flowers floated on the smooth surface of the turquoise pool, sheltered by whispering palms and purple bougainvillea.

Helen hardly noticed the rust trails from the dripping window air conditioners and the cracks in the concrete walks. The Coronado was a two-story stucco apartment complex built in 1949. Dozens like it were torn down daily to make way for condos and mini-mansions. The Coronado survived, as indestructible as its seventy-six-year-old landlady, Margery Flax.

Tonight, all the windows were dark. Pete and Peggy were asleep. So was Phil. Even Margery wasn't keeping watch out her kitchen window.

I should sleep, too, Helen thought. I have to leave for work at nine thirty. In the morning, I'll tell everyone my triumph. I can't wait to hear what they'll say.

"You were stupid enough to hit Marcella's husband?" Margery said.

"Are you nuts?" Peggy said. Pete, her green Quaker parrot, gave a startled screech.

So did Phil, the man Helen loved. "You passed up a chance to see Clapton live?" he said.

Helen's landlady was standing by the pool in purple flip-flops, fishing out dead flowers with a long-handled net. Phil and Peggy were sitting at an umbrella table. Pete was sitting on Peggy's shoulder. The table was cluttered with toast, doughnuts and coffee, but no one was eating. They were staring at Helen. Margery looked as if she wanted to throw the net over Helen and call the folks in the white coats.

"I thought you'd be pleased I finally stood up to Rob," Helen said.

"That's called assault and battery," Peggy said. She used to date a cop.

"Awk!" said Pete, her green parrot.

Peggy looked like an elegant bird, with her beak of a nose and crest of red hair. Her skin was so pale Helen could see fine blue veins. That made Peggy doubly exotic in South Florida, where so many complexions were tanned and leathery. The parrot patrolled Peggy's shoulder. Helen stretched out a finger to pet him, and he nipped it.

"Pete!" Helen said. "Are you mad at me, too?"

"Even a birdbrain knows you weren't too bright," Margery said. "Marcella doesn't like anything she owns damaged. That includes husbands."

"You said your friend Marcella was harmless," Helen said.

"I never said that," Margery said. "I said she'd never been charged with murder."

"Nice friend," Helen said. She hadn't had her coffee yet, and her head was pounding. The bright Florida sunshine hurt her eyes. Her hand throbbed, but this morning it wasn't a good hurt.

"My friends aren't nice, they're interesting," Margery said. She hung up the pool net and lit a Marlboro. She inhaled, then blew out a cloud of smoke, as if burning with anger. Not nice, but interesting—that was Margery. Her eyes were old and shrewd. Her tanned face had more wrinkles than a charity suit. Her steel-gray hair was cut in a pageboy that fell almost to her shoulders. Her purple shorts and T-shirt were nearly the same color as the bruises on Helen's knuckles.

"Look at your hand," Margery said. "You look like a prizefighter. You must have hit him good."

"I did." Helen couldn't keep the pride out of her voice.

"I can't believe you missed Clapton because you were afraid of that bald twerp," Phil said. He was stuck on that one theme.

"I wasn't afraid of him," Helen said. "I hit him, didn't I? Anyway, he's not bald. He's using Rogaine."

Helen always felt compelled to defend her ex-husband to Phil, though she never understood why. She couldn't stand the way Phil judged her. She remembered the desperate deal she'd made with Jessica to avoid her ex, and felt small and shriveled. She'd failed—twice. She'd missed the concert of a lifetime and Rob had found her.

Phil wouldn't have run like she did. He was strong. He was noble. He was totally dense when it came to understanding Helen and her ex-husband. Sometimes, she wanted to shake Phil. He really believed the system worked, and her botched divorce was a glitch that could be fixed. Helen knew better. Rob would always escape the consequences. Helen would always pay—for his sins and hers.

She wished she could make Phil understand. She wished he didn't look so handsome this morning. It was distracting. His soft blue shirt, sleeves rolled almost to the elbows, matched his eyes. His long silver hair was pulled back into a ponytail. Short hair was the fashion for men, but she loved his long. She liked the contrast between his white hair and his young skin.

His nose was slightly crooked. Helen liked that quality in a man. His mouth was set in a stubborn line. That she could do without.

"You only confronted him after you missed Clapton. Live," Phil said. The last word was almost a wail. "No wonder you punched Rob."

"I didn't punch him over Clapton," Helen said. "I hit him because of what he said. No woman would have stood for that insult."

But in the hard light of day, Rob's words seemed more silly than sinister. Why had they set her off?

"Keep your voices down," Margery warned. "The folks in 2C are still asleep. I finally have decent renters in there."

"No, you don't. They're crooks," Helen said. But she lowered her voice to a whisper. "Everyone who rents 2C is a crook."

"That's unfair," Margery hissed like a smoking snake. "And untrue."

It wasn't, and Margery knew it. Former residents of 2C were still serving time in prison. One had ads running on late-night cable TV.

"OK, we had a crook or two. But this time I had Phil check them out," Margery said. "If I have a real detective living right here, I might as well use him. George and Nancy are exactly what they said—a nice couple from Elyria, Ohio."

"Nice, or interesting?" Helen said.

"Nice," Margery said. "My other renters were too interesting. George and Nancy are dull as a church potluck supper and I like that. They've been married thirty-six years. Nancy's mother died recently, and she's selling her mom's condo and settling the estate."

"Even found the obituary," Phil said. "Her mother was definitely dead."

"Did they kill her?" Peggy asked.

Margery glared at her, and Pete shifted protectively on Peggy's shoulder.

"She died of natural causes," Phil said. "Lung cancer."

"Believe it or not, there are normal people," Margery said.

"Not in 2C," Helen said.

"They're only here for a month. They've paid me rent plus a security deposit. And you're stalling. I can always tell. What else aren't you telling us about your ex?"

"He says someone wants to kill him," Helen said.

"Besides you?" Margery said. "Let's go through this story again. I'm missing some parts."

Helen did. She told everything, from the moment Rob stepped out of the shadows till Brenda and Jessica showed up.

"You never found out who wanted to kill Rob or what he's up to?" Phil said.

"No, and I don't care," Helen said.

"I do," Phil said. "What if he winds up dead?"

"I'll cheer," Helen said.

"You'll be the number one suspect," Phil said. "And you've got a hostile witness. Brenda, the boss who gives you a hard time, saw you fighting with him."

"The fight was over by the time Brenda got there," Helen said. "Anyway, Jessica was with her. She'll counteract the poison. What can go wrong?"

As soon as she asked the question, Helen knew the answer in two words: Anything. Everything.

CHAPTER 5

Helen clocked into chaos in customer care at ten twenty-nine that morning. Jessica, Xaviera and Jackie were on the phones, placating members. Cam was nowhere to be seen. Kitty wasn't in her office. Solange's door was closed. She never helped in a crisis.

Untended phones jangled frantically. Three hulking men loomed at the front counter. They looked like escapees from a *Sopranos* episode. The leader drummed his meaty fingers on the marble top. The other two stood impassively beside him. They were used to waiting. Helen noted the bulges in the armpits of their shiny sharkskin suits and decided their needs were more urgent than the phone callers.

"May I help you, sir?" Helen asked.

The beefy leader had eyes as dead as Jimmy Hoffa. A knife scar ran down his left cheek like a lightning strike. Helen wondered what had happened to the person who cut him.

"Hey," he said. "You're new. You're cute." His *dese, dem* and *dose* accent sounded like a joke, but this man was seriously scary. He'd been pointed out to Helen before. What was his name? Angelo. That was it.

Angelo "Death Angel" Casabella didn't earn his nickname because he held hands at sickbeds. The other two men, who looked like meat sculptures, must be his bodyguards. Angelo's import-export business made a lot of enemies.

Angelo stared so hard at Helen's chest, she wanted to button her white blouse up to her chin. His bodyguards stared, too. Three pairs of evil eyes were trained on her breasts.

"Dose are da real thing," Angelo said. "I like dat in a woman."

"You know what's important," Helen said. "I like that in a man."

She saw Jessica shake her head slightly and regretted her smart remark. Rumor said Angelo left his enemies floating in barrels in Biscayne Bay.

Angelo missed the sarcasm and nodded his agreement. "I need a card for a new broad," he said.

"You're changing your DU, Mr. Casabella?" Helen asked.

"Yeah. That's what I said."

Not quite. DU, or "designated user," was the club name for a significant other. Most were very young women living with very old men. Helen wasn't sure who was using whom. DUs had the same privileges as spouses. Club members were allowed one—and only one—DU a year.

"Here. Dis is my member card." Angelo flipped it on the counter. His manicured nails were thick with clear polish. His fingers were studded with chunky gold rings.

Helen called up his computer file. Mr. Casabella had had three DUs so far this year. The two extra were approved by Solange.

"I'm sorry, sir, I can't give you another DU."

"Sure you can." The bodyguards moved in, a threatening muscle mass.

"The rules say club members are allowed one DU a year," Helen said.

"Ain't gonna happen. Lemme talk to da bimbo who runs dis place. The redhead wid the fake boobs."

"The department director is Solange," Helen said.

"I just said that," he said. "Lemme see her."

Helen knocked on Solange's door. Angelo Casabella's description was deadly accurate. Solange wiggled out of her office in a tight pink sweater and short skirt, her hair rumpled as if she'd just gotten out of bed. "Mr. Casabella," she cooed. "How may I help you?"

She ushered the mobster and his glowering bodyguards into her office with soothing sounds. Ten minutes later, they were back out. "Helen, you may give Mr. Casabella an exception," Solange said in her breathy voice. "But that's the last one, Mr. C."

"Yeah, yeah," he said. "I'll send in the new broad for her card photo."

"He needn't bother," Jessica whispered, when the Casabella entourage left. "They all look alike: skinny blondes with big boobs and little brains."

"Let me guess," Helen said. "Solange gave him an exception because he's another big spender."

"You're catching on," Jessica said.

Cam strolled in, balancing five foam cups of ice. "Look, everybody," he said. "I brought you ice."

"We don't need ice," Xaviera said, her temper as hot as her red nail polish. "We need you at your desk, answering the phones. Who gave you permission to wander off?"

"I don't have to ask you," Cam said.

"Please don't fight," Jackie said, in a small, hurt voice. Her dark hair was pulled into a painfully tight chignon that accentuated the fine wrinkles at her neck and jaw. She absently gnawed her nails.

Cam and Xaviera ignored Jackie. She seemed to expect it.

"It takes five minutes to go to the ice machine," Xaviera said. "You've been gone half an hour."

"I try to do you a favor," Cam said, "and this is the thanks I get."

Helen listened to them squabble and figured she had Cam pegged right. He was ambitious, but he'd never die of overwork.

Jessica whispered, "Helen, we have to talk." Before she could say more, the office phones all rang at once, virtually levitating off the desks.

Solange popped her head out of her office. "Girls and Cameron, answer those phones," she said, and shut her door again.

Helen dove for her receiver.

"This is Letitia Minotaur," said a soft, quavery voice. "My member number is two-six-four-one. I wanted to alert you to a little problem."

When a club member admitted to a little problem, it was a whopper. Helen called up Letitia's file, and guessed this little problem was twenty-seven years old. Letitia's son, Chadwick Minotaur IV, had been raising Cain at the club since he was sixteen. That's when he stole a member's Acura and wrapped it around a palm tree near the tennis courts.

Letitia had bought the member a better car and the club a bigger palm tree. No charges were filed against Chad. Every six or eight months, Letitia bought her son out of another scrape. Each run-in was documented in the club computers. Helen knew there was even more information in the paper files.

The Minotaurs had old money and lots of it. Letitia was a sweet widow of sixty-six who was kind to the staff, tipped lavishly and paid her club bill on time. She served on charity boards and volunteered for the duller, worthier club committees. It seemed a cruel twist that this selfless woman would have such a selfish child. Letitia had given her son everything—except character.

Helen looked up Chad's picture in the computer. Typical trust fund baby. Young women thought his heavy-lidded eyes were sexy. Helen thought they were mean. His dirty-blond hair was combed over one eye and his square jaw had a *Miami Vice* stubble. He could have been movie-star handsome, except his mouth was weak and spoiled. Chad lived in his mother's Golden Palms mansion and did not work.

The club was overrun with trust fund babies—wastrels who'd never done anything but inherit money. They spent their days charming the pants off young women and wrecking six-figure sports cars. They rarely took over the family business. Their brains were fried on coke and booze.

"It's Chad," Letitia said. Helen could hear her fighting back the tears. "I thought I'd better tell you before security calls your office. Chad's a good boy. He just gets into bad company."

Jack Daniel's, mostly, Helen thought. According to his club bar bills, Chad drank Jack and Coke, a lethal combination. The sweet soda hid the taste of the alcohol, making the drinks go down easy. The caffeine kept him jazzed long after a normal drunk would sleep it off.

"Chad celebrated a little too much last night," Letitia said. "He made off with one of the Endicott birds in the lobby."

Chad definitely needed Jack's help for that stunt. Elliott Endicott had installed a pair of fanciful wrought-iron parrots in the lobby in 1926. The birds stood four feet high and weighed a hundred pounds each. The parrots were the club's icons. Even the New York decorator didn't dare remove them. Members rubbed the birds' beaks for luck when they made a merger, a marriage, or played bridge in the club room. Generations of brides posed with the parrots on their wedding day.

Staffers were forbidden to touch the birds except to clean them, and then they wore gloves. Naked fondling by the low-paid could ruin the parrots' luck.

"I'll take care of the restoration," Letitia said. "And the divers."

"Divers?" Helen said.

"Chad threw the parrot in the yacht club basin."

"Oh," Helen said. "I see."

She didn't see how Chad had carried the bird out of the lobby with club members and staff all around. He must have been lucky. Well, why not? The kid had already won the genetic lottery: He'd scored wealthy parents.

"I'm so sorry for the inconvenience I've caused you," Letitia said.

"You didn't cause us any inconvenience," Helen said. Your son did, she thought, and he'll never apologize. "I'll note your intentions in your file and notify Solange."

"Thank you," Letitia said, with a dignity that hurt Helen's heart. "He really is a good boy."

Conventional wisdom said Letitia should try tough love, and make Chad get a job. From what Helen had seen in the Superior Club files, that didn't work. It was like turning a peacock loose in the winter woods. Trust fund babies were like the exotic birds: bad-tempered, ornamental and useless.

Helen had not seen many happy endings for young men like Chad in the files. Some ODed. Others were car crash or speedboat fatalities. One tried suicide and botched that. He was now drooling in a Miami nursing home. Another tried to claim his corporate inheritance. The crafty board stripped the arrogant kid to his shorts.

The best Letitia could hope for was that her son would exile himself to Sedona, Montana, or some other trendy place, and produce an heir. Meanwhile, she endured the pity of friends and strangers and the exquisite pain of her son's broken promises.

No one can wound you like the people you love, Helen thought.

Rob had hurt her so bad because Helen had loved him so much. Even her hate was a kind of tribute to their dead love. She should have been indifferent to his jibes by now. Helen's knuckles were scabbed and bruised from their encounter last night. She hoped Rob's mouth hurt twice as much.

Jessica was still on the phone. A worried frown creased her high, pale forehead. Her slim fingers slipped Helen a note that read, "Meet me in the restroom as soon as I finish this call. We need to talk."

Customer care staffers could use the bathrooms in the club locker rooms. Lesser staff were required to use the employee restrooms, dank affairs with antique plumbing, mottled mirrors and sickly lighting. The club locker rooms had English porcelain fixtures, marble floors, and mirrors that flattered face-lifts. The showers were stocked with luxurious towels, terry robes and slippers, and thick bars of fragrant coconut soap.

Helen and Jessica first checked the stalls to make sure no one was there.

"What's up?" Helen said. "You look worried."

"I am," Jessica said. "Kitty isn't here this morning. She had to see her divorce lawyer. Solange and Brenda spent a whole hour in Solange's office with the door shut."

"Uh-oh," Helen said. "What's Brenda the Bad plotting now?"

"Nothing good. And Kitty's not here to defend us—or herself."

"You don't think the club would be dumb enough to promote Brenda," Helen said.

Jessica looked at her. "You've seen their other decisions."

"Right," Helen said. "A place that will rip out an Elliott Endicott interior will do anything."

"There's something else going on," Jessica said. "Xaviera's boyfriend, Steven, is in club security. He calls her with the hot news. His current bulletin concerns you. Marcella, the Black Widow, reported her latest husband missing about nine this morning."

Helen felt oddly frozen in the warm, coconut-scented room. "Her husband, Rob?" she said.

"He's your husband, too," Jessica said.

"Ex," Helen said.

"Marcella told security Rob went for a walk after the Clapton concert. He didn't come home all night. The last time anyone saw him was a little before midnight."

Not true, Helen thought. The last time anyone saw Rob was after midnight. When he ambushed me in the employee parking lot. And I punched him. Ohmigod. Brenda saw us fighting. I've given her a bludgeon to use on me.

Helen's head throbbed. So did her scabbed hand.

"Xaviera told the whole office," Jessica said. "Brenda got this mean, secret look on her face, ducked into her office, made a quick call and left for almost an hour. When she came back, she was in Solange's office with the door closed. I hope I'm wrong, Helen, but I think Brenda marched over to security and reported the fight in the parking lot."

"But Rob asked her not to," Helen said.

"Rob's not here anymore," Jessica said. "I've seen Brenda in action. She'll put the worst possible spin on the incident. She'll use this against you and Kitty both. She'll claim you're dangerous and Kitty was careless when she hired you. Do you want me to go to security and make a report?"

"No," Helen said. "Not unless they ask you about it."

Jessica had been stalking back and forth in her high heels, unable to contain her nervous energy. Now she turned and faced Helen. "Let me set the record straight, for your sake. Fighting is a firing offense."

I'm only here a week and I'm going to be fired, Helen thought. After Margery called in her markers to get me this cushy job. I warned her I wasn't cut out for this work.

"I don't care," Helen said.

But she did. She'd run up a lot of debts for this new job—her car, her cell phone, her new clothes. The Superior Club paid more than most jobs in Florida. How was she going to pay those bills with another minimum-wage job? She couldn't get a better job if she was fired. She was trapped by her own greed.

"I care," Jessica said. "I like you."

"Look, why don't we wait until we know more?" Helen said. "We'll just bring trouble on ourselves if Brenda left the office for some harmless reason."

"There's nothing harmless about Brenda."

"Please," Helen said. "Don't stir things up. What happened after I left last night?"

"Nothing," Jessica said. "Brenda and I went to our cars. Rob started walking. Brenda offered him a ride, but he said it was a nice night for a stroll. But it wasn't nice at all. It was windy and threatening to rain."

"Rob loves storms," Helen said. "He didn't seem hurt?"

"He had a fat lip and a few drops of blood on his shirt. He didn't sound groggy or confused when he talked to us. I last saw him in my rearview mirror, as I turned out of the parking lot. He was heading toward the yacht club. He was walking fine."

"He probably met some woman in the bar and he's shacked up in her room at the club," Helen said. "It wouldn't be the first time he's done that."

But it might be the last time he tried it on the Black Widow, she thought.

"One more thing," Jessica said. "You don't have the Winderstine file, do you? The paper file is missing."

"No, why? Do you need it?" Helen said.

"I don't. Solange does. Apparently Mr. Sawyer Winderstine had a bit too much to drink last night. He passed out on the terrace and the valet had to load him into a cab. Solange wants to send him a letter of reprimand."

"By current club standards, his offense seems mild. Mr. Casabella has done far worse," Helen said. "I've seen his file. Chad Minotaur just threw the club's lucky bird in the yacht basin, and I doubt he'll get a letter. His mother will get stuck with the recovery and restoration costs."

"Mr. Winderstine spends a lot less than Angelo Casabella or the Minotaurs," Jessica said. "We'd better get back before we're missed."

As they walked back to their desks, Helen heard sirens screaming close by.

"Please. Not another heart attack on the golf course," Jessica said. "The paperwork will bury us."

Did someone find Rob's body and call the cops? Helen wondered. Did Marcella make herself a widow one more time?

She and Jessica ran out on the loading dock for a look. "Two Golden Palms police cars are tearing up the main drive, sirens on," Jessica said. "The members will have a fit."

"Are the cops going to the main building?" Helen asked.

"No, they're headed toward the employee lot," Jessica said. "I wonder what happened."

They didn't have to wait long to find out. Xaviera was on the phone, with her head down and her voice low, sure sign of a personal call. When she hung up, Xaviera said, "That was my boyfriend, Steven. Security found a lot of blood in the employee lot. They also found a torn shirt with blood on it back by the Dumpsters."

Helen relaxed a little. Must have been a busy night in the employee lot, she thought. There was another fight after I left.

Cameron, who'd been on the phone, poked his head up from his desk.

"They need more security in that area," he said. "It's not safe. Outsiders come over that parking lot fence all the time. Rough types. They break into the employees' cars. I've seen homeless guys camping back by the Dumpsters."

"Homeless men don't wear Tommy Bahama shirts," Xaviera said.

But Rob did. Helen felt her blood drain from her face.

CHAPTER 6

"Helen Hawthorne, could you come with us?"

Marshall Noote was used to delivering bad news. He told parents when an unruly child broke his arm running on the pool deck. He asked obstreperous club members to leave the Pink Parrot bar. He escorted freshly fired employees to their cars, then posted their photos in the gatehouse, so they couldn't come back.

Now the head of club security blocked Helen's aisle at work. He was flanked by two burly security guards with grim expressions. Unless Helen threw herself through a sealed window, she was trapped.

This was a hanging party. She could almost see the rope. Rob was missing. She'd punched him on club property. Brenda the bad boss had snitched.

Steven, Xaviera's boyfriend, wasn't one of the security guards. Helen wondered if Noote had deliberately cut him out of this assignment. These two guards were older, overweight, and uncomfortably stuffed into their Superior Club blazers.

"Just a moment," Helen said. She was stalling for time. She had one advantage. She was back in a corner and Noote didn't have a clear view of her. For once, she blessed the clutter in the customer care office. If security came after her, they'd have to squeeze past Cam and Jessica's bulky desks and tall chairs and step around purses, file boxes and wastebaskets. Three big men couldn't fit in the narrow aisle. They'd have to wait for Helen to come out.

Good. She needed a moment to think.

Noote was an ex-cop from Boston, and he'd think like someone in law enforcement.

Quick, Helen asked herself. Do I have anything that would make a cop curious?

My fake driver's license.

"Ah-hah-choo!" Helen faked a juicy sneeze and palmed the license out of her purse. Then she pretended to search for a tissue in her desk drawer. Customer care staffers could not keep anything personal, even a tissue box, on top of the antique desks.

Helen was about to slide the license into her middle drawer when she realized human resources would pack up her things if she was fired. She didn't want them finding that fake license.

"Ah-choo!" she said again. "Jessica, may I have a tissue?"

Jessica, deep in a phone conversation with a difficult member, nodded absently. The actress had incredible concentration. She could build an invisible wall around herself.

Helen slipped her fake license into a side pocket in Jessica's purse, then unzipped the purse and grabbed a tissue. She blew her nose noisily. Cam, the big hypochondriac, reached for his spray bottle of alcohol to ward off her airborne germs.

"Now, Miss Hawthorne," Noote said. It was a command.

"Sorry," she said. "Allergies." That excuse worked any time of the year in Florida.

Helen squeezed past the desks and chairs to join Noote. The security guards surrounded her. She breathed in Old Spice and sunbaked wool. She felt like all the air had been sucked out of the room.

Helen didn't trust herself to say anything else, not even good-bye to her colleagues. She was afraid her voice would shake. Jackie looked more frightened than Helen felt, as if security might come for her next. Jessica was still oblivious, locked in her phone conversation. Xaviera was frantically punching numbers on her phone, probably calling Steven for inside information. Cam was spraying his phone with alcohol.

Brenda came out of her office and gave Helen a triumphant smile.

"We'll call you if we need you, Brenda," Noote said.

Brenda, was it? Helen thought. Definitely a lynching party.

Outside, the bright sun nearly blinded her, and she stumbled on the flagstones. The burly guard on her left took her elbow. Helen shook him off.

Security escorted her around the back of the main building to a courtyard that was more like a tropical alley.

HR, Helen thought. My job is definitely toast.

Noote opened the door for her. She climbed the narrow back staircase to the office marked DIRECTOR — HUMAN RESOURCES. One security guard was in front of her. Two were behind her.

The HR office had been hacked out of a corner of the hall, an awkward arrangement of odd angles, a dusty window, and white paint thick as cake frosting. The director, Paige, sat at a beat-up wooden desk. It was old, but definitely no antique. Paige was a thin blonde with prominent teeth and a wide lipsticked mouth. The effect was oddly sexy. Helen had met her a week ago when she'd been hired. Now Paige was going to fire her.

"Let's go in here where we have privacy," Paige said, opening a door to a bare room that might have been a former closet. It was just big enough for a folding table and three plastic chairs. On the table were a blue pen and a yellow legal pad.

Paige showed her to the table and said, "Helen, we understand there was a problem in the parking lot last night with one of the guests. We'd like you to write down your side of the story. I'll be back in a few minutes. If you finish before I come back, just open the door."

Helen had worked in HR in her other life. They're going to fire me by the book, she thought. Well, I give them points for that. I'll write down my side of the story, without Brenda's embellishments. I hope Jessica will back me up, but if not, at least I'll have my story on the record.

There was no phone or computer in the room, so Helen could not contact Jessica before she wrote her statement. That was also standard procedure.

Helen wrote that her ex had surprised her in the dark parking lot and she'd swung at him. That was the story Rob had told Brenda and Jessica, and she wasn't going to contradict him. Besides, it was true enough. God knows she was surprised to see the SOB.

She added that Rob had asked Brenda to forget the incident because it was his fault that Helen hit him. (It was. It was his fault any way you looked at it.) "I didn't hit him very hard," Helen wrote. "There were only two small spots of blood on his shirt, and Rob seemed fine when I drove out of the parking lot to go home."

She reread her statement, crossed out "seemed fine" and changed it to "was fine."

Helen was about to open the door, when Paige came in with the head of security. Noote took the chair next to Paige.

Noote's here as a witness, Helen thought. They're following procedure right down the line. She wondered where the other guards were. They couldn't fit in the little room.

Paige read Helen's statement carefully and made some notes on her own legal pad. Helen tried not to fidget. Finally Paige said, "I see that you admit to hitting a club member."

"He surprised me in the dark," Helen said. "That parking lot can be pretty creepy."

"A witness says you were arguing loudly," Paige said.

"Brenda would say anything to make an employee of Kitty's look bad."

"But you were fighting with the club member," Paige said. "You know that's grounds for dismissal, no matter who started the fight. It's in the handbook. It was explained to you in detail at orientation. If there was a problem with the member, you should have called security. I understand that you were startled, but I have no choice. This is one issue where we can't give you a second chance.

"I'm so sorry, Helen. We're going to have to let you go." Paige sounded as if she meant it. She even managed a regretful sigh.

Paige handed Helen a termination statement and explained that the personal items in her desk would be sent to her home address and her paycheck would be mailed to her. Helen heard some legalese about how she was not eligible to file for unemployment compensation and something else about no health insurance.

Helen was having trouble following the conversation. She'd expected to be fired. She'd prepared herself for it. But she still felt like someone had broken a chair over her head.

"Any questions?" Paige said.

Helen had a lot of questions: How was she going to explain this to Margery? How was she going to pay the bills she'd run up? Did she have enough money stashed away for next month's rent? Helen had been spending like a Superior Club member, instead of an employee.

"No questions?" Paige said. "Well, again, I'm very sorry, Helen. Mr. Noote will escort you to your car."

The HR director stood up, the signal that the termination interview—and Helen's time at the Superior Club—were over. Helen staggered down the steps with the strange, underwater movements of a catastrophe survivor.

She was surprised to find a white golf cart with a striped awning waiting in the courtyard, along with the two security guards. Good, Helen thought. She didn't think she could make the long walk to the parking lot.

One guard climbed in the front. The guard who'd taken her elbow when she'd stumbled sat in the back with Helen, carefully adjusting the razor crease in his trousers. He wore black socks that were too short and thick-soled lace-up shoes with a military shine. Helen saw gray in his buzz cut, and wondered if he'd retired from some security job up north.

Noote, the head of security, drove. The gaily striped golf cart had a ridiculous holiday look. Helen was bone tired, and she could feel her stomach twisting itself into knots. She wanted this over. She still had to face Margery.

No one said anything as the little cart lurched over the paved paths to the employee lot. Helen studied the back of Noote's silver-gray head. He had a bald spot at the crown. He'd just had a haircut, and there were two small clipped hairs on his jacket collar. She resisted the urge to brush them off. Noote's head looked thick and square and he had almost no neck. As the cart turned into the employee parking lot, Helen caught a glimpse of his clenched jaw.

Two yellow-and-white Golden Palms police cars were parked by the entrance to the employee lot. The entrance was roped off with yellow crime scene tape. A patrol officer waved in the golf cart. "See you Saturday night, Mr. Noote," he said. The club hired a lot of off-duty Golden Palms officers.

Helen saw a yellow evidence van parked near the police cars. A woman in a white jumpsuit and booties was scraping at something on the ground.

The whole back lot by the Dumpsters—over an acre, Helen guessed—was roped off with more yellow crime scene tape. Helen wondered where the staff was parking. In the bright sunlight, the old ficus tree looked green and friendly, its branches home to twittering birds.

"My car's in the second row," Helen said.

"We have something we'd like to show you first," Noote said.

He parked the cart, then crunched through the dead ficus leaves to the edge of the yellow tape and pointed. Helen followed. At first, she thought he was pointing at a tree shadow. Then she saw dark red-black stains on the Dumpster, and more on the ground. It looked like blood. Flies buzzed around it. Helen was afraid she might throw up.

The blood on the tall blue Dumpster was in ragged arcs, and there was a small dark red puddle. A trail of fat round blood drops led from under the tree to the Dumpster. The trail was marked with numbered yellow tented signs.

Helen felt her heart seize. There couldn't be that much blood from when she hit Rob. Did her punch cause some weird, fatal injury? Did Rob die after she left? But Jessica said he was fine. He was walking toward the yacht club. Where was his body? Had they found it at the end of that blood trail?

Noote was watching her, as if he expected her to scream, faint or blurt out a confession. His hard eyes were washed-out blue. His face was red and thick and he had razor burn on one cheek, near his ear. When Helen didn't say anything, the network of wrinkles around his eyes tightened and his forehead creased into a deep frown.

He thinks I'm a hard case, Helen thought.

A police officer was standing nearby. His name tag said RULEY. I know it's a sign of age when the cops look young, she thought, but Officer Ruley should be in a Boy Scout uniform. His face was pink, smooth and hairless, except for a small blond mustache that looked like a dirty toothbrush.

Noote gave him a slight nod. The officer produced a paper evidence bag and pulled out a shirt covered in beige palm trees.

"Do you recognize this?" Ruley said.

The front was stiff with dark, dried blood. The shirt looked like the one Rob had worn, except for all that blood. There'd been only a drop or two on his shirt when Helen saw him. Also, the shirt had been intact. Now the collar was nearly torn off, and the shirt was missing two buttons.

Helen remembered her ex opening his shirt and dramatically displaying the bruises and scratches on his chest. But nothing was ripped then. Certainly not the collar.

"I didn't do that," she said.

"Didn't do what, ma'am?" Officer Ruley said. His smooth face was merciless.

"I didn't do anything to his shirt—or to him. It didn't look like that when I saw him. It was fine. He was fine."

"Where is he, ma'am?" The cop spent a lot of time in a gym. His upper arms bulged.

"I don't know," Helen said. "The last time I saw him, he was walking toward his home." Then she remembered something that filled her with relief. "Wait! May I see that shirt again?"

Officer Ruley held up the shirt, just out of Helen's reach. She couldn't touch it, but she was close enough to see it.

"It rained last night," she said. "That shirt is dry. I don't know who tore it or how it got so bloody, but the damage happened after I left and after the storm. It was just starting to rain when I pulled out of the parking lot. By the time I got to I-95 it was a deluge. The shirt would have been soaking wet."

"We got a couple of drops here at the beach, ma'am. The heavy rain was to the west, by the highway."

Florida weather was perverse. There could be a downpour in one neighborhood, and a few blocks away the sky would be clear.

"Look around the parking lot if you don't believe me," Ruley said. "Do you see any puddles of water?"

Helen just saw one puddle—of blood.

"You don't know if that's Rob's blood on the shirt," she said.

"No, ma'am. We'll run tests for that. We're also going to check and see if there's any other blood. Like yours. May I see your hands, ma'am? Hold out your hands, palms down."

It looked worse than this morning. The knuckles were red, swollen and streaked with purple and green. The scabs were the size of dimes.

"Unfortunately, you're under arrest," the young cop said.

"Arrest? What for?"

"For the domestic abuse of your husband."

"Ex-husband," Helen said.

"We have witnesses that there was an altercation resulting in trauma," Ruley said. "You were the aggressor in the situation."

"Domestic abuse! I'm not married to him. We haven't lived together for years."

"Florida law states if family members who once lived together batter each other, they can go to jail for domestic abuse."

"I didn't abuse him," Helen said. "I punched him in the mouth. He deserved it."

"That's what they all say," the cop said.

Helen's heart sank. She did sound like one of those hateful wife beaters.

"What were you fighting about? Alimony?"

"He doesn't pay alimony," Helen said.

"Your children?"

"We don't have any," Helen said.

"Your sex life?"

"We don't have any of that, either," Helen said.

"You had to be talking about something," Ruley said.

"His current wife," Helen said.

"That would be related to your prior relationship," the officer said.

"No," Helen said. "She can have him. I'm glad he married Marcella."

"So glad, you had a fight with your ex. Witnesses saw you hit him. He was bleeding. Your knuckles are bruised and scabbed, so you hit him hard. Now he's missing."

"Witnesses also heard him say that there was nothing wrong," Helen said. "Rob asked the witnesses to forget the whole episode. He said it wasn't my fault."

"That was the last thing he said right before he disappeared," Ruley said. "We have witnesses to the altercation. We have blood and physical evidence, including your own hands. I'm taking you into custody, Ms. Hawthorne. Put your hands behind you."

He began reciting the Miranda warning, "You have the right to remain silent—"

As Helen was handcuffed, she saw Jessica running up to the entrance of the lot, calling her name. The officer on guard stopped her. Jessica clung to the chain-link fence, eyes wide, hair wild, looking like a scene in a movie Helen couldn't remember.

"Helen," Jessica shouted. "What can I do?"

"Call Margery, the name on my employee contact sheet," Helen said. "My landlady, Margery Flax. Tell her I need a lawyer."

That was about the last thing Helen said for the next five hours.

CHAPTER 7

"I'm not talking until my attorney arrives," Helen said.

"That is your right," Officer Ruley said, sitting across from her in the bleak Golden Palms police interrogation room. "But silence makes you look guilty. Why not have a little chat and straighten things out? I could take off that handcuff and get you a decent cup of coffee. Or better yet, a cold bottle of water. It's hot in this room. You don't want to sit here and sweat. It could be hours before your lawyer shows up."

He looked so boyishly earnest, Helen knew he was lying.

Three years ago, she would have told the nice officer everything. He might have even let her go. But not now. The system didn't work for Helen anymore.

"I'm not talking until my lawyer arrives," she said. "This is my third request for my attorney."

"Okay, okay," Ruley said, and held up his hands.

Helen considered breaking her silence to tell him the mustache was a mistake, but he'd already left the room. It was two o'clock. She'd been here an hour already. Her stomach growled and reminded her she hadn't had lunch.

The Golden Palms police station was a small pink cube hidden behind the elaborate firehouse. The city was proud of its firehouse and the state-of-the-art equipment. Crime was something it tried to keep out of sight.

Helen had been fingerprinted and her damaged hand was photographed. Officer Ruley had asked for a DNA sample and she'd let him swab the inside of her cheek with a Q-tip. She figured he could get that with a warrant, anyway. Might as well seem cooperative. She guessed the police were looking for her blood either on the Tommy Bahama shirt or in the parking lot. She had the awful feeling they would find it.

Now she sat alone in the hot, windowless room, her left hand cuffed to a ring on the metal table. That hand chafed. The other itched from the scabs on her knuckles. The air stank of fear-sweat and despair. She hoped her own terror wasn't part of the smelly atmosphere.

Helen had been set up, and she knew it. Ruley, the young cop, knew too much about Helen's fight with Rob and Brenda's statement to security. That was Marshall Noote's doing. The club's security chief was way too cozy with the Golden Palms police. Noote had given that little nod and Ruley had waved the bloody shirt at her, hoping to shock Helen into some kind of admission.

Ruley also knew about Rob's disappearance.

It was too soon for the police to be concerned. The cops usually didn't care about missing adults for at least twenty-four hours—any Court TV buff knew that. The Black Widow reported Rob missing to club security at nine this morning. Her errant husband hadn't been gone half a day yet.

Why wasn't the eager young cop asking the Black Widow some serious questions? Marcella had more missing husbands than Helen did.

Helen knew the answer to that question: The Black Widow was a Superior Club member. It was Noote's job to protect and serve those members. Helen was a minor clerk and nonresident of Golden Palms. She was easy to sacrifice. That was how the system worked in the world of the rich.

Helen used to believe in the system. Its rules had worked for her. She'd dressed for success—and succeeded. She bought the right home in a safe suburb. Her granite kitchen counters and Pella windows said the right things about her: She was ambitious but no risk taker. Let the crazy folks in advertising buy Victorian mansions in dicey city neighborhoods. Helen lived sensibly.

She never wanted children. She embraced her career instead. Everyone knew Helen always worked late. Especially her husband. That's why Rob was stunned when Helen came home from work early and found him with another woman. But he was not as surprised as Helen.

Helen had expected the system to right this wrong. Instead, the divorce judge awarded half of Helen's income to her unfaithful ex. That's when something broke inside Helen. She couldn't believe anymore. Once Helen didn't believe in the system, it didn't believe in her.

Her ex-husband was the cosmic monkey wrench tossed into her life. Rob knew how to work the system and he knew how to work her. Rob had cheated on her and destroyed their marriage, yet the judge rewarded him and punished her.

Rob had chased her across the country, trying to get that miserable money. When he finally tracked her down, the cosmos rewarded him with a fabulously rich wife. The Black Widow was probably a serial spouse killer, but Helen knew Rob would cheat death the same way he cheated on his wives.

Her new life handed her one more surprise: Helen liked living outside the rules. She actually enjoyed her new world. She no longer ate rubber chicken dinners with balding bigwigs to advance her career. Now she sat by the Coronado pool with her blue-eyed lover. Instead of breakfast meetings, she had sunrise picnics on the beach. She traded in her business suits and sensible heels for sandals and T-shirts. She no longer clawed her way up the ladder to make a hundred thousand a year. Instead, she took home minimum wages and toasted the sunset with cheap wine.

Her new job at the Superior Club had been a partial return to respectability. Margery had urged her to make some decent money. Now Helen was confined in a tailored uniform and panty hose. She also had a car, a credit card, a cell phone and a debt load that kept her awake at night.

Look where it landed her: broke, busted and in jail.

By her old standards, Helen was ruined. Even now, she felt shame and anger. She wanted to blame Rob, but it was her fault. If she'd left him alone, she wouldn't be sitting in jail. She shouldn't have hit her ex, no matter how good it felt.

And Phil—what would he think of her? She wished she'd asked Jessica to call him, but there wasn't time. She'd barely managed to shout Margery's name before she was shoved into the cop car.

Helen checked her watch for the hundredth time that afternoon. Four o'clock. Where was Margery? What was taking so long? The lawyer should have been here hours ago. Jessica had delivered the message. She wouldn't desert Helen.

Maybe Margery wasn't home. Maybe Colby, the criminal lawyer Margery called when there were emergencies, was in court or out of town.

Maybe Margery was sick of Helen and her self-inflicted problems. Margery had warned her that Rob wasn't her business. He belonged to Marcella. The man wasn't worth worrying about. He was pampered as a pet poodle.

Until he disappeared.

Where was Rob? Where had that blood come from? And the torn shirt? Did Marcella follow her husband last night and kill him? Rob knew how to bring out the rage in a wife. But why attack him in the parking lot? It would have made more sense to lure him onto the yacht and shove him overboard.

Helen remembered the bruises and the ugly wound on Rob's chest. Did those really come from Marcella? Rob hinted he'd made some very bad people angry. There were plenty of them around, including more than a few club members. Did he make some sort of dirty deal with the mobster, Angelo Casabella? His thugs could have easily beaten Rob to death, then hauled off the body.

If her ex was dead, Helen didn't know how she felt about that. She'd wished him dead so often. But if he really was gone, would she be free?

Free wasn't the right word to describe her current circumstances. Her growling stomach let her know she'd been hours without food. Her tongue was dry and cottony. Her imagination ran wild. She saw herself in a courtroom, on trial for Rob's murder with only a bumbling public defender. Then the door to her room was opened.

Helen stared. This must be a hunger hallucination.

A lawyer was standing in the doorway. It wasn't Colby Cox. This lawyer didn't have to introduce himself. Helen had seen him a hundred times on Court TV.

She recognized that bulldog walk, the outsized head with the leonine hair, the hand-tailored suit. It wasn't shiny, like Angelo Casabella's suits. It had a burnished glow. The lawyer was shorter than Helen expected, the way famous Hollywood actors are short.

But he was definitely a big man.

He was Honest Gabe Accomac, the most famous trial lawyer in America.

"Officer," Honest Gabe called out. "Could you uncuff my client? And bring her some water, while you're at it."

A subdued Officer Ruley entered, looking even younger. He also seemed to have shrunk. He unlocked Helen's cuff without looking at her. He put down a bottle of water on the table carefully, as if Honest Gabe were armed and dangerous.

When you had Gabe Accomac for a lawyer, the nation assumed two things:

You were guilty.

Gabe would get you off.

You might never be received in polite society again, but you also wouldn't sit on death row. Honest Gabe got the Sutton Place Needle Artist, the socialite accused of injecting his rich druggie wife with an overdose of heroin, off on a technicality. He convinced a jury that Handsome Harry Balfour would never have sex with three underage girls, then beat them to death. He successfully defended a number of East Coast crime families.

There was a third assumption: You had to be incredibly rich to afford Honest Gabe. Helen knew Margery had pulled some fast ones in her life, but sending in Gabe was a miracle.

Helen took a drink of water, then started to gush. "I know you. I mean, I've seen you. You're Gabe Accomac."

"I am," he said, as he took a seat at the table. He opened a briefcase made of some soft, strange leather, possibly the skin of losing lawyers.

"I would have been here sooner, but the plane couldn't take off because of bad weather. Took an hour for the storm to clear."

"Plane?" Helen said. The gush was over. She could barely manage that one word.

"My office is in New York, but I came as soon as I got the call. Now, let's not waste time. The misunderstanding about the domestic abuse has been cleared up. I spoke with the attorney general of Florida."

"You did?"

"Well, an assistant attorney general. You should have never been arrested. No experienced police officer would have arrested you because the alleged victim wasn't there. The key word here is *experienced*. Officer Ruley is two months out of the police academy. In return for a written apology, we promised not to sue."

"We did?" Helen said.

"I'm sure you're wondering what happens if your ex suddenly shows up and wants to press charges."

Helen was too dazed to wonder anything, but she managed a nod.

"The domestic violence law is a little ambiguous," Gabe said. "But it seems you can be arrested only if the fight was brought on by feelings engendered by or related to your prior relationship. A discussion of your ex-husband's current wife would not be part of that law, as the attorney general sees it. For that reason alone, the officer exceeded his latitude when he arrested you.

"None of the witnesses heard the actual fight, but they did hear Rob say that there was no problem. You are free to go."

"I am?" Helen tried to gather her scattered wits. She couldn't be more surprised if Gabe wore chiffon and waved a magic wand.

"The assistant attorney general is a member of the Superior Club. We both agreed this kind of publicity would be bad for the club. Your job will be restored. The unfortunate incident will be expunged from your record. The club regards you as a valuable employee."

"It does?" Helen said.

"Shall we go?" Accomac said.

"Thank you," Helen said. "I don't know what to say. I can't afford you. I have five hundred dollars to my name. I know that probably wouldn't cover an hour of your time, but it could take care of your plane ticket home if you don't mind flying coach. I'll pay the rest off at twenty-five dollars a week but it will take some time."

"It's being taken care of," Gabe said. "There is one condition. You'll have to have a chat with the woman who arranged this."

"Of course," Helen said. "I want to thank her."

He stood up and opened the door. They walked through a seething quiet. No one in the station would look at Helen or Honest Gabe.

Helen staggered out into the flower-scented twilight and breathed in the warm evening air. She expected to see Margery's big boxy white Lincoln Town Car. Instead, a long black limo was waiting in front of the police station. The chauffeur jumped out and opened the door. The little lawyer slid in. He didn't have to duck his head.

"Come, Helen," he said. "Let's thank the woman who set you free."

"Margery sent a limo?" she said. "For me?"

"Margery didn't arrange this," Gabe said. "Marcella did."

CHAPTER 8

Marcella? The Black Widow had rescued Helen?

Something was wrong.

Helen figured she'd misheard Gabe Accomac. "Did you say Rob's *wife* hired you to save me?"

"I did indeed," the little lawyer said.

"Why?" Helen said.

"I've found her to be very generous," he said. "But she can answer that question herself. We're going to her yacht. We'll be there in a moment."

The yacht. Not the club. Of course. There would be no witnesses on the yacht. Helen was on her way to meet South Florida's foremost husband killer. She shivered. The limousine's teak-and-black leather interior closed in around her. Helen felt like she'd been shoved inside a hearse. She put her hand on the door handle. Fat lot of good that would do. She couldn't jump out at this speed.

Gabe Accomac reached for a teak cabinet. The sudden movement made Helen jump.

"Drink?" he said. "You could probably use one after that exhausting afternoon."

"Yes," Helen said, then realized she'd need her wits with Marcella. "I mean no. Any water in there?"

"Evian?" he said, checking the cabinet's interior. "Fiji? Sparkling?"

Helen wondered what those three words had just cost Marcella. Gabe's hourly rate had to be stratospheric.

"Fiji," Helen said.

The most expensive bartender in Florida put three frosty cubes in a crystal glass and poured the water for Helen. His white shirt cuffs took on a ghostly glow in the limo's softly lit interior. He caught Helen staring at his cuff links: a skull with three bloody teardrops.

"A gift from a grateful client," Gabe said. "Platinum and rubies. Not in the best taste, perhaps, for a man accused of a triple murder. But he was grateful when the jury found him innocent."

Helen noticed the careful wording. Gabe didn't say that his client was innocent.

"Interesting," she said.

"Yes, he was." Gabe's theatrical mane of white hair made his head look too big for his small body.

He can't hurt me, Helen thought. Not physically, anyway. I'm bigger than he is.

She gripped her water glass and tried to steady her shaking hand, but the ice cubes rattled. She was rattled, too. What was going on? Why would Marcella rescue her?

The Black Widow had to know that Helen was a suspect in her husband's possible murder. Marcella must have aroused suspicion herself. So why would she try to clear Helen? The Black Widow was off the hook if Helen was accused of Rob's murder. Marcella should have hired Honest Gabe to make her drinks and walk her through the police interrogation—not give him to Helen like an expensive present.

They turned into the yacht club basin. The gravel crunching under the tires sounded like little bones breaking. The long black limo pulled in front of the *Brandy Alexander*. Up close, Marcella's yacht seemed big as an ocean liner.

The chauffeur opened Helen's door. She abandoned her glass and slid out. The little lawyer hopped out after her, hauling his heavy briefcase after him. He moved briskly up the yacht's gangway, unholstering his cell phone as he walked.

Helen trailed after him. She was met by a strapping white-coated steward with a shaved head. "Miss Hawthorne, I'm Bruce. Would you like to freshen up?"

"If you'll excuse me," Gabe said, "I have some phone calls to make."

"Thank you," Helen said.

"Thank Marcella." Gabe disappeared into a doorway, or whatever it was called on a boat.

Helen gratefully entered a bathroom designed for a woman. There were thick face towels, a lighted makeup mirror, hand lotion, mouthwash, fresh flowers and a flush toilet. No pump commodes on this yacht.

Helen winced at herself in the mirror. She was finally going to meet Rob's new wife. Marcella was sixty, with all the beauty money could buy. Helen was eighteen years younger and slightly shopworn. Her long chestnut hair needed a good cut. She wanted a manicure and a facial.

She wasn't going to get it.

You aren't in competition with Marcella, she told herself. You have the one thing she's killed for—a good man. With all her billions, Marcella couldn't find a lover like Phil. Instead, she'd married Helen's discard.

Helen smiled at herself in the mirror. Maybe I don't look so bad. I have interesting hazel eyes, good skin and terrific legs. She wiped the grease off her face with a warm, scented washcloth and put on fresh lipstick. Enough.

The shiny-domed Bruce escorted Helen to a deck on the back of the boat. Helen saw the nighttime panorama of the yacht basin. The water was black silk, the sky was black velvet, and the moon was mother-of-pearl.

Soft candles lit the white table where Marcella sat, twirling the stem of a champagne goblet. From this distance, in that light, she looked glamorous.

"Join me in a drink?" she said.

"Water's fine," Helen said.

"For washing," Marcella said. "But if that's what you want, you can have it."

"It is," Helen said and sat at the table.

Up close, even in the flickering candlelight, Marcella looked like a caricature of herself. Her hair was dyed the too-dark black of her youth. The rich natural color had long since fled her face, replaced by bright red lipstick and harsh black eyeliner.

"Care for a sandwich?" Dainty crustless sandwiches were arranged on a silver server. Two hours ago, Helen would have devoured them. Now, she'd lost her appetite.

"Not hungry," she said. "But thanks."

Bruce silently appeared with water in a wineglass and three more champagne goblets. Each contained a yellowish liquid and a lemon peel.

"You can go now, Bruce," Marcella said. "This is between us girls." She tossed off the goblet's contents in one gulp.

Bruce removed the empty glass, lined up the three champagne goblets in front of Marcella and bowed.

"Odd champagne," Helen said. "It doesn't bubble. I've never seen it served with lemon peel."

"It's a James Bond martini," Marcella said. "Remember the lines from *Casino Royale*? 'A dry martini in a deep champagne goblet . . . three measures of Gordon's, one of vodka, half a measure of Kina Lillet.' The Lillet gives it the yellow color. It's sweeter than an American martini. My husband taught me how to drink these when we lived in London." Her red mouth curved into a surprisingly sweet smile.

Helen didn't ask which one. She knew it was Marcella's first husband. Perhaps he was Marcella's only husband.

Helen studied the woman whose fatal beauty had lured men for decades. She looked embalmed. Her hair was carefully arranged to cover the face-lift scars. She had the stretched eyes of frequent eye jobs. There wasn't a wrinkle anywhere. Those would have made her seem younger.

Helen saw where the surgeons couldn't reach—the crooks of Marcella's arms and the backs of her blue-veined hands. She wore white linen pants and a navy blazer. Good tailoring couldn't quite hide Marcella's fight to control her weight.

"Thank you for sending the lawyer," Helen said. "That was very generous. But I'm not sure why you want to help me."

"Margery is a good friend of mine," Marcella said.

That still didn't explain it. "The police think I'm a suspect in your husband's murder," Helen said.

"You didn't kill him," Marcella said. "I know that."

I bet you do, Helen thought. She stared at the black water and wondered if Rob was down there wearing concrete overshoes instead of Gucci loafers.

"You aren't a killer," Marcella said, "or you would have whacked him instead of his Land Cruiser." She started twirling the stem of the first goblet.

"You know about that?" Helen said.

"He never stopped talking about it," Marcella said.

Good, Helen thought. Then she realized Marcella was talking about her husband—their husband—in the past tense.

"I also know that Rob is dead," Marcella said. She stared at Helen, almost daring her to say something.

You have the right to remain silent, Helen told herself.

"I feel it in my heart," Marcella said. "A wife knows."

So does an ex-wife, Helen thought. I feel nothing, so I know Rob must be dead. If he was alive, I'd want to kill him.

"I need your help," Marcella said. She twirled the martini glass faster. Her painted fingertips looked like they'd been dipped in blood.

Here it comes, Helen thought. Here's why Marcella paid thousands of dollars to get me released.

"I know Rob was a crook," Marcella said. "He was up to something at the Superior Club. I want you to find out what it was. I need to know how deeply he was involved and how far he dragged my reputation into his nasty mess."

"Surely you could hire a private investigator," Helen said.

"There's no such thing as a discreet inquiry at a country club," Marcella said. She polished off the martini. "That place is worse than a small town. You're in the customer care office. You have access to all the club records. I need you. You can look through things without arousing suspicion."

"But I wouldn't know where to start," Helen said. "We have thousands of present and former members in our computers. We have still more information in a storage room packed with paper files. It would take years to go through all that."

"I don't have years," Marcella said. She picked up the third goblet and started twirling the stem. "I'm afraid whatever he did will come back to haunt me very soon. I think Rob was involved with some tough customers."

Like you, Helen thought. "Rob showed me the cuts and bruises on his chest," she said. "He said you liked to play rough."

Marcella threw back her head and laughed. "You know Rob and the truth are strangers. How could I inflict that kind of damage? I only weigh ninety pounds."

Marcella and the truth had only a nodding acquaintance, Helen thought. She was used to sizing up women from her time working in dress shops. Lots of fourteens claimed to be sixes. The Black Widow weighed one-forty minimum. But she had a point. Rob was bigger, stronger and younger than his wife.

Marcella took Helen's careful silence for agreement. She was spinning the martini goblet faster. The lemon sliver bobbed around. "I can tell you what I've found out so far. He was in contact with someone in your department."

"Customer care?" Helen said. "Who was it?"

"I have no idea. But he slipped that person cash. Small amounts—a thousand here, two thousand there."

"That's big money when you make eleven bucks an hour," Helen said. "Do you know the name of this person?"

"No." The martini glass was whirling on the ends of Marcella's blood-tipped fingers.

"What extension did the person use? I can identify the employee that way."

"She—I'm assuming it was a woman, it usually was with Rob—used a pay phone on the club grounds. I don't know what he was buying from her."

"Drugs?" Helen said.

"Rob was a drinker," Marcella said, and downed a third martini. "You know that. I'm sure she was selling information. And he was buying."

She picked up the fourth martini and wrapped her blood-tinged fingers around the stem.

"The club files contain all sorts of information," Helen said. "Credit card numbers, car license plates and VIN numbers, billing records, home addresses and phone numbers, office addresses and vacation homes, the dates when members are in Florida and when they're traveling."

As she rattled off her list, Helen felt sick. The dates when a rich person was away from home were closely guarded—and extremely valuable to burglars. They'd want to know the best time to spirit away the art, jewelry and silver.

No wonder the Black Widow wanted to know what her husband was doing. Society could overlook Marcella disposing of a few unimportant husbands. Stealing from her rich friends was unforgivable. If Rob had brought thieves into their protected world, Marcella would be ostracized.

"Marcella, it could be anything," Helen said. The martini glass was spinning until Helen was sure the lemon peel would be launched into space.

"It was something in particular," Marcella said. "I want you to find out what it was."

"But that's impossible. There's too much."

"I'm sure you can do it if you put your mind to it." Marcella gulped down the last martini.

"What if I can't?" Helen said. "Are you going to send me back to jail?"

"Only if you're lucky," Marcella said. She stood up. "I expect your first report shortly."

Bruce appeared to clear away the empty glasses and Helen.

Helen's head was spinning like the champagne glasses when Marcella's black limo took her back to the Superior Club. Too much had happened.

She checked her watch. Seven thirty. The customer care office was closed. "Please drop me off at the employee parking lot," Helen told the driver. She still had to retrieve her car.

The crime scene tape was gone, along with all trace of the blood. The Dumpsters had been freshly painted.

"Which car is yours?" the driver said.

Helen was ashamed to point out the Toad. "Just drop me off at the gate," she said.

As the luxurious limo pulled away, Helen heard the putt-putt of a golf cart. Marshall Noote rode up on his cart, looking like grim death under the gaily striped awning.

The director of security stopped in front of her, blocking her path with a shower of gravel.

"My friends on the force asked me to deliver a message," he said. "They want you to know they can't be bought. They're going to find out the truth no matter how many fat cat lawyers protect the guilty."

"I'm not guilty," Helen said.

"Right," the security director said. His massive foot crushed the gas pedal as he drove away.

CHAPTER 9

"You ask me, you're damned lucky," Margery said.

Helen's landlady blew a cloud of cigarette smoke over the Coronado pool, as if putting it under a spell. Her cigarette glowed in the dark like a one-eyed demon.

"Lucky?" Helen said. "I was arrested, I lost my job, I've been threatened by a serial killer and the cops—all in one day."

"You need wine to see this clearly," Margery said. "I opened a bottle of the real stuff. Here. Have some."

Helen's landlady had uncorked a bottle of Fat Bastard merlot. Corks were rare at Coronado wine parties. Usually they drank cheap box wine from the supermarket. This merlot had probably seen an actual grape. The wine glugged into her glass and Helen took a generous gulp.

"This is good." Of course, her standards were low.

Helen had found some Greek olive hummus in her fridge and brought it out to the pool. Phil had contributed a bag of spicy hot Doritos. The chips were salty and strangely orange. Helen thought the unnatural flavor of the Doritos blended nicely with the bland, healthy hummus. She also thought she might be getting slightly looped on the wine.

"We have some time to talk before the others arrive. Let me explain why you've just won the lottery," Margery said, sounding like a professor. Her purple poncho could be an academic robe, if you overlooked the lavender short-shorts—and there wasn't much to overlook. Her red-orange nail polish matched the glow of her lit cigarette. "First, you were arrested by a baby cop straight out of the academy. He didn't know what the hell he was doing."

"The cops normally don't arrest a person for one sock in the mouth, especially if the complaining party was AWOL," Phil said. He was stretched out on a chaise, drinking a Heineken. "They might have asked you some questions, but no experienced cop would have arrested you."

"Except Marcella and Rob are members of the Superior Club," Helen said. "And Golden Palms is a company town."

"Exactly," Margery said, and blew a long hiss of smoke. "That means you should have been seriously in the soup. Those little police forces don't like to admit they've made a mistake. Instead, your arrest was expunged and the cub cop apologized. That was lucky.

"Second, you got your job back, and you know that fighting for any reason is an automatic firing offense. You should have been canned regardless of what happened.

"Third, and it's a big third, Marcella flew in Gabe Accomac, for god's sake—and paid all your legal bills. I'd have to sell the Coronado to cover his fees."

"And that's what doesn't make any sense," Helen said. "Marcella is setting me up. If Gabe is so good, why didn't she hire him for herself?"

"If Marcella was setting you up, you'd still be sitting in the Golden Palms jail," Margery said.

"I agree with Margery," Phil said. He reached for another handful of Doritos.

"I bet you do," Helen snapped.

"No, hear me out," Phil said. Helen found his sweet reason irritating.

"You and Marcella have the same goal. You both need to find Rob to clear your name. You can't go around under a permanent cloud of suspicion. Your colleagues won't want to work with a suspected murderer."

"I'm telling you, Marcella's interest is a lucky break," Margery said. "Otherwise, you'd still be in jail."

"Why didn't you just get Colby Cox to represent me? She's good. I could have afforded her," Helen said.

"Could you now?" Margery said.

"Well, if I paid her twenty-five dollars a month," Helen said.

"Neither of you is going to live that long," Margery said. "Anyway, she was in North Carolina. Colby's a good attorney, but I don't think she could get you out of that jam *and* get your job back. The attorney general doesn't take her calls."

"Assistant attorney general," Helen said.

Helen didn't feel lucky. She felt angry, trapped and resentful. She took another drink of wine and glared at Margery and Phil. Margery's cigarette glared back.

"Why won't anyone believe me?" Helen said. "Rob's wife is up to something."

"She probably is," Margery said. "But right now, your interests intersect. When you help her, you also help yourself. You both need to find Rob, dead or alive."

"You aren't alone in this, Helen. I'll help you," Phil said. "Tracking down people is what I do best. I'm a private investigator. You find out what Rob was doing at the club, and I'll find him—or his body."

"Do you think he's dead?" Helen said.

"Don't know enough to speculate," Phil said.

"There was an awful lot of blood for him to be alive," Helen said.

"You don't know if the blood was all his," Phil said.

"What I saw looked scary," Helen said. "Especially those arcs of blood on the Dumpster, like a Jackson Pollock painting."

She saw Phil wince.

"That's bad, isn't it?" she said.

"That could be an arterial bleed," he said carefully.

"Then he's dead," Helen said.

"We don't know," Phil said. "It could also be castoff from a club-bing or stabbing and he might survive that."

Might, Helen thought, and took another gulp of wine.

"The amount of blood isn't always an indicator of death," Phil said. "I've read a lot of expert testimony on blood. Blunt force trauma can kill with one blow and not leave any blood if the skin isn't broken. A few good whacks with broken skin, especially on the head, can leave lots of blood because head wounds bleed freely—but the victim will survive. An ice pick will do lots of damage, but the thin, narrow in-strument will leave a self-sealing hole. Not much blood, if any. You can't always tell by the amount of blood."

"Maybe it was a scam," Helen said. "Rob is a con artist. We all know that. Maybe he froze his own blood and stockpiled it. I saw that on a TV show. *Desperate Housewives,* I think. This woman wanted the real killer to go down for her sister's murder, but there wasn't enough evidence to get the police interested, so she stockpiled her own blood in the fridge. Then she threw it all over the killer's floor and cut off two of her fingers and hid out. The police thought her sister's killer had murdered her."

Even as she said it, the scenario sounded improbable.

"That wouldn't work in real life," Phil said. "Once blood leaves the body, it clots. If Rob stockpiled his own blood, he'd be throwing around globs of blood—blood clots. You wouldn't get spray or pooling. If he used an anticlotting factor, it would show up in the testing. The cops would know he'd faked his disappearance."

"Oh," Helen said.

"How hard did you hit Rob? Did you take out a tooth?" Phil crunched on another Dorito at exactly the wrong time.

"Did I what?" Helen asked.

"Knock out a tooth," he said, through fiery orange crunches.

"Of course not," Helen said. "I just popped Rob in the lip. His teeth scraped my knuckles, but he didn't lose any. He hardly bled at all."

She looked at her battered hand. It still hurt. Hitting Rob didn't seem nearly so satisfying now. How come when you finally got what you wanted, it wasn't what you needed?

"Sounds like you hurt yourself more than you hurt him," Phil said.

"The story of my life," Helen said.

"I don't understand why you are so convinced Rob is dead," Margery said. "Is it because you want him dead?"

Spare me the cheap psychology, Helen thought. But she didn't say it.

"Yoo-hoo. Is it too late to join you?"

Helen heard a soft, fluttery voice.

"I've brought some chicken salad sandwiches and a lovely wine I found at the grocery store."

It was Margery's sweet, dithery friend Elsie. Helen's eyes crossed when she saw Elsie's outfit. Elsie dressed like Miss Marple with a makeover from Mr. Blackwell. Today, she wore what looked like a pirate costume crossed with the Arabian Nights.

Phil's eyes bugged out. Margery blew a cloud of smoke, possibly to cover up the vision.

"What do you think?" Elsie spun in her thigh-high black leather boots, and the exposed skin on her upper legs wobbled. So did her chins. "It's a knockoff of a Prada outfit I saw in *Vanity Fair.*"

Helen suspected the model in the magazine was a good half century younger than Elsie. Besides the pirate boots, Margery's friend wore a black leather miniskirt, a burgundy satin blouse with a plunging neckline, and a green satin turban.

"It's amazing," Helen said, truthfully.

"I should get a gentleman's opinion," Elsie said. "What do you think, Phil?"

He gulped. "I've never seen anything like it." Phil took a big drink to avoid any further comment.

"I think the belt may be a mistake," Elsie said. "I'm having a little trouble locating my waist."

Helen thought it was probably somewhere under Elsie's large breasts. They'd slid south over the years. "Maybe so," Helen said.

"I didn't dress exactly like the magazine model," Elsie said. "I had to make some allowances for my age. She was wearing pale pink lip-stick, which makes me look washed-out." Elsie's red lipstick crept into the cracks around her mouth.

"It's quite colorful," Helen said.

"Awk!" said Pete the parrot. Peggy and her green sidekick drifted into the party. Peggy carried a platter. "Hi, everyone. I brought cheese, crackers and grapes."

"Does Pete get a cracker?" Helen said.

"No, he's on a diet. He gets a grape." Pete examined the green grape in sullen silence.

"Speaking of grapes, I have wine," Elsie said. "Fat Bastard. I found it at the grocery store."

"Good. You can add it to the stash we already have," Margery said.

"Don't you love the name?" Elsie asked. "When I was a girl, we couldn't have said it."

"That's what we call my boss," Peggy said. "Good name for a wine. That fat bastard drives everyone to drink."

Nancy and George came out of 2C, and Margery waved them down-stairs. "Come join the party," she said. "We have snacks and wine."

"I like wine," Nancy said.

"I like snacks," George said, patting his round stomach. "I'll get a beer out of the fridge and join you."

It was the first time Helen had seen Margery's nice normal couple from Ohio. They were amazingly ordinary in khaki shorts and navy golf shirts. Even their gray hair matched.

Nancy gulped a little when she saw Elsie's outrageous outfit, but she recovered enough to shake Elsie's hand, then Helen's, and make small talk about the weather.

"And what do you do back in Ohio, George?" Elsie said.

"I'm in investments."

"Maybe you can help me then," Elsie said.

"Elsie!" Margery said. "Let the poor man alone. He's not at work now."

George looked grateful for the reprieve.

"Well, maybe the rest of you can help me," Elsie said. "I need some advice. I'm worried about money. My son Milton is a good boy, but he won't increase my allowance. He says I'll just fritter it away on worthless junk.

"I'm actually very careful with my money. I bought this new skirt and blouse at Marshalls. The boots were a bit of an extravagance, but they were on sale. I'd never pay full price. I made the turban myself with fabric remnants." She patted the green satin. "I wasn't going to pay two hundred dollars. I do know how to stretch my pennies. But I'm tired of cheeseparing. I'm still young. I like nice dinners and pretty clothes. I need more money fast. I'm willing to invest my entire next Social Security check."

"I don't think investments are the answer," George said carefully. "Anything high-yield is too risky for the small investor."

"Maybe you could get a job," Nancy said.

"Doing what?" Elsie said. "I haven't worked in years, and I never enjoyed it. I don't want to bag groceries at Publix. That's about all that's open to someone of mature years. That and hostessing at the all-you-can-eat buffet, and I don't want to spend eight hours on my feet."

"Maybe you could buy a lottery ticket," Peggy said. "I play every week."

"Awk," said Pete, and dropped the unwanted grape.

"How much have you won in the lottery, Peggy?" Margery asked.

"Nothing yet," Peggy said. "But I've had a lot of fun losing."

"Fun," Elsie said. "That's what I need. More fun."

"You don't need to lose more money, Elsie," Margery said. "Make sure you buy a winning ticket."

"Awk!" said Pete.

The poolside party was in full swing. Elsie was asking Peggy where she bought her lottery tickets. Nancy was making cooing sounds to Pete. George was happily munching Doritos.

"Nice party," Phil said, "but I'd better go. I want to make some phone calls to my friends on the force. Maybe I can find out something useful about Rob. They're more likely to talk at night when the brass isn't around."

He gave Helen a kiss. "I'm glad you're home safe. We'll celebrate later."

Helen watched Phil disappear into the dark.

"Are you going to let that man get away?" Margery said.

"You heard him," Helen said. "He has to make some phone calls."

"I wasn't talking about tonight. I meant are you going to marry him?"

"He hasn't asked me," Helen said.

"He has, too," Margery said.

"Well, he hasn't asked in a while."

"Any woman worth her salt goes after the man she wants," Margery said. "Don't be a fool. I'd marry him myself if I wasn't so damn old."

Helen thought Margery could still marry Phil. He seemed half in love with her landlady.

"I've got a few other things on my mind right now," Helen said.

"Yeah, well, don't let a live one like Phil get away."

"While pursuing my dead ex?" Helen said.

CHAPTER 10

Yesterday, Helen left the Superior Club in handcuffs.

This morning, she came back in a neatly pressed uniform and a crisp white blouse. Inside she felt worn, wilted and afraid. She dreaded opening the mahogany doors to the customer care office. If her colleagues cold-shouldered her, Helen would have to find another job. Even a lawyer like Gabe Accomac couldn't make them want to work with her.

She heard the angry shrilling of the phones. Cam was ignoring his ringing phone and cleaning his desk with alcohol spray. Xaviera was talking on her cell to her boyfriend. She gave Helen a friendly wave. Jackie was writing down some convoluted complaint and chanting into the phone, "Yes, ma'am. No, ma'am. I'm sorry, ma'am."

Jessica was finishing a phone apology. "I'm so sorry you had to go through that," she said. She hung up as Helen slid into her desk chair.

"Did you hear the latest scandal?" Jessica said.

I'm the latest scandal, Helen thought. But she was wrong.

"Mr. Casabella was caught with a hooker at the Superior Club restaurant last night." Jessica's eyes were wide with actressy wonder.

"No," Helen said.

"Yes. They were having sex in the men's restroom. The handicapped stall."

"Yuck. There's a romantic spot," Helen said.

"Here's the best part: Solange was at the restaurant. The waitress told me all about it. Solange was having dinner with four members of the Old Guard, trying to reassure them that the Superior Club had not lowered its standards. They'd finished dinner and were drinking coffee—no after-dinner brandy for that bunch—when the members started in criticizing the club. One said, 'Your new policies are bringing in a crude clientele with whom we do not wish to associate.'"

"Definitely Superior people," Helen said. "They'd never end a sentence with a preposition."

"Solange told them, 'Those were just summer people. Our regulars are a different class. Now that the summer people are gone you'll see a completely different tone.'"

"'This club admits too many NOKs,' the second member said."

"What's an NOK?" Helen said.

"Not our kind," Jessica said. "A third member said, 'Some of them didn't even wear jackets at dinner in the Superior Club.'"

"'The club remains a Superior place for Superior people,' Solange said, as two huge security guards charged through the restaurant door. They burst into the men's restroom. Everyone could hear the loud argument. Then security marched a disheveled young blonde and a grinning Mr. Casabella out of the restaurant. The woman barely looked twenty. And she was barely dressed. It was clear what had been going on. Mr. C's zipper was down."

"What did Solange do?"

"She pointed out that Mr. C was wearing a jacket. Then she offered the Old Guard a free dessert. They turned her down."

"A club member refused free food?" Helen found that more astonishing than sex in the restroom.

"All four of them. They left the club immediately and turned in their resignation papers this morning." She pointed to a three-foot stack on Cam's desk. "It's part of a growing trend."

"I thought Mr. Ironton wanted rid of the old members," Helen said.

"He's succeeded beyond his wildest dreams."

"What's going to happen to Mr. Casabella?" Helen asked.

"Not much. He'll get another letter of reprimand from Solange."

"I'd love to see the wording," Helen said. "Was he entertaining his DU in the john?"

"No, a call girl brought in by limo."

Helen groaned. Nothing would set off the remaining genteel members like hookers at the club. "How are we going to keep this mess quiet?"

"We can't. It happened in front of the whole restaurant. By last night, all of Golden Palms knew. By today, the news will have spread as far north as Palm Beach and from there it will go straight to New York. It's the talk of the country club set. I thought I'd better give you a warning, in case you get calls about it.

"That's not the worst." Jessica paused dramatically. "Last night was the ice cream social."

"And that's a problem?" Helen had visions of women in fluttery pastel dresses and flowered hats, men in linen suits, and little children frolicking.

"A big one," Jessica said. "We had to bring in security to handle the complaints."

"At an ice cream social? What could the members possibly complain about?"

Jessica picked up a pad on her desk and started reading: "The ice cream was too cold. The ice cream was not cold enough. A member couldn't bring in a guest, even though he offered to pay her way. Security was called and the member shoved the guard."

"A fight over ice cream?" Helen asked.

"Soft-serve," Jessica said. "This isn't even the good stuff. Between Mr. Casabella and the ice cream social, the phones have been ringing off the hook.

"Oh, one more thing. Solange is still looking for the Winderstine file. Are you sure you haven't seen it?"

"Positive," Helen said.

"So is everyone else. I can't imagine what happened to it, but she'll make our lives hell until she finds it. By the way, how are you?"

"Fine," Helen said. "Thanks for calling my landlady."

"I'm glad it worked out," Jessica said. "Oops. There's my phone again."

That was it. Helen was accepted back. Jessica didn't ask for the juicy details of Helen's day with the police. She was barely a footnote in the club's chronicle of gossip. She'd spent the night dreading her return to work, wondering how she'd face her co-workers after her shameful departure. Things were back to normal—almost.

Helen waited until Jessica's back was turned, then slipped her fake driver's license out of her co-worker's purse. Jessica never noticed. She was too busy watching the front counter drama starring Jackie.

A hard-faced woman came to the counter in a red Escada suit that made her look like a fireplug. "Jackie dear," she cooed. "Why don't we see you for bridge on Tuesdays anymore?"

The face-lifted fireplug knew why. Jackie simply said, "I don't have Tuesdays off, Estelle."

Helen admired the cool way Jackie handled the sly dig, but it must have hurt. The pencil Jackie was holding snapped in two. How many times a week did the poor woman have to endure those slights? Her nails were bitten to the quick.

Helen's phone rang, and her ear was assaulted by a loud, insistent New York voice.

"This is Mrs. Amos Sherben." The voice bored into her brain like a corkscrew. Where did people learn to talk that way? Mrs. Sherben owned miles of South Florida beach. She could afford elocution lessons. "I'm calling to complain."

"Of course you are," Helen said.

"What did you say?" Mrs. Sherben's words seemed to latch on to Helen's ear with iron grappling hooks.

"How may I help you?" Helen said.

"I'm calling to complain about the ice cream social. The bowls are too small. The ice cream dripped on my linen pants. If you had bowls the proper size, this would never happen. It's your fault. The ice cream was chocolate. The pants were D and G."

"I'm sorry, ma'am," Helen said. "What do you want us to do?"

"Pay for my dry cleaning," Mrs. Sherben said. The words were now razors, slicing into Helen's eardrum.

"I can't do that, ma'am. You filled the bowl yourself. The ice cream is self-serve. You eat it at your own risk. But I'll make a note of your complaint about the bowls. What's your member number, please?"

"Look it up," Mrs. Sherben said. "That's what you're paid to do." She slammed down the phone.

"You old bat," Helen said to the disconnected phone.

Jessica burst into applause. "Now you're officially one of us. On the phone with a smile, off the phone with a snarl."

Xaviera shook out her long hair. "I think she deserves to go to lunch first today, don't you? It's Jackie's turn to eat early. Go with Jackie, Helen. You need to be with someone nice and calm."

"What about my blood sugar?" Cam whined. "I have a medical condition. I should go first."

"A convenient medical condition," Xaviera said. "You've spent the whole morning cleaning your desk. You can wait."

"A clean desk is important. Brenda said so."

"Your phone is really clean," Xaviera said, pointing at it with a manicured nail like a bloody dagger. "You never pick it up."

"And you never use yours except to call your boyfriend," Cam said.

"Want to compare phone logs?" Xaviera said.

"Please, don't fight," Jackie said. She looked pained. "Shall we go, Helen?"

She reached for a Chanel bag that was beautifully made. Helen saw the leather was worn gray on one corner.

It was the first time Helen had spent any time with Jackie. She was about forty, with fine bones and hair pulled into an elegant chignon. In Helen's hometown of St. Louis, Jackie would be a knockout. But here in Florida, among the very rich, Jackie was considered past her prime: There was a slight droop to her eyelids, with small lines around her mouth and larger lines on her forehead. Jackie couldn't afford an eye job or Botox.

The two women clocked out and threaded their way through the dingy back halls. "I need to be careful," Jackie said. "I'm wearing open-toed slingbacks. I could get written up for improper footwear. My other pair of heels is at the shoemaker for new soles. They won't be ready for another day."

"Kitty won't mind," Helen said.

"Brenda will," Jackie said. "And she has it in for me. Well, let's not spoil our meal talking about Brenda."

"What's for lunch today?" Helen studied the cafeteria board.

"Roast beef. So fattening," Jackie said. "I brought my own food. I'll get us a table."

Helen came back with a plate piled with beef, string beans and fruit salad. Jackie carefully unwrapped a single hard-boiled egg. Poverty food.

"How are you settling into the job?" Jackie said.

"It's OK," Helen said. The beef was tougher than the club members. Maybe she'd bring her own food, too.

"What do you think of the members?" Jackie asked. She nibbled her egg.

"I don't understand how people with so much can be so unhappy," Helen said. "They live in paradise."

"Adam and Eve weren't happy in paradise, either." Jackie delicately wiped her mouth with a paper napkin and took a small sip of the free water from the cooler. "We have two groups of members here. The young ones, the trust fund babies, have no concept of work. They inherited their money. They are rude, arrogant and demanding."

"That's for sure," Helen said.

"The old ones earned the money. They're usually in poor health. Their spouses are either sick and old, or divorced and living with someone younger. Their children are gone. Their choices are gone. Their families are sitting around waiting for them to die so they can get the money. There's nothing left for them to do. That's why they spend all day quibbling their bills and complaining. We shouldn't envy these people."

"I don't," Helen said. "They're so unhappy. I always thought I wanted to be rich. Now I realize I just want enough money. They have too much."

"But when do you know you have enough?" Jackie said. "That's the key."

I didn't know in St. Louis, Helen thought. I was almost as unhappy as the club members.

"I used to have a house in Golden Palms." Jackie sounded wistful. "I loved to entertain. I had a dinner service for eighty, with silver, plates and linens. I never had to rent anything for my parties, not a single wineglass. My house had a view of the ocean and a big veranda where I could entertain. The worst part is, I thought we had a happy marriage. I had no idea anything was wrong until he came home and said he wanted a divorce."

"Another woman?" Helen asked.

"No. He said I wasn't any fun anymore. I did everything he wanted, I went everywhere he wanted and I wasn't fun. He wound up marrying someone who ordered him around. I guess that's his idea of fun. Never give a man everything he wants—you'll get nothing."

"Did she get the house?" Helen asked.

"No, he bought her a newer, bigger place," Jackie said. "No point in talking about the old days. It's all gone now. I didn't do well in the divorce."

"Me, either," Helen said.

"I'm so tired," Jackie said.

"This job takes a lot out of you," Helen said.

"I'm tired of the struggle," Jackie said. "I'm not sure I can afford to live in Golden Palms anymore. The rent is going up on my apartment."

Ohmigod, Helen thought. Jackie lives in those little servants' apartments by the Dixie Highway. She's gone from a beachside mansion to a one-bedroom box.

"Maybe you could get some place cheaper in Fort Lauderdale or Miami," Helen said.

"But I've lived here all my life," Jackie said. "I don't want to leave the only place I know. My friends try to get me to date, but so far, nothing's worked. A gentleman I knew from before has asked me out to lunch on my day off."

Before. Jackie's life, like Helen's, was divided into BD and AD—before the divorce and after.

"He is interested in charity causes, like I am. He's recently divorced. We were in the same circles before."

"Sounds interesting," Helen said.

"It's too soon to plan our wedding," Jackie said, but Helen could tell she had hopes. "I haven't even gone out with him yet. But I feel I know him so well. We were part of the same social circle for years. I'd like to live the way I did before."

I wouldn't, Helen thought.

"You know the worst part of being single?" Jackie said. "There's no one to share your thoughts with. No one cares whether you wake up in the morning. There's no one to find your body if you die in the night."

Helen shivered. She liked being single, but then she wasn't really, was she? She had Phil. Jackie's loneliness surrounded her like a thick perfume. Jackie carefully rolled the aluminum foil that she'd wrapped her egg in and put it in her purse. She reuses it, Helen thought. She's that hard up.

"That can't be true," Helen said.

"Oh, but it is," Jackie said. "I have no children."

"But your friends are fixing you up with dates."

"They feel sorry for me. They don't come around the way they did before. Well, things will get better." Jackie put on a too-brave smile. "They have to."

There was an awkward silence. Jackie, in her loneliness, had revealed too much too soon. Now she was embarrassed. "Guess we'd better get back," she said.

Helen clocked in early. She was glad to be at her desk, away from

Jackie's sad desperation. She reached for her insistent phone almost gratefully.

"Hello," said a soft, pleasant voice. "This is Demi Dell."

The wife of the hairy, horny plastic surgeon.

"I misplaced my club member card," Demi said. "I took it out of my wallet before I went to New York, and left it on my dresser. Now it's gone."

"No problem," Helen said. "Would you like me to freeze your account?"

"No, I don't think the card was stolen," Demi said. "It's lost somewhere in the house. I'm coming by to play tennis shortly. I'll stop by and pick up a new one."

"I'll make sure it's ready."

"Thanks," Demi said.

There was a word Helen didn't hear much from the members. She printed out the new card and examined the photo. Helen had seen many hard, rich faces at the club. Demi was a surprise. Everything about her seemed soft and sweet: her curly dark hair, her plump lips, her big brown eyes. How could the ugly surgeon cheat on such a pretty woman?

"Hello? Is anyone alive here or am I in a wax museum?"

Helen looked up from the card machine. The young woman at the counter wore a pouty expression and a tight halter top. Her cantaloupe breasts looked as though they were fighting for room in the tiny top.

"How may we help you?" Jessica asked. Frost should have formed on the young woman's shirt.

"I want to return this useless shit," the young woman said, and threw a Superior Club shopping bag down on the counter. Jackie gasped.

"When did you buy it?" Jessica said.

"I didn't," the young woman said. "Dr. Dell bought it for me last month. I have the receipt."

Helen wondered whether this was the infamous staffer who'd caused Dr. Dell's recent tirade over the bill. She looked a bit chubby to be some doctor's new cookie. They usually liked flat-stomached babes.

"Are you a member here?" Jessica asked, though she already knew the answer.

"Of course not," the young woman said. "I wouldn't join this old folks' home if you paid me."

"What is your name, please?" Jessica said.

"Mandy," the young woman said. "Now, are you gonna give me my money back or not?"

Jessica studied the receipt. "I'm afraid all I can do, Mandy, is direct you to the Superior Togs shop, where they will issue Dr. Dell a credit for the clothing."

"You mean I can't get any freaking cash?"

"Sorry," Jessica said. "But you didn't buy the items."

"Screw that," Mandy said. She grabbed the bag and flounced out.

"Is that Dr. Dell's new cookie?" Helen said.

"That's her," Jessica said. "And what a piece of work she is."

"I've never seen two people who deserved each other more," Helen said.

There was a soft "excuse me," and Demi Dell was standing at the front counter in fresh tennis whites. Helen recognized her from her club photo.

"I'll handle this," Helen said to Jessica. "Demi Dell wants to pick up her new member card. I've already run it off the machine."

The staff studied their desks or suddenly grabbed their phones. No one knew if Demi knew about the scene her husband created trying to get the bill or the infamous day of relaxation he'd bought for Mandy, his nasty staffer.

Demi signed the paperwork for her new card and left with good-byes and thank-yous. Helen could almost hear the audible sighs of relief when she was finally gone.

"She's a nice person," Xaviera said. "She doesn't deserve him."

"Who does?" Jessica said.

"Ms. Halter Top," Helen said. "I wonder if Dr. Dell installed those outsized breasts."

With that, Brenda with the hatchet-blade hair blew in the office. "We aren't paying you to hold a cocktail party," she said.

"Oh, boy," whispered Jessica. "She's in a mood."

"Cam!" Brenda shouted. "What is that pile of files doing on your desk?"

"They're resignations. I just got them this morning."

"You should have processed them by now. You know Mr. Ironton hates desk clutter."

Cam resentfully picked up the files.

"I'm going to reorganize the supply cabinet," Brenda said. "It's a mess."

"Terrific. We won't be able to find anything for weeks," Jessica whispered. "I hate it when she starts straightening things. She always loses something important."

The staff worked in sullen silence, except when they were on the phones. Helen could almost see the black clouds over their heads. She could hear slapping and thumping as Brenda worked in the supply cabinet.

By three o'clock, Helen was hungry. She sneaked an energy bar out of her purse and took a bite, then hid the rest by her phone.

Brenda emerged, carrying a box of envelopes. "Helen! What's that thing on your desk?" She pointed a nearly meatless arm dramatically at the half-eaten energy bar. "Throw it away. You know it's against the rules to eat at your desk."

Helen picked up the bar and shoved it in her purse. She wasn't tossing it.

Brenda wheeled around and said, "Jackie, what's that on the floor behind your desk?"

Jackie swivelled in her chair to check. "A piece of paper," she said.

"Pick it up. This office is a pigsty. And why are you wearing open-toed slingbacks? You know they are against regulations."

"My shoes—" Jackie began.

"No excuses. I'm writing you up."

Jackie cowered miserably at her desk.

"And you, Xaviera. Why do you have those unsanitary daggers? Your nails should not be longer than half an inch. And red polish is strictly forbidden."

"Go to hell," Xaviera said. "You're jealous because my nails are real. So are my boobs."

"You can't talk to me like that," Brenda said. "I'm an assistant manager."

Kitty came running out of her office, Kewpie-doll curls bouncing. "And I'm Xaviera's supervisor. I'll discipline my people. That's not your job."

"You aren't doing your job," Brenda said. "You're letting them get away with murder."

"Obviously, Brenda, you have a lot of time on your hands if you can interfere with my staff. Maybe I should ask Solange to give you additional duties."

"She's not here," Brenda said.

But the office door opened, and Solange was there. She still looked like she'd just gotten out of bed, but after a sleepless night. There were dark shadows under her eyes that even concealer couldn't cover.

"I had a horrible meeting with Mr. Ironton. Horrible." Solange nervously ran her fingers through her tousled red hair. "But first, I have another issue to address. Has anyone found the Winderstine file?"

"We would have told you," Kitty said. "We've looked everywhere."

"The file room is a mess," Brenda said. "I don't see how you could find it."

"We've searched the file room four times," Kitty said.

"Then make it five," Solange said. "I need that file. I have to write the letter of reprimand within seven days of the incident. The missing file is part of a larger problem. Mr. Ironton has received a detailed report that there are multiple staff abuses in our office. It gave dates and times. Our staff has been dressing improperly!"

She glared at Xaviera's red nails. Xaviera glared back. Jackie tucked her illegal slingbacks under her desk.

"And eating—yes, eating—at their desks. You know how Mr. Ironton feels about that."

He should get over it, Helen thought. This place has a lot bigger problems than my energy bar. That damned Brenda. She's been keeping notes on us. Her latest attack was to underline her spy memo.

Jackie looked ready to burst into tears. Xaviera seemed about to explode.

"Worst of all, someone stole company time by conducting personal business during working hours," Solange said.

"That's a lie," Cameron said. "I needed to go to the title company for my new condo, but I cleared it with Kitty first. I came in early off the clock to make up the time."

"I didn't mention your name," Solange said.

"You didn't have to," Cam said. "We all know Brenda wrote that memo. Why does Mr. Ironton listen to that Botoxed bitch?"

"Why, indeed?" Kitty said. "Our department just finished a huge customer care mailing without overtime. We're operating below budget. We rank higher than any other department in customer satisfaction. I hope you told him that, Solange."

"Well, no," Solange said. "I was so shocked and surprised I didn't say anything."

"Were you really?" Kitty said. "You know what a backstabber Brenda is. Why would you be shocked when she snitches on us?"

"I think we'd better have the rest of this conversation in my office," Solange said.

"Fine." Kitty's small determined chin was stuck out in battle mode. She grabbed a notebook and followed Solange into her office. Brenda tried to follow them, but Kitty slammed the door in her face. Brenda had a smug smile when she retreated to her office and shut the door.

"Miserable bitch," Xaviera said. "I'll get her for that."

"We all will," Cam said.

CHAPTER 11

"Honey, I'm home," Helen called when she opened the door to her apartment.

Thumbs, her six-toed cat, was waiting for her at the door. The big gray-and-white cat with the golden eyes twined himself around Helen's feet, then led the way to the kitchen.

"I'm just a drudge," Helen said to the cat, as she followed his plume of a tail. "Someone who fixes your meals and cleans up after you. Do you really care about my feelings?"

Thumbs patted his food dish with his enormous six-toed paw. When Helen didn't immediately fill it, he stared at her, then deliberately flipped the empty metal dish. It clanged and clattered on the floor.

"Apparently not," Helen said. She righted the dish and poured dry food into the bowl, then changed the cat's water. Thumbs gently nudged her out of the way so he could get to his dinner.

"I'm not getting much sympathy here," she said to the cat's back, as he methodically chomped the brown pellets. "Guess I'll have to look for satisfaction outside our home. Just remember, if I stray, it's your fault."

Helen rummaged in the fridge for a box of red wine. That's all it said, RED. There was no mention of grapes. Instead of a vintage year, it had an expiration date. She changed into jeans and one of Phil's white shirts, picked up the box of wine and half a bag of pretzels, and padded out to the Coronado pool to salute the sunset.

She could hear her landlady, Margery, laughing with Phil. Helen thought if Margery were twenty years younger, Phil would run off with her. Sometimes, Helen wondered if he might anyway. Margery was old and made no bones about it. She scorned the nip-and-tuck work of the Superior Club crowd. It made her seem sexier and younger than they did. Margery wore her age like an achievement.

She also wore purple. She always did. Helen never had the nerve to ask why. Today, Margery was in lavender from her cotton top to her flowered flats. She had fired up a Marlboro and was blowing smoke rings across the pool.

How did she do that? Helen wondered. Could you take smoke ring–blowing lessons? Maybe the community college had a class.

Phil was stretched out on a chaise next to Margery, dressed in a white shirt and jeans. The shirt looked much better on him than on her, Helen decided. The jeans matched his blue eyes.

"So how was your day?" Margery said.

"Lousy," Helen said. "All I did was listen to complaints."

"So what?" Margery said. "I hear complaints all day, too, and nobody pays me. People bend my ear for free."

"Yeah, but you don't have to listen to 'Do you know who I am?' If I had a dollar every time I heard that, I'd be rich enough to join the Superior Club," Helen said.

Margery sent another smoke ring skimming over the pool. "They aren't asking you that question," she said. "They're asking themselves. They don't know. They've never had the chance to find out. You're the lucky one."

"Oh, please," Helen said. "These people have everything. I have nothing. I know who I am: a failure. We're all failures in that office. Jessica is a failed actress. Jackie is the failed wife of a rich man. I'm a failed corporate wonk."

"To fail, you have to try something first," Margery said. "They'll always be cushioned by mummy's money and daddy's lawyers. If they screw up, their parents will rescue them and find them a safe place in the family business. They can't even fail."

"Lucky them," Helen said.

"Not really. Look, Helen, learn to handle those people, so you don't upset yourself. Anybody who works customer service has a few key phrases they use to handle the screamers. Here's my favorite: Next time Mrs. Rich screams at you, tell her, 'Rest assured that topic will be brought up to the staff.'

"It will, too. You'll warn them she's a bitch on wheels. But she doesn't know that. Mrs. Rich is happy because she thinks she got someone in trouble."

"Here's another good one," Phil said. "I use it all the time: 'Don't you worry, ma'am. There will be a note in the file over this incident.'

"You're not lying. The note will warn the staff that Mrs. Rich is a real problem."

"If the complainer is halfway reasonable," Margery said, "you try this one: 'I understand. I agree with you. But the rules say . . .'"

"How do you handle the line that always makes me grit my teeth?" Helen said. "'I'm a doctor.' The doctor acts as if he expects the yacht club basin to part so he can walk across it. I'd like to say 'So what?' but that would get me fired."

"No, no," Phil said. "You have to tweak their noses, not hit them on the head with a brick. Next time someone says, 'I'm a doctor,' you say, 'PhD or MD?' Deliver it very seriously. That always flummoxes them."

Helen laughed.

Phil looked at her. "You don't believe a word of this, do you?"

"I hate this job," Helen said. "I hate these pointless people."

"But you like combat," Phil said. "Why do the members upset you so much?"

"I don't know," Helen said, miserably. "I don't understand them. I don't understand myself. I guess I'm not a Superior person."

"Well, then, let's talk about the less than Superior Rob. I found out some things."

Helen was grateful he'd changed the subject. "You made those phone calls, just like you said you would." She leaned over and kissed him.

"I've been working all last night and most of today. I found out quite a bit." Phil expected to be paid for his work with praise and undivided attention. Margery stubbed out her cigarette. Helen put down her wineglass. They both listened carefully.

"Apparently, Rob didn't take any clothes or personal items with him," Phil said. "There's no new credit card activity. His last charge was for lunch at Joe's Stone Crab the day he disappeared. Your ex spent two hundred fifty dollars for lunch."

That's almost what I make in a week, Helen thought.

"Rob has about ten thousand dollars in a local bank," Phil said. "There have been no withdrawals since he disappeared. He wrote a check for seventy bucks the last morning he was seen alive."

"He probably used it for tips at the restaurant and the valet stand," Helen said. "Rob liked to throw money around, especially if it wasn't his. I'm sure that ten thousand came from his wife."

"You're talking about him in the past tense," Phil said.

"He has to be dead," Helen said. "Otherwise, he would have cleaned out that bank account. Rob ran through a lot of money when he lived with me. I don't think the Black Widow put him on a tight budget. I guarantee that seventy dollars was gone long before I belted him in the club parking lot."

"What about his cell phone?" Margery said. "Any calls?"

"Police found it in the parking lot. There was a bloody fingerprint on the call button."

Helen felt a rush of guilt. Had Rob been calling for help when he died? Did he wander around dazed and fall into the water? Did he collapse by the side of the road and fall into a ditch? Where was his body?

"Any interesting phone numbers?" Margery said.

"Several calls from pay phones."

"Who makes pay phone calls anymore, except for Helen?" Margery said.

"At least three other people in South Florida," Phil said. "Rob had calls from pay phones at the Superior Club, the Miami airport, and the main library in Fort Lauderdale."

"Sounds like people who didn't want to be traced," Margery said.

"The numbers were dead ends," Phil said. "I ran into a lot of those. I covered some of the same ground the police did, trying to find Rob. No John Does at the hospitals in Miami, Lauderdale or Palm Beach. No dead men matching his description at the morgue. No bodies pulled out of the water from here to down south to Key West or up north to Palm Beach County.

"Rob hasn't rented a car, or bought a plane, train or bus ticket in his name. I'm not ruling out a passport and credit cards under another name.

"Helen, you can do one thing for me. Do you have access to the club security reports?"

"Sure," she said.

"See if there are any missing dinghies or small boats in the yacht club. There's a chance Rob may have stolen a boat from the marina and escaped that way."

But Helen knew he didn't, even before she checked the reports. Rob was dead. All Marcella's husbands were dead. Rob's killer had dropped him into the ocean. Or sent him to the bottom of the yacht club basin. Or fed him to the alligators in the Everglades. His body would never be found. Her name would never be cleared. She'd always be a suspect.

She knew her ex would end this way. Rob didn't even have the decency to die right.

"You're staring off into space," Phil said. "Penny for your thoughts."

"Not worth the money," Helen said.

"You're brooding," Phil said. "You're going to sit here all night in a dark fog." He checked his watch. "It's not too late."

"Too late for what?" Helen said.

"The sunset cruise on the *Jungle Queen*," Phil said. "We can still make it if we hurry. Don't bother changing. You look fine the way you are."

Helen made a face. "That boat's kind of touristy, isn't it?"

"Yes," Phil said. "That's exactly why we're going. Nobody important takes a cruise on a tourist boat. It won't impress anyone. Most of the yachts at the Superior Club are bigger than the *Jungle Queen*. You won't meet a single club member. We'll just be two people, enjoying the night and each other. Three, if Margery wants to join us."

"You kids run along and have a good time," Margery said. "I'm staying here and enjoying my smoke."

The *Jungle Queen* was everything Helen thought it would be: a big fake hunk of gingerbread tricked out like a Mississippi River boat, docked near the beach in Fort Lauderdale. Helen felt ridiculous as she boarded the boat with couples from Tampa and Tacoma. Their clothes were too new, bought for this vacation. Their skin was burned a brutal red and reeked of coconut sunscreen. They snapped pictures of palm trees, wild parrots and sailboats and yelled, "Look at that!"

Helen and Phil slid onto a metal bench on the upper deck. A honeymoon couple from Akron sat next to them, nuzzling each other. They could have been on a bus back home, for all they saw of the view. The other passengers waved and cheered as the *Jungle Queen* pulled away from the dock and the guide began his narrated tour of the sights along the New River. It was hopelessly corny.

Phil put his arm around Helen and whispered in her ear, "Lighten up. Or I might mistake you for a Superior person."

"Please, I want to get away from that place," Helen said.

"Then do it," he said.

Helen stared at the sunset-stained water and wondered if Rob was down there somewhere. "You asked what I was thinking earlier this evening. I'm afraid Rob is going to be as big a pest dead as he was alive."

"We'll find him," Phil said.

"How?" Helen said. "Florida has a million places to hide a body."

The nuzzling couple stared at Helen, then edged away down the bench, clutching each other even tighter.

"Finding people is my job," Phil said. "I'm good at it. And you're good at your job. We'll do it together. The two of us."

"Against the world?" Helen said.

"A big chunk of the world wants to help us. Now sit back and enjoy your cruise."

Helen did. She oohed and aahed at the outrageous mansions lining the waterway. She waved to the people on shore and cheered the drawbridge tenders. She liked the idea that traffic on the city streets was held up while the *Jungle Queen* sailed through the open drawbridges.

When the boat docked at the "private island," she sat on another bench and stuffed herself with sauce-smeared ribs and boiled shrimp. She found yet another bench and laughed at the old-fashioned variety show. For a few hours, she forgot the Superior Club, the Black Widow and Rob. She told a nice couple from New York about other sights they should see on their vacation.

The cruise back home was quiet. The narrator hung up his microphone and the friendly groups divided once again into couples. The soft darkness seemed to wrap itself around them like a warm blanket. Helen cuddled with Phil and watched the moonlight shimmer on the water. He smelled of shaving lotion and barbecue sauce. He kissed her forehead, then her eyes and lips.

"Do you know who I am?" he whispered.

"Yes," Helen said. "The man I love."

CHAPTER 12

Helen awoke to Sunday morning sounds: a newspaper rustling and coffee perking in the kitchen. The bed was empty. Phil must already be awake.

She stretched luxuriantly and surveyed the wreckage of her bedroom. A lacy bra hung on the bedpost and her panties were flung on the dresser. The sheets were pulled loose and the comforter was pooled on the floor. The mattress was crooked.

That made her smile. Helen remembered what she and Phil had done to get them that way.

She turned over and caught herself in the mirror. She hardly recognized this abandoned woman. Her dark hair trailed over one eye and her lips were bruised from Phil's kisses.

"Do you know who I am?" she whispered to the woman in the mirror, and laughed.

The sun seemed extra bright this morning. That made her sit straight up in bed. What time was it? She checked her clock: eight twenty-seven. She had to leave for work in half an hour. Thumbs usually woke her up long before, demanding breakfast. Phil must have fed him.

Her apartment smelled of sex and coffee. Hot love at night, hot coffee in the morning. What more could a woman want?

Money to pay the rent. She'd better get moving if she was going to make it to work on time. Helen hummed a little tune as she got out of bed. She splashed water on her face, brushed her teeth, combed her hair, and slipped into one of the white shirts she found on the floor. She tripped over her teddy bear, Chocolate. She kept part of her stash hidden in Chocolate's fat tummy. Alas, her bear was a lot thinner these days. Helen's new job had turned out to be expensive, and she constantly robbed her stash for gas and lunch money and never replaced it. The money always went for something else she needed.

Phil was sitting in her kitchen with a steaming coffee mug. The Sunday paper was spread open on the table. Thumbs was sitting on the national news. Phil was reading the business section and scratching the cat's solemn, round head.

"Hi, sexy," he said to Helen. "You look like someone who's been sleeping with her boyfriend."

"I didn't get much sleep," she said. "Any more of that coffee?"

"Half a pot. Want to go out to breakfast?"

"Yes, but I can't. I have to be at the Superior Club by ten, which means I need to get dressed and hit the highway." She kissed Phil on the ear and he held her close.

"Can't you call in sick?" he said. "Dr. Phil thinks you need another day in bed."

"Sorry," she said. "There's no one else working in the office today. I'm on my own on Sunday."

"Think you can handle the meanies by yourself?" he said.

"After last night, I can handle anything," she said. "I won't let them get to me."

That was her mantra as the Toad rumbled and belched through pristine Golden Palms, drawing disgusted glances from the rich women walking their dogs. Helen waved to the guard at the club's employee entrance.

"I won't let them get to me," she repeated, as she parked the car and walked to the customer care office.

She didn't get a chance to say it again. Blythe St. Ives, the notoriously nasty golfer, was pacing by the office door in an outfit no serious sportswoman would wear on a dare: short pink skirt, belly-baring pink designer top and silly pink golf spikes. A ruby-and-diamond bumblebee perched on her perky pink visor.

"Where have you been?" Blythe said. "I've been waiting here ten minutes."

"We don't open for another fifteen," Helen said.

"Do you know who I am?" Blythe said.

Her face was set in a dissatisfied frown. Helen wondered if she could put up a sign: CAUTION: FROWNING CAUSES WRINKLES.

"The rules do not permit me to unlock the door for members before the appointed time," Helen said. It was technically true, but the staff made exceptions for some members, like nice Mr. Giles who brought them roses. He could walk in anytime he wanted.

"That's outrageous," Blythe said. "I spend a lot of money at this club."

What did Margery tell her to say? Oh, right. "Rest assured that topic will be brought up to the staff," Helen said.

"It better," Blythe said. But she seemed satisfied with Helen's answer. Maybe Margery's customer service phrases really did work.

Helen unlocked the door and quickly shut it in Blythe's face. Then she turned on the office lights, opened the curtains, clocked in and booted up her computer. The phone was ringing already.

Blythe was staring at her watch when Helen unlocked the door at precisely ten o'clock.

"Finally," Blythe said. "I need a guest pass for eleven tomorrow morning. I'll be golfing with two friends and what's-her-name in your office."

"Brenda?" Helen asked.

"She doesn't need a guest pass, of course, but my friends do," Blythe said. "They're from out of town."

That explained it. No one in Golden Palms would golf with Blythe.

Helen printed out the passes, then ran for the ringing phones.

"What took you so long?" screamed a woman with a New York

honk. "I had to call twice." She said this as if she'd had to swim the English Channel.

"My guest is coming in fifteen minutes," she said. "I want a guest pass. Now." No please or thank you. "Hurry up. I don't want them waiting."

Helen hurried. It went like this all morning: last-minute demands for guest passes and members' friends who had to be called in at the gate. If the members had called yesterday, when the office was fully staffed, they would have had faster service. But they wanted what they wanted when they wanted it.

The flurry of phone calls stopped about eleven thirty. Helen felt frazzled. She'd forgotten all of Margery's advice. Her good mood was gone, buried by the problems of people who had no problems. She took a deep breath, and then prepared herself to tackle the phone messages. She knew those would be extra rude.

"I want to speak to a human being," a petulant woman said on the tape. She slammed down the phone without leaving a number.

"Me, too," Helen said, and picked wilted rose petals off her desk. The roses from nice Mr. Giles had all died. Helen couldn't remember the last pleasant conversation she'd had with a member.

She flinched when her phone rang again. She recognized that cold voice immediately. Mrs. DeVane must have a layer of permafrost on her phone. She never wasted time on pleasantries, or even hello. Each frigid word conveyed that she was forced to speak to a servant.

"I haven't received my copy of the *Superior Magazine,*" Mrs. DeVane said, in a voice like wind off a glacier. "This is the fourth time I've called this month. You promise that you'll send it, but you never do."

"I do?" Helen said.

"I mean those people in your office." An icicle pierced Helen's ear.

She checked the database. Jessica, Xaviera and Cam had taken Mrs. DeVane's calls. They all noted that Mrs. D was "very nasty" and reported that they mailed out the magazine.

"Perhaps the problem is with your mail carrier," Helen said.

"It is not," Mrs. DeVane said. "The problem is with you people. I want my magazine. I've paid for it." Another layer of frost settled on Helen's phone.

"Which address should I send it to?" Helen said.

"The only address I have."

Helen wondered if acid could freeze. "Many of our members have two or three homes," she said. "I was checking if you had multiple residences." She enjoyed inserting that little needle. "I'll note your request in the file and send out the magazine today."

"See that you do," Mrs. DeVane said. "And get it right this time." Her glacial voice disappeared into a cold soundless sea.

Helen made the same notes in her computer as Jessica, Xaviera and Cam, then didn't send the magazine. She suspected her three co-workers did the same thing.

That small revenge cheered her. She wondered if Mrs. DeVane would call poor Jackie next. Jackie might actually send the magazine. Mrs. D passed through the customer care office at least three times a week on her way to the tennis courts, but she wouldn't sully her fingers by picking up the club magazine. It had to be mailed to her.

Helen poured herself a cup of coffee, then looked at the clock. It was nearly three. The phone calls and last-minute requests for passes had slacked off. The phone messages were all returned.

Finally, Helen had time to do some work for Marcella. She wanted to search the staff desks. One of her co-workers had been in touch with Rob, and she had to find out who it was. Her ex had paid big money—a thousand dollars a pop—for information in the customer care files.

What did she know about the people she worked with? Only that they all needed money. But then, so did she.

Helen felt guilty going through Jessica's desk, but her friend was a loser in the Florida hurricane lottery. She and her husband, Allan, did not get hurricane insurance, which was horribly expensive.

"We figured what we would have paid in premiums could be used for repairs if we got hit," Jessica had said. The plan would have worked, except they spent the premium money instead of saving it.

Hurricane Wilma did thirty thousand dollars' worth of damage to their townhouse. They were saddled with massive bills. Jessica was driven nearly crazy dealing with city inspectors and contractors.

Helen found bills and work orders stashed in an envelope in the top drawer. The painters wanted seven thousand dollars. The hurricane glass estimate was for ten thousand dollars. There were second notices from the painters and a carpet company.

Poor Jessica. What a load of worry was stuffed in that envelope. A thousand dollars would go a long way toward staving off her hungry creditors.

In another drawer, hidden under a stack of blank guest passes, was a photo of Frank Langella signed, "To my elegant Jessica. Here's to our next success." Jessica had one line in a Broadway hit he'd starred in five years ago, when her acting was on the upswing.

Jessica's acting career was another victim of the hurricane. The lucrative commercials and movie parts were gone. Florida no longer looked as lush after Wilma stripped the trees and blew away their branches. The movie and commercial makers wouldn't come back until the trees grew back and the damaged signs, roofs and windows were repaired.

Searching Jessica's desk was easy. Outside, it was as bare as Mr. Ironton demanded. Inside, it was a moil of paper, pens, broken pencils and paper clips. Helen wouldn't have to worry about putting things back precisely. She opened the rest of the drawers and pushed around more papers, but found nothing else except a list of casting agents.

She felt like a rat when she closed Jessica's last drawer, but her search had just begun. It was four o'clock and she had to hurry.

Jackie's desk was harder to search. Everything was lined up with neat precision inside and out. There were special holders for sticky notes, paper clips and stationery.

She couldn't find anything personal in Jackie's desk. There were no photos of her former glamorous life, but Helen hadn't expected those. Jackie was a loser in the marriage sweepstakes. What must it be like to be a servant at the club where you were once a queen?

Brenda, a bully who sensed an easy target, made Jackie's life miserable. Jackie probably kept her desk free of personal items so she wouldn't give the assistant manager more ammunition. The staff knew Brenda searched desks when no one was around.

Like I'm doing, Helen thought.

Buried in the back of Jackie's last drawer, Helen uncovered a small cardboard box. Inside were coupons, a hosiery club card from a discount store and a small bottle of run-stopper.

Helen remembered the hard-boiled egg lunch. Jackie was so desperate for money even a run in her panty hose was a financial disaster. She didn't drive to work, except when it rained. Jackie walked to save gas. Helen knew she worried about paying her rent. She struggled to hang on to this last vestige of her old life.

A thousand-dollar bribe would buy salvation.

The phone rang. It was Jim in security, asking for information on a member. Helen looked up the man in the computer.

"He's in good standing?" Jim asked.

"Definitely."

"OK, I'll note that when I file my report."

"What did he do?" Helen said.

"The member gate wasn't working," Jim said.

"Again?" Helen interrupted.

"That's what he said. When the electric arm wouldn't go up, he rammed it with his BMW. Took out the arm—and the gate camera. Ruined his car's front fender, too."

"Mr. Ironton is not going to be happy," Helen said.

The phone call and paperwork cut into her snooping time. The office was only open until six on Sundays, and she couldn't stay late without alerting security.

Cameron's desk was next. Helen thought he was smart and ambitious with a tricky streak. She didn't trust him.

Cam had a small leather-framed photo in a cubbyhole on his desk, out of sight of Mr. Ironton, but in plain view of Cam. The woman in the picture had to be Cam's mother. She had the same girlish features and plump body as her son. But on her, they were pretty. Cam towered over his mother in the picture. She was holding a small fluffy dog and staring at her son adoringly. Cam's father was not in the picture.

Inside, Cam's desk was somewhere between Jessica's and Jackie's in neatness. Helen found the usual office supplies in the first drawer. Under a yellow legal pad was some paperwork for the infamous "stolen time" condo loan Brenda had reported to Mr. Ironton. Cam was buying a three-hundred-thousand-dollar condo on the Intracoastal Waterway. Helen couldn't tell how much he was putting down or what his monthly payments were. But three hundred thousand was a staggering amount of money for a young man making eleven dollars an hour, even if Cam was single.

A steady supply of thousand-dollar bribes would help make those loan payments.

Cam's bottom drawer was locked. That was odd. No one locked their desks in customer care, except Solange—and that was only the petty cash drawer. Everyone in the office knew she kept the key under her philodendron.

Helen didn't have time to deal with it now. It was after five. These old desk drawers could be opened with a skeleton key. Margery had one. Helen would open the mysterious locked drawer later.

She moved on to Xaviera's desk. The fiery-nailed Latina had a heart-shaped framed photo of her boyfriend in the cubbyhole on her desk. Steven looked more like a lifeguard than a security guard. With his blond hair, blue eyes and muscles, her man was definitely scenic.

She could see why Xaviera was worried. She was turning thirty, and suddenly time was moving too fast. She wanted to marry her handsome Anglo boyfriend, buy a house and start a family. In her desk, Helen found three *Modern Bride* magazines, a ticket to a bridal fair, and a sheet of real estate listings for houses. Most were in the four- to six-hundred-thousand-dollar range. Even with two jobs, the couple couldn't afford that. Not on Superior Club salaries. Was Xaviera taking bribes to get that down payment?

Helen checked the clock: forty-five minutes till she closed the office, and she still had to do her end-of-the-day chores. Helen had just enough time to search Brenda's desk. Solange and Kitty's offices would have to wait, but she came in early tomorrow morning. Maybe she could take a quick peek then. Usually, the rest of the staff didn't show up until nine a.m. or later.

Brenda's office, as befitted her status as assistant manager, was smaller than Kitty's and Solange's. It was painted ice white and decorated with photos of Miami Beach. There was just room enough for the antique desk and her golf clubs.

Helen picked up the seven iron, removed the stupid pink cover and swung the club in the office. She hit Brenda's desk chair with a loud *thwack!* Fortunately, it was a padded chair. The swing didn't take a chunk out of it. Helen put the club back and started a serious search of Brenda's office.

Brenda had left her appointment calender on her desk. Helen paged through it and saw sixteen doctors' appointments during the last three months. Brenda had her surgical enhancements and checkups on company time.

Interesting.

Helen would copy Brenda's calendar first thing tomorrow. Kitty could use some ammunition next time Brenda complained that the customer care staff wasn't working hard enough.

The phone rang, and Helen jumped. She bumped Brenda's desk pad, then saw something underneath that made her forget the ringing phone.

Brenda had the lost Winderstine file hidden under her desk pad.

CHAPTER 13

Helen stared at the missing Winderstine file. Solange had driven them crazy, demanding that manila folder. They'd searched their desks again and again, trying to find it.

All that time, it had been hidden on Brenda's desk.

Helen knew what that meant: Brenda was Rob's spy. She was selling him club information.

"Yes!" Helen said out loud, and pumped her arm in the air. Could any story have a happier ending?

This was beautiful. This was perfect. Helen would get the Black Widow off her back. She'd make her report to Marcella. Then her obligation would be finished and she'd never have to speak to the Black Widow again. The woman gave her the creeps, with her spooky makeup, silent staff and dead husbands.

Helen could guess what Phil would say: She was jumping to conclusions. He'd give her a dozen other reasons why Brenda would conceal that file under her desk pad.

But Helen knew better. Something in this file was worth a thousand dollars.

She picked up the battered legal-sized folder with a coffee ring on one side. There were some five thousand files like it in the club storage room.

At first glance, its information seemed routine: Mr. Sawyer Winderstine III had had a few small problems at the club. But he was nowhere in the mobster Casabella's league when it came to outrageous behavior.

The worst was a report written by Xaviera two years ago. Helen waded through her co-worker's convoluted English. The short version was that a club bartender had refused to serve Mr. Winderstine another double scotch and offered to call a cab for the tipsy member.

"When Mr. Winderstine became *belligionerent*"—Helen winced at Xaviera's free-form spelling—the bartender had called security. Security had confiscated Winderstine's car keys and escorted him to a waiting cab.

The incident didn't even rate a letter of reprimand. It was noted in the file and forgotten.

Last year, Mr. Winderstine was sixty days behind paying his club bill. He'd owed eight hundred dollars, a measly amount at a club where people ran up ten and twenty thousand dollars a month in charges.

The club sent Mr. Winderstine a sixty-day overdue notice. He paid by check immediately and sent a letter explaining that he'd been traveling and forgotten the bill. Again, it was a minor problem. No further action was taken and he was now a member in good standing.

Helen went through his club charges:

Mr. Winderstine rarely spent more than five hundred dollars a month, usually for business lunches or drinks. He was one of the "fifteen-dollar hamburger people" that Mr. Ironton sneered at. Except for that one past-due notice, he paid his bills on time.

Otherwise, Mr. Winderstine had stayed off the club radar until recently, when he called a Superior waitress a "stupid bitch" because she was slow with his salad. That incident hadn't yet made his paper file.

Maybe I'm wrong about Brenda, Helen thought. Rob would never pay a thousand bucks for this information. The Winderstine file was a big yawn.

But she remembered all those expensive nip-and-tuck procedures on Brenda's calendar. Her medical insurance wouldn't cover them, and Brenda didn't make enough money to pay for them. She had to be taking a bribe.

Helen knew valuable information was hidden in that file folder. She had to find it. She read and reread each page until the words blurred. Then, in "spouse information," she found it: Winderstine was a dull corporate type, but he'd married an heiress. Sonny Hamptin Winderstine wouldn't inherit major money until Daddy died, but in the meantime, he'd given her three Early American paintings by Jared Poole. Sonny had loaned them to the club for its Art of the Americas exhibit last September. The paintings were valued at between five and six hundred thousand dollars each. The exhibit was not open to the public or covered in the newspapers. Club members didn't want their art exposed to the risk of theft. The club was a safe place to show off their possessions.

More than a million and a half dollars' worth of art was in a starter mansion at Lighthouse Point. The Winderstines spent one month each year in Paris. The date varied. Sonny Winderstine had sent a note on thick cream Crane's stationery to customer care, asking that any club correspondence be forwarded to the Paris address for the month of February.

That information was definitely worth money to the right people—or the wrong ones. The Winderstines would be out of the way for a whole month. Helen was pretty sure they didn't have live-in help. Most houses in that neighborhood weren't big enough. The property would be unguarded, except maybe for a burglar alarm—and any decent burglar could get around one of those.

Gotcha! Helen thought.

She surveyed Brenda's ice-white office and those silly pink slip-covered golf clubs leaning against the wall. After tomorrow, this room would be empty. Blythe St. Ives would have to find herself another golf partner.

Helen checked her watch. Yikes! It was five forty-five. She had to finish up and clock out by six or security would be on her doorstep.

Her office phone had stopped ringing, but the message light was on. Helen knew who it was. Mrs. Buchmann wanted a guest pass. She always wanted one right before closing. Helen checked the message and there she was. "I don't know why I can't get anyone in this office," Mrs. B whined.

Helen typed up Mrs. Buchmann's guest pass and saw she was running low on the right forms. She rummaged in the supply cabinet for more guest passes, but they were gone from their usual spot. Damn Brenda. She must have moved them during her last crazed cleaning. Well, the terror cleanings would come to an end, too.

Helen uploaded the computer files, then closed the office curtains and clocked out at precisely six. She turned off the lights, shut the office door and waved good night to Julio, the weekend valet parker.

She was halfway to her car when she wondered if she'd locked the office door. She thought she did. She could picture herself turning the key in the lock. But was that a memory of another night, or did she lock the door this time? She knew she'd torment herself if she didn't go back and check.

She ran past the splashing fountains and velvety green lawns of the Superior Club. Even when she was in a hurry, she was struck by its beauty. If only it didn't have such ugly members.

Julio was at his valet stand, a fit coffee-skinned man who ran to retrieve members' cars as if it were an Olympic competition.

"Back so soon?" Julio asked. She liked his soft island accent.

"Couldn't stay away," Helen said. "I'm checking to see if I locked the door."

"Of course you did," Julio said. "You are not careless. But go put your mind at ease."

Helen jiggled the door handle. The office was definitely locked.

"Was I not right?" Julio said, when she walked past him again.

"Yes," Helen said and waved good night again. On the walk to the car, she saw a fat round raccoon washing its food in a marble fountain. Even the animals here lived a superior life, Helen thought.

Her life in customer care was about to improve. Brenda, the woman who delighted in disrupting and tormenting the staff, would be gone.

Helen couldn't wait to spring her surprise tomorrow. They would be free of Brenda at last. Helen would be a hero.

She steered the rumbling Toad homeward, singing, "Freedom! Freedom!" all the way up I-95. She did a little dance on the sidewalk at the Coronado. Thumbs greeted her at the door and she gave him an ear scratch.

"How about a can of tuna, old buddy?" she asked. "You should celebrate, too."

Phil, bless him, had made the bed and washed the coffee cups. He left a note propped on the pillow, next to her teddy bear, Chocolate: "Out by the pool with Margery, Peggy and Fat Bastard. Come join us when you get in."

She changed into the new white shorts and flirty sandals she bought as a present to herself when she got this job. It was time to celebrate her victory with her friends. Later, she and Phil could have a private celebration back here.

She was still smiling when she reached the pool. Margery, Phil, Peggy and Pete were stretched out on chaise lounges. Damn, her man looked good. Peggy was pale and weary. Pete was nuzzling her neck protectively. Margery looked like a grape Popsicle in her purple clam diggers. She was surrounded by her usual cloud of smoke.

"What got into you?" Margery said.

"I'm about to get rid of half my problems at the Superior Club." Helen kissed Phil, poured herself a glass of wine, pulled over another chaise, and told them she'd found the missing Winderstine file—and the information inside was explosive.

"Isn't that stuff in the computer?" Margery said.

"I checked. There were only brief notes on the drunken incident at the bar and the sixty-day past-due notice," Helen said. "There was also a comment about the change of address during February. But I wouldn't have understood what it meant unless I'd seen that information about Sonny's art collection in the file folder.

"That was the crucial part: There's expensive—and relatively unguarded—art in the Winderstine home. That's the kind of information Rob would buy.

"Rob really needed someone combing the files for full documentation. Those paper files have incredibly damaging information: whose lover is banned from the club for selling drugs, which members started drunken fights in the bar, whose children destroyed club property.

"I've seen letters of reprimand and revocation of privileges. There are copies of court orders when ex-boyfriends stalk club members—or in one sad case, ran off with a lover's jewelry. I've seen death certificates, divorce decrees and child custody agreements."

"Don't you think someone might want to know that this Winderstine person got behind paying his bills?" Peggy asked.

"It was only eight hundred dollars," Helen said.

"It would take me more than a year to pay off a credit card debt that big," Peggy said.

"Me, too," Helen said. "But that's pocket change for the club members. They often forget to pay their bills when they switch banks or go on a long trip. That's what Mr. Winderstine said happened to him."

"What did you do with the file?" Margery asked.

"I left it where I found it, hidden under Brenda's desk pad. Kitty needs to see it in place. I'll show it to her first thing tomorrow. She'll go ballistic. You can't believe what we've had to listen to. Solange has been demanding that file for days and Brenda's been hanging on to it all that time. It will be the end of one rotten assistant manager."

"How are you going to explain you were snooping through Brenda's desk?" Margery asked.

"I wasn't snooping," Helen said. "I'll say I was looking for the missing guest pass forms. Brenda rearranged the supply cabinet again and I couldn't find them. I still haven't."

Phil had been silent until now. He'd listened carefully while Helen told her story and Margery and Peggy peppered her with questions. When he finally spoke, he said exactly what Helen thought he would.

"Helen, aren't you moving a little fast here? You found that file hidden on Brenda's desk, but she might have another reason for it to be there. She's devious. She doesn't think like you. She could even have a legitimate reason. Maybe you'd better wait until you know more. You have to be careful before you attack an ambitious boss."

"The only other reason she would have that file would be to make trouble for our department—and she did that already with her memo to Mr. Ironton," Helen said. "She has to be Rob's source, Phil. She's been selling him the information in the files. She kept this file because she was waiting for his call. Except he never called. That's more proof Rob is dead. No wonder Brenda was so eager to report my fight with Rob to security. She has to find Rob to get her bribe money. Nailing me is a bonus."

"Is she in debt?" Margery said.

"I know she's had a lot of expensive cosmetic surgery that's not covered by our medical insurance. She has to need money," Helen said. "I got her, fair and square. I can't prove to Solange that she's been selling club secrets, but this will be good enough for Marcella. And no matter what, once Solange finds out that file was hidden under Brenda's desk pad, she'll be fired for sure. Solange has been looking for an excuse for a long time."

"Well, if you're really sure," Phil said. He didn't sound sure. But Helen was.

"You know, without Brenda stirring up trouble," she said, "I think I could handle the nasty members. I could learn to like this job.

"Tomorrow, Brenda will be gone for good. My whole life will be different. I'm right. You'll see."

Helen raised her wineglass in a triumphant salute to herself.

She was absolutely right. Her life would be different. It would be a whole lot worse.

CHAPTER 14

Monday morning, the sun was shining. The birds were singing. And so was Helen. Today she would nail Brenda.

Helen leaped out of bed with a few choruses of "Freedom! Freedom! Freeeeeeedom!" Too bad those were the only words she knew. After she exhausted the song's artistic possibilities, she switched to Meat Loaf's "Paradise by the Dashboard Light." Helen knew all the words to that song.

By the time she'd reached I-95, Helen was wailing Steppenwolf's "Born to Be Wild." The words, as mangled by Helen, were a good accompaniment to the Toad on the road, especially the line, "I like smoke and thunder." The Toad was smoking and thundering. Also rattling and shaking.

Helen was supposed to open the customer care office at eight this morning. She wanted to get there early for half an hour of off-the-clock snooping, but a small red Pontiac derailed that plan. It slid into a blue minivan near Ives Dairy Road and blocked three lanes of traffic.

Helen's song died on her lips, replaced by cajoling curses. The Toad rumbled along at high speeds, but stalled in slow traffic. "Come on, you stupid car," she said to the bucking, belching Toad. "Don't die on me now. It's not fair. I haven't paid off the last repairs."

She alternately pumped the gas and slammed on the brakes as the traffic slowed and stopped, slowed and stopped. She prayed the worthless rust bucket wouldn't die and block the last open lane.

Finally, the highway opened up and Helen zigzagged in and out of traffic, trying to make up for lost time. She wasn't late after all. Helen waved to the guard at the employee gate. Seven forty-five. Still time to do a second quick search of the office.

The path to customer care was like her own private nature walk. Long-legged white egrets waded delicately in the reflecting pool. Fat black ducks with red beaks paddled in the golf course pond. Mourning doves cooed softly in the shrubbery. There was the comfortable drone of a mower on a distant lawn.

Helen pulled out her key, but the office wasn't locked. Odd. She'd checked that door last night. Double-checked. Helen knew she'd locked it. She remembered her conversation with Julio, the weekend valet. Maybe Cameron came in early to work off the time he'd spent on his condo closing.

Then she remembered. The golf course opened at seven. Brenda had a game with Blythe St. Ives. But that wasn't until eleven, was it? She wouldn't come in this early. Did Brenda have to practice to lose those games with Blythe?

Helen hoped not. It would ruin her search plans.

Then she had a horrible thought: What if the missing file wasn't on Brenda's desk this morning? What if the proof against Brenda was gone? It would be just like the treacherous assistant manager to come in early and hide the Winderstine file somewhere else—or even put it back where it belonged.

Damn, Helen thought. I should have called Kitty at home last night and told her what I'd found. But no, I had to savor my triumph. I had to hold on to it like a miser. Now I've lost it.

The office door swung open at Helen's touch. The lights were on. Helen knew she'd turned them off yesterday.

"Hello?" she said.

Silence.

The curtains were still closed. Her co-workers' desks were undisturbed. Cam wasn't in yet.

"Hello?" Helen said again.

She looked in Solange's office, then Kitty's. Their offices had the heavy stillness of busy rooms before the day's work began. Kitty still had Mr. Giles's dying roses on her desk. One petal had fallen on her teddy bear.

Kitty and Solange weren't in yet. It had to be Brenda. She'd come in early and discovered someone had searched her desk.

I'm a dead woman if she finds out it was me, Helen thought. She will, too. One look at the schedule and she'll know I was here alone Sunday.

Helen checked Brenda's office. Her desk seemed untouched, but there was a pile of clothes tossed on the floor. A white blouse and a black suit. She saw the Superior Club crest on the jacket: a customer care uniform. There was something else. A white hand.

No. That couldn't be right.

Helen moved around the desk for a closer look. A half-naked Brenda lay on the floor behind the desk. She was wearing only a pink golf skirt. Her skinny stick arms were splayed. Her new breasts were obscenely perky. There was a bloody golf club next to her head and red arcs and spatters on the ice-white walls.

Brenda had been beaten to death with her own seven iron.

She wasn't alone. Brenda was lying next to the philandering plastic surgeon. The hirsute Dr. Rodelle Dell was fully clothed in his golfing togs. Helen wouldn't be caught dead in that yellow-and-green plaid.

The doctor was reaching for Brenda's bare breast, like a dead god trying to touch his creation one last time.

Helen heard an odd high-pitched sound, somewhere between a scream and a whine. She realized she was making that noise. She backed out of the office and called the club's emergency number from her desk. Her fingers felt numb and clumsy.

"Security," a man said.

Helen took a deep breath. Her voice was frighteningly calm. "This is Helen in customer care. We have a problem. A big one. Two people are dead. In the office. One's a member and one is an employee."

"This is Steven," the man said. "You know me. Xaviera! Please tell me she's OK."

Helen could hear his fear. "She's fine. She's not here. No one's here but me and—" Her teeth were chattering. She couldn't say the names.

"Helen? Are you still there?" Steven said. "You are alone in that office?"

"Yes. I think so. I just reported for work and found them."

"Get out of there now. Lock the door and don't let anyone in. Don't let any of the customer care staff leave the area. Keep them there. I'll be right over. I'll bring help. You're going to be OK."

Helen's hands shook so badly, she could hardly turn the key in the lock. She paced up and down the veranda outside the office while she waited. She took deep breaths and tried to think.

Brenda was dead. Brenda was dead. The words were a drumbeat in her head.

Yesterday, she'd wanted her sneaky boss dead. The whole office did. But not like this.

Who killed her? Everyone on the staff had a key to the office. Was Helen working with a murderer? Was anyone in her office angry enough to bludgeon two people?

She couldn't see Cam killing them—too many germs.

Jessica or Jackie? Now there was a joke. Meek little Jackie was too frightened to argue with Brenda. Jessica never fought. She was too laid back.

Xaviera? She had the fury, but she wouldn't beat two people to death and run. Xaviera was no coward. She'd stood up to Brenda. She'd kill them and confess.

There was Demi, the doctor's long-suffering wife. She played tennis and had quite an arm. Dr. Dell was notoriously unfaithful. Would Dr. Dell have an affair with Brenda when he had a sweet wife like Demi?

Of course he would. He not only cheated on his wife, he was unfaithful to his mistress. What about the staffer who "relaxed" at the club?

Helen didn't find Brenda's stringy body and surgically enhanced breasts attractive, but a surprising number of men fell for fake boobs. Brenda was the doctor's own personal do-it-yourself project.

But their affair was only gossip. It might have ended long ago—or never happened. Once a man had a reputation as a hound, every woman he said hello to was labeled a conquest. Suppose Dr. Dell had simply seen the open door and cut through the customer care office to the golf course, the way so many members did? He'd walked in at the wrong time and wound up murdered. What a stupid death.

Helen had another scary thought: Was Brenda killed by the same person who'd murdered Rob?

The Winderstine file! Where was it? Was it still hidden under Brenda's desk pad? Helen had to know fast. Security would arrive any moment. She unlocked the office door with fumbling fingers, then stopped abruptly at Brenda's door. She couldn't see anything but that hand and those dark red spatters on the wall, but she felt some force push her back.

It's your own fear, she told herself.

There was a powerful stink when she entered the room. How could I have missed that the first time? she thought.

But she knew. The mind couldn't take in all the room's horrors at once.

She tiptoed over to Brenda's desk and moved the desk blotter. The Winderstine file was gone.

Oh, no, Helen thought. No, no, no.

She backed out of the room and managed to lock the office door again.

Brenda wasn't whacked by an irate wife or a jealous lover. She was killed for that file. Helen couldn't say anything to anyone. She couldn't even prove she'd seen it.

She heard the putt-putt of the golf carts, and four security guards swung in front of the office. Steven was riding shotgun with Marshall Noote, the head of security. Noote dismounted and hitched up his trousers: John Wayne in a club blazer.

"What seems to be the problem?" Noote asked. He could barely hide his dislike of Helen.

"There are two dead people," Helen said. "I found them when I came in to work."

"What did you touch?" It was an accusation.

"The door. My phone to call you. That's all, I think."

"Stay out here," Noote said.

Helen never wanted to go back in there again.

She heard a flurry of footsteps. "Helen, what's going on? Why is security all over the place? Was there a break-in?" It was Jessica, looking fresh and rested on Monday morning.

"No, much worse. It's—"

Noote interrupted. "No talking. Not until the police question you."

"The police?" The color drained from Jessica's face. "What's happening?"

"You'll find out soon enough," Noote said. He turned to a thick-necked security guard. "Take them over to the main building and put them in separate rooms. Don't let them hang out together and compare notes. That's the fastest way to screw up an investigation.

"You!" He pointed to the other guard with a neck like a tree trunk. "Do the same thing with the rest of the customer care staff as they arrive. A different room for each one and no talking. We're following procedure. I run this department by the book."

"But what about the office?" Jessica said. "Who'll take care of the members?"

"They can take care of themselves for one day. This office is closed. It's a crime scene."

"Oh, man," Jessica whispered. "Those phones will be radioactive tomorrow. What's happening?"

"I said no talking!" Noote barked, and Jessica clamped her mouth shut. She looked frightened.

Helen and Jessica rode off in silence in the silly striped golf cart. The guard made Helen ride up front. Jessica sat alone in the back, clutching her purse like a security blanket. Helen saw Xaviera and

Cam strolling down the path together, laughing and chatting. Their day was about to be ruined, too.

At the hotel, security confiscated Helen's cell phone. She was stashed in the Granada Room, a poky meeting place that was almost never used. It had been stripped of everything but a folding chair and a bare table.

Helen stared out the window at the parking lot. She could hear the sirens baying. It looked like half the police cars in South Florida were out there, parked at haphazard angles. There were also crime scene vans, unmarked cars and vehicles whose purpose she couldn't begin to identify.

She paced up and down on the worn carpet, too restless to sit. The room was warm, but her teeth were still chattering. Shock, she thought. I'm in shock. She unwrapped an energy bar, took two bites, then remembered Brenda's last angry words to her about eating in the office. She saw Brenda's battered, bloody body and lost her appetite. Helen threw the rest of the bar away.

She wished she could feel bad about Brenda, but she was glad the woman was dead. That made her feel worse. She couldn't feel anything about Dr. Dell. He'd been a bully, too. If nice Mr. Giles had died, she'd be weeping buckets. This numb hatred made her feel sick and dirty.

Helen counted the cracks in the plaster ceiling. She counted the dead flies on the window sill. She'd started counting police cars when she was called in for questioning by Golden Palms homicide.

A uniformed officer escorted her to another meeting room. Helen didn't know Detective O'Shaughnessy, but he seemed to know her. He treated her with respectful contempt, as if she could do a lot of damage—like a ticking bomb. She guessed that's what happened when you had Gabe Accomac for your lawyer.

The homicide detective could have been Marshall Noote's younger brother. His hair was sandy blond instead of gray, but he had the same military haircut, thick neck and beefy face. She'd bet O'Shaughnessy's father and grandfather had been cops, too. The detective never mentioned her missing ex, but Rob seemed to be there, spreading suspicion and discord, the way he did when he was alive.

Now he'd caused the deaths of two more people. Helen was convinced Brenda was murdered for the Winderstine file. She didn't say that, of course. She didn't mention the file at all. She didn't want to talk about her deal with the Black Widow.

She had trouble concentrating on the detective's questions. He asked if Dr. Dell had any enemies. Helen said she didn't know. She'd only met him briefly when he had a question about his bill.

Was the doctor having an affair with Brenda?

"I don't know," Helen said. Well, she didn't. Not for sure.

Did Brenda have any enemies?

Helen knew she'd better answer this truthfully. "She didn't have a lot of friends among the customer care staff. But that was office politics. I don't think anyone would kill her for that."

"Then why would they kill her?" the detective asked.

"I don't know," Helen lied.

He didn't believe her. He asked her the same questions again and again. She tried to keep her answers straight. She wanted to put her head down on the table and sleep. Finally, O'Shaughnessy let her go after she signed a statement. A tech took her fingerprints "for the process of elimination." Helen wondered why the police bothered. They'd find staff fingerprints on every surface in the office.

She retrieved her cell phone from security and found a text message: "We're all meeting at Cam's condo after."

Helen didn't have to ask after what. The message had the address to Cam's new condo in Fort Lauderdale. He lived in a big pink building on the Intracoastal Waterway. Cam's building had all the signs of Florida luxury: bubbling fountains, pricey landscaping, acres of awnings and a grumpy security guard who made her hide the unsightly Toad behind the garage.

Helen signed in at the front desk and took the oak-paneled elevator to the tenth floor.

"Come in, come in," Cam said. "You're the last to arrive."

The apartment was a knockout—a sweeping view of the Intracoastal Waterway. Cam's apartment was furnished in Tropical Guy: a fat brown leather sofa and big comfortable chairs, wicker lamps, a teak elephant footstool and a woven sea-grass rug.

"Nice," Helen said.

Cam looked at home here. His big, awkward frame blended well with the oversized furniture. The sofa seemed to swallow Jessica and Jackie. Both sat pale and silent, clutching their water bottles. Xaviera drummed her long painted nails on the chair arm.

Kitty perched on the teak elephant, sipping a diet soda. The woman who'd tried to undermine the manager was dead, but Brenda's murder had brought Kitty more trouble. There were dark circles under her brown eyes.

Cam was too jittery to sit. He kept using his puffer. "My asthma is triggered by stress," he said.

Xaviera rolled her eyes.

Jessica, the peacemaker, made them compare notes about the morning. Helen knew the most.

"You actually found the body?" Xaviera said.

"What did she look like?" Cam asked. "Was she all bloody and bashed in?"

"Please, no." Jackie started making tiny hurt-mouse sounds. Her eyes were a raw red. Helen knew this wasn't the first time she'd cried today.

Xaviera came over and hugged her. "Please, Jackie, do not cry. Brenda's murder is a good thing. Whoever killed her did us all a favor. She can't torment us anymore. She's dead and I'm glad." She looked defiantly around the room, daring anyone to disagree.

"I am, too," Cam said.

"I won't miss her," Jessica said.

"I would have killed her myself, sweetpea, if she was in that office much longer," Kitty said. One brown curl had collapsed on her forehead. "I'm in serious need of relaxation. Cam, do you have any wine?"

"I have something better," Cam said, and carried out a hookah—the first Helen had seen outside a movie. "Wait till you try this. I use a mixture of half pot and half tobacco. A few puffs and you're so incredibly mellow. You won't care what happened today."

"I don't do drugs," Jackie said.

"Oh, Jackie," Xaviera said. "If anyone needs to relax, it's you."

"No, I prefer not to." Jackie gathered up her battered Chanel purse and fled.

"What about you, Helen?" Cam said. "You don't object, do you?"

"Of course not," Helen said. "Can I use your john?"

"Down the hall," Cam said.

Helen didn't care about a little pot, but she didn't like Cameron having a hold over her. The club had strict rules about drugs and could order random drug tests. She wished Kitty would leave now, before the hookah started bubbling. If their boss ever needed to discipline the crafty Cam, she wouldn't be able to after a pot party.

Helen sat on the commode in Cam's tasteful slate-gray bathroom and called Margery. "I have a situation," she whispered into her cell phone. "I'll explain later. I need you to call me back on my cell in about a minute. I have to get out of here. Make up an excuse."

"I won't have to," Margery said. "Marcella wants to see you. Now."

CHAPTER 15

Monday started with a murder. Now it would end with the Black Widow. Could it get any worse?

Helen couldn't see any way to escape meeting Rob's wife again. She'd asked Margery to get her out of Cam's condo. Her landlady had granted her wish. Some escape. The alternative was far worse than a silly pot party. Now Helen had to walk back into Marcella's private, perfumed hell alone.

This time, no lawyered limo took her to the yacht club. Helen parked the rumbling Toad in the Superior Club's employee lot and followed the path to the yacht basin.

It was dusk. Purple night clouds were sliding across the sky. The January air was cool. Flocks of black birds were settling in the trees for the night, twittering to each other. The hibiscus were closing. Their red ruffled parasols opened for one day in a great, gaudy show. Then it was all over.

It was also over for Brenda and the doctor. They'd gone out in a horrific splash of red. Then there were the arcs of blood all over the parking lot where Helen had last seen Rob. There was too much death in this little paradise. Helen shivered, but not from the cold.

Marcella's white shark of a yacht loomed above her, dwarfing the club building. Once again, Helen was greeted on deck by the silent, shiny-domed Bruce. This time, she noticed the *Brandy Alexander* had five radar domes, shaped like Bruce's round head.

She almost blurted that out, then reconsidered. Bruce had serious muscles. She didn't think Marcella kept him around because he was ornamental.

Marcella was sitting on the back deck at the same white table with the flickering candles. Two outdoor heaters, like the ones used in expensive restaurants, warded off the night chill. Three more champagne goblets were lined up in front of Marcella—another trio of Bond martinis.

Bruce brought Helen a crystal glass of water with a thin lemon slice. It was exactly what she wanted, until the glass was in front of her. Then she wanted something, anything else.

Helen wondered if this was what it was like to be fabulously rich: Your every wish was anticipated, until you began to wish for something you couldn't imagine.

Tonight, Marcella looked old and powerful. She hadn't bothered putting on her harsh, bright makeup and her dark dyed hair washed the color from her face. Helen could see the predatory intelligence in the woman's eyes. She wished she knew what Marcella was thinking—or maybe not. She'd seen eyes like Marcella's only once, on a shark.

"I heard you found the bodies," Marcella said, studying Helen with those flat eyes.

The club had clamped down on any information about the deadly scandal. The murders hadn't made the news yet and Helen's role would probably never be public. But Marcella could afford the finest spies.

Helen told her everything she knew: the half-naked Brenda and the fully dressed doctor, the missing file, which was missing again, and the bloody golf club.

While Helen talked, Marcella started spinning the champagne goblet between her red nails. "So do you think these murders are about sex or money?" Marcella went straight for the heart.

Spin. Spin. The martini goblet was whirling. Helen stared at it, hypnotized by the movement.

She shook herself free, then said, "Money. I think the killer tried to make the murders look like sex, but they were really about money. That missing file has valuable information."

"Sonny Winderstine's art collection?" Marcella asked.

"Yes. It gives the dates when Sonny and Sawyer will be out of the country and the collection will be easier to steal. I'm pretty sure that's it, though there are other possibilities worth paying for in that file."

"You mean the eight hundred dollars in arrears?"

"Yes," Helen said.

"Ridiculous," Marcella said. "No one here would care about that." Helen felt the insult in those words: You might worry about petty cash, but my world doesn't. The Black Widow's martini whirled madly. Helen had to pull her eyes away from it to concentrate on the conversation.

"And you think Rob was buying this information?" Marcella asked.

"Absolutely," Helen said. "I also think he's dead. Otherwise, that file would be back where it belonged, Brenda would have her bribe money, and no one would be the wiser. It was just bad luck that Winderstine mouthed off in the club restaurant and Solange needed to see his file. It could have sat unnoticed under Brenda's desk pad for months. Do you know Sawyer Winderstine?"

"Who?" Marcella said.

"Sawyer Winderstine," Helen said. "The name on the file."

"I've heard of his wife, Sonny," Marcella said. "He's nobody. Some tiresome climber who joined the club because it was good for business. I try not to associate with those people. Do you think this Winderstine person killed Brenda and that doctor?"

"No," Helen said. "Winderstine is a corporate wonk. He wouldn't have the nerve."

"You'd be surprised how far a man will go to get what he wants," Marcella said.

Helen gulped her water. The Black Widow knew exactly how far a man—or a woman—would go. She'd gone there.

"Winderstine didn't need to kill anyone," Helen said. "If he found out a member was selling information, he could complain to the club. Rob would be banned and Brenda would be fired. That's easier, and more effective, than killing anyone."

"So it would make more sense if Rob killed Winderstine," Marcella said.

"No," Helen said. "That wouldn't make any sense at all. Rob had no reason to kill anyone."

Why am I defending my ex? she wondered. Because he's an adulterer and a leech, not a killer.

"Rob needed a mole inside customer care," Helen said. "He wouldn't kill Brenda. He'd use her and pay her. But I don't think he bought that information in the Winderstine file yet. There's no evidence that anyone has acted on it. I can check, but I'm sure the Winderstine art collection is still safe at home."

"Well, somebody killed that woman and the doctor," Marcella said. "I need to know why. There are too many cops poking around that office. If this art thing leaks . . ."

She didn't finish the rest of the sentence. She didn't have to. If her husband was selling club information, Marcella would be shunned by the only society that still accepted her.

She stopped spinning the martini and tossed it off in one gulp. "I need to find Rob."

The Black Widow gripped the glass so hard, the fragile stem snapped. "I need to know what he's done." A thin red line of blood ran down her fingers.

Marcella didn't notice.

CHAPTER 16

Helen drove home, feeling like she'd been wrapped in ice. The January night and the double murder were chilling. But that wasn't what left her cold. The Black Widow froze Helen down to the bone. The woman wasn't human.

Helen had seen Marcella slice her fingers till the blood ran, yet she didn't react. Could the Black Widow even feel pain? Did she know what she inflicted on herself and other people?

Helen had left Marcella staring into the dark water. The silent, servile Bruce had guided her to the dock. Then Helen ran for her car as if the devil were after her.

I have to get free of this woman, she thought. I was so close. Then Brenda got herself killed and ruined everything.

No, I let that file sit there overnight and lost my chance. And Brenda lost her life.

Who killed Brenda? And why? Helen pounded the Toad's steering wheel in frustration. She couldn't think of a single reason. Brenda's death made no sense. Neither did the doctor's.

Helen was relieved when she finally saw the warm yellow glow of the

Coronado's windows. She pulled the lumbering Toad into the parking lot and sat there in the dark. She felt overwhelmed and defeated. The day had been too long and it had held too many horrors: the battered bodies, the missing file, the meeting with Marcella. She put her head down on the hard steering wheel and closed her eyes, too tired to move.

"Helen? Are you OK?"

Helen sat up suddenly. Phil was knocking on her car window. His silver hair formed a halo around his long thin face. Peggy and Margery stood behind him, looking worried. Peggy's skin was paper white in the streetlights. She looked like a beautiful wraith. Margery's wrinkles were deep as furrows in a dry field.

Helen cranked down the Toad's window. "Sorry. I must have fallen asleep."

"When's the last time you ate?" Margery said.

Helen remembered the energy bar she'd thrown away. Lunch had been lost in the police interrogation.

"Breakfast," Helen said.

"That was twelve hours ago," Margery said. "You need food."

"I'll heat up some chicken soup," Peggy said.

"I'll make you a sandwich," Phil said. "I have turkey and rye bread."

That sounded good to Helen, until she remembered that Phil's sandwiches often had strange, smelly surprises. "No sour cream or raw onions," she said.

"But those make it interesting," Phil said.

"No ketchup, red pepper flakes or hot sauce," Helen said.

"You like it too bland," Phil said.

"Just slap some turkey on bread and don't argue," Margery said, shooing Phil toward his apartment. She waved her lit cigarette like a cattle prod. "Helen is light-headed from stress and hunger. Two bodies in one day are too much."

Helen hadn't told her landlady about the murders. She wondered if Marcella had filled her in.

"I'm taking her to my place," Margery said. "Bring the food there."

Margery's soft purple recliner felt like welcoming arms. Helen sank into the old easy chair, and Margery brought her hot coffee. Helen wrapped her hands around it to warm them. She heard the beep of a microwave, and her landlady came back with a heated brownie.

"Eat dessert first," she said. "Life is short."

"It certainly was for Brenda and Dr. Dell," Helen said.

The brownie was gooey and sweet. She ate it in three bites and felt better. By that time, Peggy returned with a bowl of microwaved soup in her hands and Pete on her shoulder. The parrot was clutching a cracker and had no plans to share it.

Phil handed Helen a thick turkey sandwich on a plate. It was plain, the way she liked it, with a dill pickle on the side and no surprises. Helen didn't like surprises. She'd had too many unpleasant ones. She surveyed her meal and gave a little sigh of satisfaction. Between bites, she told them about her day.

Margery poured wine for herself and Peggy. Phil opened a beer and perched on the recliner's arm. Pete nibbled his cracker.

When Helen finished, Peggy said, "And you really believe the murders are related to Rob's disappearance?"

"They have to be," Helen said. "That missing file clinches it. I just can't figure out how they fit together."

"We need to know more," Phil said. "I've been doing some follow-up work. There's still no sign that Rob is alive. There's no activity on his credit cards or bank account."

"He's definitely dead," Helen said. "That man lived to spend money."

"Marcella throws it around, too. It's possible he accumulated a stash from her petty cash and he's living off it now," Phil said.

"Sort of the way my grandmother used to buy herself little luxuries with the pocket change my grandfather left on the dresser," Peggy said.

"Exactly," Phil said. "If Rob is alive, he'll lie low for a while, but eventually, we'll flush him out. People develop habits, and they return to them once they start to feel safe. That's how we catch them. I traced one woman because she loved a particular spiced tea from a shop in St. Louis.

When she relocated to Alaska, she held out for six months. Then she ordered her tea online, and that's how I tracked her down.

"That's how we'll find Rob, too, if he's still breathing. But I need your help, Helen. Did Rob have any special needs? Was he asthmatic or diabetic? Any medicine he had to take? Anything he couldn't live without?"

"Rob was healthy," Helen said. "When I knew him, he didn't even take cholesterol pills. He did tell me he used Rogaine for his hair."

"That won't help," Phil said. "You can buy it at any drugstore without a prescription. I need something unique."

"I don't know what new habits he developed since he lived with Marcella," Helen said, "but the Rob I knew sponged off rich women. He liked to hang around where they gathered—upscale hotel bars, fancy restaurants and expensive malls."

"I've been checking those," Phil said. "No sign of him in Lauderdale, Miami or Palm Beach County. But it's too early for him to surface in those places. He knows people are looking for him."

"Does he?" Helen said. She was convinced her ex was dead. The unused credit cards and bank account were proof.

Margery stayed oddly silent. Pete gnawed his cracker, dropping crumbs on Peggy's shoulder.

"Help me out here," Phil said. "What are his luxuries? What does he drink?"

"Wine or beer, but when he had the money, he preferred Laphroaig single malt scotch."

"Good," Phil said. "That's unusual enough I can track it."

"He drank a lot of coffee, but he wasn't a Starbucks fan," Helen said. "He was addicted to Ronnoco coffee. That's a St. Louis brand. You can buy that online, too."

"That helps," Phil said. "He'll chug along with supermarket coffee for a while, and then one day the craving for his favorite will hit him hard and he'll need a caffeine fix."

"If he's alive," Helen said, "Rob won't forgo his indulgences for long. I doubt if he'll hold out six months."

"The sooner we find him, the better," Phil said. "Talk to Marcella next time you see her, and see if he's developed any new indulgences."

Helen paled at that thought, and saw Margery studying her. Helen took a comforting sip of her cooling coffee.

"I'm going to check with my police contacts to see if I can learn anything more about the double murders at the club," Phil said. "I still have things I can look into that could help turn up Rob."

"Maybe the girlfriend killed him," Peggy said.

"Awk!" Pete said.

"What girlfriend?" Phil said.

"The dead doctor's." Peggy had changed the subject with lightning speed. "Didn't he send a staffer to your club for a three-thousand-dollar day of relaxation?"

"Yep," Helen said. "The doctor didn't want his wife, Demi, to see the bill and made a big scene. I'm sure the police are checking out the wife and girlfriend. But I can do some snooping on my own."

"How are you going to find out anything about the doc's love life?" Phil said.

"I have my ways." Helen managed a grin, her first since she'd left the Black Widow.

"Yoo-hoo, anyone home?" Dithery Elsie was knocking on Margery's jalousie door.

"I'm not sure I'm ready for Elsie tonight," Margery said, softly.

"She's sweet. Let her in," Helen said. "It's been a horrible day. Elsie will cheer us up."

Margery opened the door. Elsie breezed in wearing a sheer red top over a black-sequined bustier. Helen thought there was a wide pink belt around her hips, and then realized that was Elsie's bare skin. She'd forced her considerable self into black velvet lowriders, and they were stretched to the limit.

"Awk!" Pete dropped his cracker.

"Wow. Look at you," Margery said. "Those clothes are brand-new. Did you win the lottery?"

"I'm going to," Elsie said. "I have the winning ticket." She held up a bottle of champagne. "You're going to help me celebrate."

"Are you sure you've won?" Margery said. "Have you turned in the ticket yet?"

"I know this ticket is a winner," Elsie said in her soft, feathery voice. "There's no doubt. The numbers match the ones printed in the paper."

Margery set her wineglass down with a thump. "Well, why are you standing there? Let's go claim your winnings."

"Oh, no, not yet. I'm waiting for the young woman to come back with the ticket. She wasn't feeling well. I'm going to meet her tomorrow."

There was a frozen silence. Then Margery said, "What young woman?"

"The one I bought the winning ticket from," Elsie said.

"Awk!" Pete said.

"You'd better explain." Margery looked grim.

"You told me to make sure I bought a winner," Elsie said, clutching her champagne by the neck. "There's this nice young man who does odd jobs in our neighborhood. I told him I needed to win the lottery and he said his girlfriend from Haiti had this week's winning ticket. It's fourteen million dollars. But she couldn't claim it because she was an illegal immigrant. It's awful how people discriminate. This young woman—her name is Maria—"

"I bet," Margery said.

"Maria sold me half of her winning ticket for fifteen thousand dollars cash. Not a bad investment, is it? Seven million for fifteen thousand. And lucky for both of us."

Everyone groaned.

Elsie looked sweetly befuddled. "Aren't you happy for me?" she asked.

"Where did you get fifteen thousand in cash?" Margery said.

"I gave them my mother's diamond engagement ring. It's worth about thirty-five thousand, but they'll have to pawn it to get the money. The nice young man told me the pawn shops are in bad neighborhoods, so he'd do the pawning for me."

"Elsie!" Margery said. "You didn't!"

"It's OK," Elsie said. "He gave me a receipt for the ring. I'm not a complete ditz."

"Awk!" Pete said.

Margery put her head in her hands.

Elsie dithered on with her story. "I have the receipt right here," she said. "It's signed Juan Garcia."

"That's Spanish for John Smith," Peggy said.

"We have a lot of John Smiths, too," Elsie said. "Most are perfectly trustworthy. If I may continue my story, Juan gave me a receipt. He promised to pawn the ring, and then he and Maria were going to meet me in the park and give me the winning ticket. Except at the last minute, the young woman called. Maria sounded really sick. She said she had the flu. She promised they'd meet me tomorrow morning, first thing.

"If you ask me," Elsie said, dropping her voice to a confiding whisper, "I don't think it's the flu. I think she's in the family way."

"I think you're screwed," Phil said.

"No, no," Elsie said. "They're a nice young couple. They wouldn't do anything bad."

"They already did," Phil said. "It's a scam, Elsie. An old twist on the pigeon drop."

"You're the pigeon," Margery said.

"Awk!" Pete said.

"No," Elsie said, but now her old eyes were dark with fear. The celebration champagne was abandoned on a side table. Elsie was wringing her hands. "No, that can't be right. I saw the ticket. The numbers matched."

"They were altered," Phil said.

"I'm sure if we go to the park—"

"They're gone," Phil said. "You gave them enough for a first-class ticket out of town."

"It's my mother's ring," Elsie said. "I promised it to my granddaughter when she graduated from college. Now I've given it to a stranger. I'm such a fool."

She sat down heavily on the couch.

"This is all my fault," Margery said. "I told Elsie to buy a winning lottery ticket and she got scammed."

"It's my fault, too," Peggy said. "I told Elsie to buy the ticket in the first place."

"No, you're very kind to share the blame, but it's all my fault," Elsie said, miserably. "I've been had again. I can't believe I was so trusting."

"We'd better call the police," Margery said.

"No, please," Elsie said. "My son Milton will find out and have me declared incompetent. He'll put me in an old folks' home. I have to get my mother's ring back or he'll find out."

"We'll help you," Margery said. "Phil will find it. He'll check the pawnshops. Do you have a description of the ring?"

"I have a photo," Elsie said. "Milton made me photograph my valuables for insurance purposes."

"Thank god he's a tight-ass," Margery said.

CHAPTER 17

"I am Mrs. Hadley Kent-Jones. I've been a Superior member for twenty years."

Helen winced and held the phone away from her abused ear. The woman had a well-bred accent and a screech like a wild parrot. "I demand to be placed at the top of the list. The top! Do you hear me?"

"Yes, ma'am," Helen said, her ears aching. I'd have to be deaf not to, she thought.

"First, it was that disgraceful sex in the club men's room," Mrs. Kent-Jones said. "Mother was there."

"She was?" Helen said.

"She was having dinner with me in the restaurant while that—that behavior—was going on. She saw the security guards escorting the woman out the door. I was mortified. How could I explain it to Mother?"

Unless Mrs. Kent-Jones was delivered by FedEx, Mother probably knew about sex. Helen suspected the scandal thrilled the old lady to the tips of her Pappagallo flats.

"Now it's murder," Mrs. Kent-Jones said. "Two murders! Put me at the top of your resignation list. I want my refund *now.*"

Her shriek hit a pitch so high, Helen thought every dog in Golden Palms would start howling.

"I promise you are at the top of my list," Helen said, as the screecher slammed down her phone.

"But it's not the list you want to be on, you old witch," Helen said to the dead phone.

She took Mrs. Kent-Jones's resignation letter off the top of the stack, where it had been resting comfortably, and buried it at the bottom under some sixty letters of resignation.

"You should have kept your big mouth shut, Mrs. Kent-Jones," Helen said to herself. "Now you'll have to wait an extra two months for your refund."

Jessica let out an unladylike snort. "Talking to yourself already this morning?"

"Do rich people take special obnoxious voice lessons?" Helen asked.

Jessica laughed. "It comes naturally, darling. Let me guess. Another resignation. I've had four so far this morning."

Helen tried to keep her eyes on Jessica during their conversation, but it took effort. She was irresistibly drawn to Brenda's still-sealed office. She couldn't stop staring at the dark door draped with yellow crime scene tape. She couldn't get the picture of that blood-spattered interior out of her mind. How many coats of paint would it take to cover those awful red splotches on the walls? Who would use that coffin-sized desk again? Helen saw the white hand reaching around it, and shuddered. Could office furniture be haunted?

Kitty had scented candles burning on the marble-topped counter to hide the awful odor from Brenda's office. Helen thought she could still smell it, but wondered if that was her imagination.

Kitty and Solange were in Mr. Ironton's office, discussing how to deal with the fallout from the murders. The managers had already briefed the customer care staff on funeral information (nothing at this time) and where people could send donations to the victims' favorite charities. So far, no one had asked.

Instead, the staff fended off irate calls from members and curious calls from other departments. They were all on edge. Cam kept wiping down his desk with alcohol spray until Xaviera finally said, "Murder isn't catching, Cam."

"I know that," he said. "But it's brought a lot of strangers into this office, and that means more germs."

"How can a big man be afraid of a little germ?" Xaviera said.

"They kill bigger men than me," Cam said.

"Please, stop. I can't take the bickering," Jackie said. She'd snapped another pencil in two, and her blue-veined hands shook. Stray hairs escaped her normally impeccable chignon.

Cam and Xaviera looked like two children who'd been caught fighting. Cam actually picked up the phone when it rang and talked to another angry club member.

Xaviera drummed her long painted nails until Helen wanted to grab her hands and make her stop.

Jessica was paler than usual, and the fragile skin under her eyes looked bruised. "These murders have everyone spooked," she said. "Staff and members both. People say the craziest things. One caller told me she was shocked that we had a double murder—she thought this was an exclusive club."

"It is," Helen said. "Only one member was killed. How exclusive is that?"

"Exclusivity is such a joke at this club," Jessica said. "We charge our members twenty thousand a year for air. They pay us to come on the property. That's all we give them, the right to drive through the member gate."

"When the gate works," Helen said.

"The poor fools think they're getting exclusivity. They don't realize we're a third-rate club. We have no board and no membership committee to vet new people. Our admission fee of fifty thousand dollars sounds like a lot of money, but it's cheap in this world. The really exclusive clubs start at a hundred thousand and they have strict standards. Members must be people of wealth, education and achievement. We have no standards, except that members must have money."

"This place is as exclusive as Sam's Club," Helen said.

"But the members aren't as nice," Jessica said. "There go the phones. Back into battle."

Helen had to listen to another complaint, this one in a clipped British voice. "I am Mrs. Jacob Rialto. I believe you closed the customer care office yesterday. How did you expect me to get my guest passes?"

"I'm sorry, ma'am," Helen said, "but the police would not permit us to open the office."

"That's the other reason I'm calling," Mrs. Rialto said. "The club entrance was blocked by police vehicles. The police should use the service entrance. It sets the wrong tone."

"I'll make a note of your complaint," Helen said.

She'd barely hung up before the phone rang again. Either she was tired, or the ring tones were starting to sound angry. "This is Mrs. Adriana Capetto. There were two murders at the club yesterday." The voice was an accusation.

"Yes, ma'am," Helen said carefully, while she searched the computer for the Capetto file. Mr. Capetto was big in trash hauling in New Jersey, she read. His mail was sent to a post office box in the Bahamas. Helen recognized the hallmarks of a mobster.

"I didn't join this club to associate with criminals," Mrs. Capetto said.

"Yes, ma'am," Helen said, and hung up the phone with a sigh.

"You look upset," Jessica said.

"I can't believe this. Two people were horribly murdered in this office, and the members don't care. Not one person has asked about the victims' families, funeral services, or if they should send flowers or food. All they care about is how it affects them."

"That's what they're like," Jessica said. "They can't help it."

"Doesn't anything human happen here?"

Xaviera popped up from her desk like a gopher from a hole. "My boyfriend, Steven, said old Mr. Smithson got caught having sex in the pool this morning. He's eighty-nine and the woman is forty-two."

"Is he going to get a letter of reprimand?" Helen asked.

"I think he's going to get a medal," Xaviera said.

Even Jackie managed a smile.

Helen's next phone call wiped away any trace of good feeling. It was Blythe St. Ives, the nasty lady golfer.

"I was unable to play golf at the club yesterday," Blythe said. "Because of the problem."

Because of the murders, Helen wanted to say. Because your golf partner, Brenda, who always let you win, lost big-time. Her head was bashed in with a seven iron. You played golf with her once a week. Aren't you going to say anything?

"I hope I'm not going to be charged for the tee time," Blythe said.

"I'll note it in your file," Helen said. Then, before she could stop herself, she added, "By the way, you can make a donation in Brenda's name to the cancer society."

"Why would I do that?" Blythe said, and hung up.

Helen was about to tell Jessica about Blythe's heartless reaction. Then she heard her desk mate deep in a whispered argument on her phone.

"What do you mean the city inspector didn't approve the new air conditioner?" Jessica said. There was a long pause. "My fault! It's not my fault that the contractor didn't use tie-down straps that could withstand hurricane-force winds."

Jessica began shaking her head and slapping the desktop. "No, I am not staying home to deal with the problem. It's your turn. *You* take off work for a change. I've had—"

Helen slipped down the hall to let Jessica argue with her husband in privacy.

I need some air, she thought. The club walls are closing in on me.

The only place staff was allowed to linger was the loading dock. It wasn't a garden spot, but it was outside. Well, sort of. Helen could see a slice of green lawn and tennis court over the Dumpsters.

Helen had barely cracked the door to the loading dock when she heard Xaviera, arguing with her blond surfer boyfriend. The two were facing each other, red-faced and rigid with anger.

"When are you getting that promotion, Steven?" Xaviera said. "I'm not getting any younger. I want a house. I want a baby." Helen could hear her desperation.

"I'm doing everything I can," Steven said. "I'm in line next for a promotion at the club. I've also applied for a job with the Lauderdale police. It's more money and better benefits. But I won't hear anything for a while."

"How long?" Xaviera stamped her foot. "I'm tired of waiting."

"Why don't you try for a promotion for a change?" Steven said, raising his voice and shaking his streaked blond hair. "There's a slot open in the club billing office."

"I will," Xaviera said. "But if I get it, I'll have to work longer hours."

"Maybe it's a good idea if we don't see so much of each other," Steven said. "At least we'll fight less."

Xaviera wheeled away and threw open the door with such fury she nearly hit Helen in the face. She didn't notice Helen as she pushed past, leaving a trail of perfume and hurt feelings. Xaviera's heels tapped her anger all the way down the hall.

Oh, boy, Helen thought. This is going to be one of those days. No point hanging around outside. The air is toxic. She went into the restroom, splashed cold water on her face and headed back to her desk. Her phone was ringing.

"Do you know who I am?" the caller screamed.

"Yes, ma'am," Helen said, as she looked up the woman's club number. But I'm starting to forget who I am, she thought.

By two o'clock, Helen felt like she'd been beaten by pros. There were no visible marks, but she hurt all over. She popped two Tylenol and broke out an energy bar. She ate her snack at her desk, with pleasure—or as much pleasure as she could get from something that tasted like sawdust and dried cranberries. Brenda wouldn't be lurking nearby, making her throw it away.

Except Brenda was there. Her restless, angry spirit seemed to fill the room. Helen's eyes were once more drawn to that sealed door.

The mahogany door to customer care swung open and Marshall Noote marched in with O'Shaughnessy, the Golden Palms detective who'd interviewed Helen before. Once again, she was struck by the resemblance between the two men. O'Shaughnessy could have been his thick-necked son.

"Uh-oh," Jessica said. "Trouble."

"I need to see Helen Hawthorne," Noote said.

Helen's heart was pounding. They're going to arrest me, she thought. Did they find Rob? Or is this for Brenda's murder?

"We have a few more questions," Noote said. His smile showed teeth like yellowed tombstones.

"Do I need to call my attorney?" Helen said. Her attorney. What a joke. She could afford maybe an hour of Gabe Accomac's time. That wasn't enough to fly him in from New York.

"Of course not," O'Shaughnessy said. He gave her a boyish smile. It was nicer than Noote's. Helen wondered if he practiced in front of the mirror. "This is a friendly chat. Just to clear up a few minor points. We don't have to go to the police station."

"We can use my office in security." Noote beamed like a proud father.

"If we use the security office, I'll definitely want my lawyer," Helen said. She was bluffing, but she didn't want to sit in Noote's office. It was his territory, and to her, it was the same as the police station.

"Let's find a nice quiet conference room," O'Shaughnessy said.

"Do you want me to call Margery?" Jessica whispered. She looked worried.

"Couldn't hurt," Helen said.

"I hope it will help," Jessica said, squeezing Helen's hand. "Good luck."

Helen followed Noote and O'Shaughnessy to the same room where the detective had interviewed her about Brenda. There was something dismal about an unused conference room, with its bare tables and dusty chandeliers. A half-filled coffee cup with a drowned cigarette was sitting on the table. Helen's stomach turned.

Noote and O'Shaughnessy took seats on one side of the table.

Helen was on the other. The message was clear. Noote considered himself on the side of the Golden Palms police.

"Where were you at eight Monday morning?" O'Shaughnessy asked.

"Is that the day Brenda died?" Helen said. "I was stuck in a traffic jam on I-95. I told you that last time."

"Did you have anyone with you who can verify that?" the detective said.

"I ride to work alone. You can check the accident reports. It was near Ives Dairy Road. Besides, you know what time I arrived. The camera at the employee gate was working."

"The camera showed us when you went through the employee gate," O'Shaughnessy said. "But that might not be when you arrived at the club. You could have heard about the traffic jam on the radio."

"But I didn't," Helen said. This friendly chat was turning decidedly unfriendly. "What are you really asking, detective?"

"Do you play golf, Miss Hawthorne?"

"Me? No. I hate golf."

"Did you ever touch the victim's golf club?"

Helen started to say no. Then she remembered that stupid swing she'd taken in Brenda's office, when she'd whacked the chair. They must have found her prints on the club. No point lying.

"Once," she said. "Brenda kept her clubs in the office and I took a practice swing."

"When?" O'Shaughnessy said. "Was she in her office at the time? Did she give you permission to use her clubs?"

"No," Helen said. "It was Sunday." She left out "the day before she died." "I was alone in the office. I saw her clubs and wondered what they felt like. I took a swing."

"So you have time to work on your golf swing at the office?" O'Shaughnessy said.

Noote sat across from her and stared. Was he going to make a re-port that she was a goof-off, as well as a murder suspect?

The more Helen said, the worse she sounded. Taking a swing with

Brenda's seven iron had seemed harmless at the time. How could it land her in such deep trouble?

"No, I just wanted to see what her clubs felt like," Helen said.

"Why use her seven iron?"

"It seemed like a lucky number," Helen said.

"It wasn't for Brenda," O'Shaughnessy said. "What were you doing in her office? Your desk isn't there."

"I was looking for guest passes," Helen said. "Brenda had rear-ranged the supply cabinet. I was running low and couldn't find them."

"The passes weren't hidden in the victim's golf bag," O'Shaughnessy said.

"I also checked her desk," Helen said.

"We know you did," O'Shaughnessy said. "We found your prints there, too. Now, would you care to tell us what you were really looking for in Brenda's desk?"

"Guest passes," Helen lied.

"Are you sticking with that story?" he said.

"Yes," she said.

"That's all, Miss Hawthorne," O'Shaughnessy said.

But Helen knew it wasn't.

"Am I free to go?" she asked.

"For now," O'Shaughnessy said. This time, his smile wasn't warm or friendly. "Don't leave the area."

Helen looked at her watch. She was off at four today, and it was three fifty-five.

"I'll drive Miss Hawthorne to the employee lot in the golf cart," Marshall Noote said.

"I can walk," she said. "Besides, I have to clock out at customer care."

"I'll wait," Noote said. "There's a killer loose on the club grounds. I wouldn't want you hurt."

They drove in the striped cart in silence. Jessica waited for Helen at the customer care door. "You're back. Are you OK?" she asked.

"I'm fine," Helen said.

"You are not. Is there a problem?" Jessica asked.

"No, no. The police had a couple of questions."

Jessica knew Helen was lying, too.

Helen clocked out and tried to leave by the loading dock. But Noote had anticipated that move. He was waiting for her there. She was trapped. She sat down wordlessly in the cart.

The silence continued as they drove to the lot. It grew heavier and heavier, until Helen thought it would crush her. Noote pulled up in front of Helen's car. It unnerved her that he knew the Toad was hers.

She climbed out of the cart without thanking him. "Remember my message," Noote said.

"Stay away from me, or I'll tell my lawyer," Helen said.

"Tell him this," he said. "I think you're lying. I think I'll prove it."

CHAPTER 18

"I have news about Rob," Phil said, "but I don't know if it's good or bad."

"It must be bad, or you wouldn't be getting me drunk," Helen said.

She was on her second glass of white wine. For the first time today, Helen felt relaxed, even mellow. Phil and Helen were sitting outside under the awning at Beachie's Beachside Inn, a funky bar in Fort Lauderdale, eating greasy cheeseburgers and watching tourists on the wide stretch of yellow-tan sand.

At five o'clock, the air was growing chilly. Long purple shadows stretched across the cool sand. Sunburned parents were calling to cranky children, folding beach umbrellas and shoving sandy towels into canvas bags.

Seagulls rummaged through the fast-food wrappers in the trash cans, looking for dinner. One flew off with a limp french fry. An elegant fish hawk was diving for its dinner, plummeting straight down into the turquoise water. It brought up a struggling fish and flew high with its prize. The fish flopped and twisted so hard to escape it slipped out of the predator's claws and fell back into the sea, dropping four stories into the water. Helen wondered if it could survive that fall.

"Helen," Phil said. "Are you there?"

"Sort of," she said. "I was watching that struggling fish and wondered if it was better to die quickly in a fall instead of getting your guts torn out by a hungry bird."

"I'll take the quick fall," Phil said.

"I read somewhere that it doesn't hurt when a predator kills you," Helen said. "It hypnotizes you, so you don't feel the pain."

"I bet whoever wrote that never met a real predator," Phil said. "That fish fought hard to escape, even though it could die in the attempt."

Helen remembered Marcella's flat eyes and her spinning goblets. She'd been hypnotized by a predator, and she found it terrifying. She'd do anything to escape the Black Widow.

Helen had come home after a hard morning of verbal abuse at the Superior Club, and an even worse afternoon being interrogated by the Golden Palms police. Then there was the threat from Marshall Noote—and the knowledge that he knew she was lying.

When she'd straggled into the Coronado, Phil had insisted that they go out. "Don't bother dressing up," he'd said. "Let's sit on the beach."

Now she knew why. Beachie's was a soothing spot. The soft *shussh* of the ocean waves calmed her. The wine and food cushioned the blow. Now Phil had to deliver the bad news. She knew what it was. She braced herself. This won't be so bad, she thought. Rob's death will set me free at last. I'll finally be able to escape him and his awful wedded wife.

"You're making small talk because you don't want to tell me," Helen said. She downed her wine. "OK, I'm ready. Get it over with."

"A body washed up on the beach," Phil said. "Some tourists found it early this morning."

Helen saw a tiny blond girl in a pink bikini run into her father's arms. The proud father settled her on his shoulders. The little girl giggled and patted his balding head while they walked through the waves.

"They weren't children, I hope," Helen said. Please, don't let some innocent child find him.

"No, two adults. A couple from New York was jogging on the beach."

"Welcome to Florida," Helen said. "Was it Rob?" She tried to squeeze the hope out of her voice.

"The body was too badly decomposed to tell."

Helen winced and wished she had more wine. Phil saw her pale face and signaled the waiter for two more drinks.

"But they think it's him?" she asked.

"It's a white male fitting Rob's description, late thirties or early forties."

"Rob was forty-two," Helen said.

"There's still some hair on the scalp," Phil said. "It's similar to Rob's color. The dead man is about Rob's weight, though that's hard to determine."

"Where did they find him?" Helen asked.

"On the beach about three miles south of the Superior Club. If Rob died at the club and was dumped in the water, the body would drift in that direction."

"Do they know how he died?"

"Not yet," Phil said.

Helen felt pleasantly numb. This wasn't bad, she decided. Not bad at all. She was taking the news just fine. She felt good. Better than good. She was relieved.

The tide was going out, and Helen could see little crabs scurrying along the wet sand. That reminded her of something, but she couldn't remember what. The waiter appeared with more wine. Helen took another drink, and then it hit her.

"If you're in the ocean for a while, don't you get eaten by things?"

"The body has been nibbled on," Phil said. "I don't think you want the details."

"They eat the eyes first," Helen said.

Phil looked slightly green. "Can we change the subject?"

Helen clutched her wine, as if Phil might take it away. "I'm not supposed to talk this way, am I? You expected me to cry, scream and faint at the news. Rob's dead and I'm glad. He made my life hell when we were married—and it got worse when we divorced. If he provided dinner for some hungry crab, it's the only useful thing he ever did."

Phil was staring at her.

"I've said too much," Helen said. "You think I'm horrible."

He reached for her hand. "I think you're honest," he said. "That's why I love you. Only a woman with a taste for abuse would still love Rob—and you're way too healthy for that. Rob is a bad man. I hope whatever happened to him, he can no longer hurt you."

"I can see why you talked me out of the crab appetizer, though," Helen said.

Phil choked on his drink. Helen pounded his back and gave him her water to sip, until he stopped coughing. She thought he might be laughing, but she wasn't sure. There were tears in his eyes.

"Why is this washed-up body bad news?" she said. "I thought we wanted to find Rob."

"A live Rob would be a lot better than a dead one," Phil said. "If the body turns out to be his, the police will start asking you awkward questions again."

"Oh." Helen felt her stomach drop and flop like that fish. "Right." She wasn't that drunk. She knew she was the last person seen with Rob, and they'd fought in front of witnesses.

Ohmigod. Brenda was a hostile witness. Now she was dead, too. This was looking worse and worse. "You think the police will charge me with his murder?" she said.

"I don't think there's enough evidence," Phil said. "At least not now. But if the coppers pick you up again for questioning, promise me you won't talk to them without a lawyer. Call Margery or call me, and we'll find you a lawyer. I'm serious, Helen. A mistake like this could land you in prison—or worse."

"What's worse than prison?" she said.

"Florida is a death penalty state. I know you don't like Marcella, but you can't afford to be choosy. If she sends Gabe Accomac when you're taken in for questioning again, tell her thanks and do whatever he says."

When. Not if. Phil really thought the police were going after her.

Helen watched the waves surge in on the sand, swallowing everything in their path. She was never going to be free of Rob. Her ex-husband's suspicious death would follow her like a slime trail.

"How soon before they get a positive ID on the body?" she said.

"It shouldn't be long. It will have to be identified by dental records."

"I guess those are in St. Louis," Helen said. "I think I can remember the name of our dentist, if the police need it."

"You won't have to. Marcella had Rob's dental records on board her yacht."

"She what!" Helen sat up so fast, she nearly overturned her wine. The beach was empty now. The tourists were gone. Their fellow drinkers had gone inside to the warm pub. "You think that's normal?"

"It is for rich yachters," Phil said. "They sail all over the world. Marcella explained that they carry their medical records with them on CDs in case they need emergency work in a foreign country. She says it can be awkward tracking down important medical information in a hurry, especially on some remote island."

"It also makes it easier to identify her dead husbands," Helen said.

"True," Phil said.

Helen's mellow mood was gone. She was suddenly cold—and stone sober.

"She killed Rob," Helen said. "Marcella killed him and she's going to set me up for his murder."

Phil took her in his arms. "No," he said, fiercely. "That won't happen. I won't let it happen."

"Do you really think we can beat the Black Widow?" Helen said.

"She's not your enemy," Phil said. "Not yet. She's only dangerous if the police go after her. Right now, you're useful to her."

"Can we solve this before she turns on me?" Helen said.

"We haven't any choice," Phil said.

CHAPTER 19

Xaviera clicked into the office in killer heels—black spikes with silver buckles.

Helen suspected it wasn't new shoes that put that dreamy smile on her face. Xaviera had made up with her boyfriend, Steven.

Helen guessed Xaviera had bought the shoes when she was down in the depths after their fight. Then she made up with her man. Now Xaviera had the best of both worlds: new shoes and an old love.

"Where's Kitty and Solange?" Xaviera asked.

"The bosses are meeting with Mr. Ironton and the club lawyers," Jessica said.

"Again?" Xaviera said.

"They're going to be tied up all morning."

"Good. Put the phones on automatic answer and meet me in the ladies' room in five minutes," Xaviera said. "I have information about the murders."

"Hey, what about me?" Cam said.

"We'll sneak you in," Jessica said. "It's the only private place for a staff meeting. A club member could walk in anytime and overhear us. Anyone could listen in at the staff cafeteria."

"But the bathroom is full of germs," Cam whined. He pouted like an overgrown baby.

"OK, don't come with us. But don't say we didn't ask you," Xaviera said. She tapped her way out of the room in her saucy heels, swinging her round bottom provocatively.

Helen took one more call, then put her phone on automatic answer and slipped down the back hallway. Jessica and Jackie followed. Cam trailed behind them, grumbling and clutching a bottle of hand sanitizer in his huge paw.

The OUT OF ORDER sign was already hanging on the women's locker room door.

Helen knocked three times and Xaviera opened it. "It's clear," she said. "But we can only get away with closing it down for ten minutes. I'll talk fast."

Helen noticed Xaviera had a new manicure—bright purple polish with rhinestones on the nail tips. Brenda would have gone ballistic if she'd seen it.

Jessica, Helen and Jackie perched on the marble vanity. Cam stood in the middle of the room, as if he expected the germs to jump out and grab him.

"Oh, come on, Cam," Jessica said. "You're bigger than those little germs."

"This room is loaded with staph and other things that can kill you," Cam said.

"I promise to get you out of here alive," Xaviera said. "I have news. My boyfriend, Steven, overheard the head of club security talking about the murders with the cops. Marshall Noote is friends with the Golden Palms chief of police."

Nobody asked where Steven was when he overheard the information. Listening at the office door, Helen figured.

Xaviera stood in front of them, looking like the cool high school teacher the boys fell in love with. All she needed was a blackboard and a pointer.

"Here's what the police know so far. It's confidential, so if you start telling other people, you'll get Steven and me in trouble."

"We wouldn't do that," Jessica said.

"Just talk," Cam whined. "I don't want to be in the ladies' room. I'm a guy."

Xaviera looked like she had a snappy comeback, but she swallowed it.

"The police believe the murder scene was staged. The victims had been dead only a short time before Helen found the bodies.

"Julio, the weekend valet, said Helen locked the door when she left Sunday night. She even came back to check it. Steven had night security. He reported that all the customer care doors were locked and the lights were off.

"The police believe Brenda opened the office early Monday morning. She wasn't due in until eleven, when she was supposed to play golf with Blythe St. Ives. But she came in the employee gate at seven thirty-three. The police don't know why. There was no early morning appointment in her desktop diary. Her killer may have been waiting in the building or walked in after her. They think he surprised her.

"As you know, there are no cameras in this building. But security analyzed the employee gate tapes. All the employees coming in Monday morning both before and after the murder arrived at times that fit their scheduled work hours. No one else came in unusually early, except for Brenda."

For once, Helen was glad that she'd been delayed by the car crash on I-95. An early arrival would have made her a prime suspect in Brenda's murder.

"What about the club members?" Jessica said. "Are the police checking their arrival? Or are they only going after the staff?"

"Yeah," Cam said. "The cops should hear the members' phone calls. Those people are mean."

"Some are killers," Jessica said. "Mr. Casabella's with the mob."

"We have a number of mobsters," Jackie said. "As well as other unsavory types. This new management lets in people who could have never joined in my day."

Helen was surprised Jackie spoke up. Maybe, now that Brenda wasn't browbeating her, she'd feel more at ease with her colleagues.

"The police aren't ruling out anyone," Xaviera said. "But they can't rule anyone in, either. Did I say that right? Can you rule someone in?"

"We understood. Go ahead," Jessica said. "If we're in here much longer, the members will start screaming."

Cam sneezed. "It's unhealthy, too."

Xaviera looked at her watch and started talking faster. "There's a problem. The camera was out of order at the member gate."

"I was here Sunday when it happened," Helen said. "A club member got mad when the gate wouldn't open automatically. He rammed it with his car."

"He took out the gate arm and the camera," Xaviera said. "So there are no camera or computer records for the gate Sunday night or Monday morning. It was wide open and unguarded."

"Anyone could have come in and killed Brenda—even a nonmember," Jackie said.

"That's pretty much it," Xaviera said. "Here's what we know about the murder. The police believe Brenda was killed first, and she was the intended victim. The employee gate guard saw her arrive in her golf outfit. The gate camera tape confirmed that she was wearing a golf shirt and visor, not her club uniform.

"There was not enough blood on Brenda's body for her to be killed topless. The police believe she was wearing her golf shirt and the murderer cut it off with the scissors in Brenda's desk. The golf shirt was not found on the club property, though there was an extensive search of the Dumpsters."

Helen thought of the huge old buildings with their warren of back passages, nooks and closets. There were a million places the killer could hide a bloody shirt, then take it away later.

"The police believe the killer wanted to humiliate the victim. Whoever killed Brenda was very angry. She was beaten nearly fifty times with the golf club. The doc got hit only once or twice."

"The killer wasn't teed off at him." Cam laughed loudly at his own joke. His laughter echoed hollowly off the bathroom marble. No one else joined in.

"The doctor was killed by number two," Xaviera said.

Cam snorted at Xaviera's mildly mangled English.

"He was killed second," Jessica corrected.

"Right. That's what I said. Dr. Dell had a club billing statement in his pocket. He withdrew thirty-five hundred dollars in cash from the bank yesterday afternoon. The money wasn't found on his body. Police think the killer took it. They say the doctor saw the office was open early and tried to pay the bill before his golf game."

Helen suspected that the doctor had filched the statement out of the family mailbox and wanted to pay off the incriminating bill before his wife saw it. Talk about a fatal attraction. His fling with a staffer had cost him his life.

"The police think the doctor wandered into Brenda's office during the murder and got himself killed," Xaviera said.

"I'm confused," Jessica said. "Was this a robbery?"

"No. The police think the killer just helped himself to the money."

"Or herself," Jessica said. "The killer could be a woman. Nobody would pass up that much free cash."

"The police say the killer then tried to make the murder look like a jealous spouse had attacked the two. But Brenda wasn't married and didn't have a serious boyfriend. The doctor's wife was in New York on a shopping spree. Demi knew about the doctor's affair. That's why she was on the shopping spree."

"Then why was the doctor trying to pay off the bill before his wife saw it?" Cam asked.

"It's one thing to *know* something, and another to see it in black and white," Jessica said.

"Yeah. That could drive a woman to—" Helen stopped. She could tell everyone automatically finished her sentence.

"What about a hit man?" Cam said. He watched a lot of movies. "Maybe Demi hired some guy to kill the doctor."

"The police say Demi was not the jealous type. The doctor had strayed before and Demi had the same solution for her pain: retail therapy. She took a major shopping trip to New York or Paris. If she decided to get rid of Dr. Dell, she might hire a cutthroat divorce lawyer, but she wouldn't murder her husband."

"So the doctor was in the wrong place at the wrong time," Helen said.

"Right. The real target was Brenda."

"Maybe if he'd stayed home with his sweet wife, he'd still be alive," Jessica said.

"The police have any idea why someone would kill Brenda?" Helen said.

"It's more like who wouldn't kill Brenda," Cam said. "We all hated her guts."

"Do we have to go to her funeral?" Jessica said.

"I want to go," Cam said. "I'm going to dance on her grave."

Jackie had turned whiter than the Superior Club towels, and started nibbling her nails. Helen felt sorry for her. Just the mention of Brenda's name seemed to sicken her.

They heard someone pounding on the restroom door. The staffers held their breath, and the door pounder went away.

"We'd better get back to work," Helen said.

"Any more questions?" Xaviera said.

Helen had a lot of questions, but she couldn't ask them.

Was Rob's disappearance connected to Brenda's murder? Was he dead, too? What had her wandering ex gotten himself into? Was that his body the tourists found on the beach? What happened to the missing Winderstine file? Was Brenda killed because of it?

Then Helen had a thought that made her heart freeze.

When did the killer leave the customer care office?

How close did Helen come to making the death scene a threesome?

CHAPTER 20

"The service at this club is intolerable." Blythe St. Ives's shriek was shrill as a steam whistle. Helen held the phone away from her seared ear.

"Yesterday was the absolute limit," Blythe screamed. "The locker room had an out-of-order sign on the door. I couldn't use it for an hour. An hour, I tell you."

"I'm sorry, ma'am," Helen said. "But I'm sure the restroom wasn't out of order that long." We only hijacked it for ten minutes, she thought.

"I pounded on the door until my hands were bruised, but no one answered," Blythe said. "Then I went for help in customer care. No one was in the office. Not one person. What were you people doing?"

Meeting in the restroom, Helen thought. Blythe made it sound like she was abandoned in the wilderness.

"Someone must be on duty in the office at all times during business hours," Helen said. "We are required to keep it staffed."

"Don't you *dare* call me a liar!" Blythe shrieked. "Let me speak with Solange."

Helen put Blythe on hold and knocked on Solange's door. The department supervisor looked like she'd had a sleepless night. Her red hair had gone from artfully tousled to unfashionably tangled. Her skin was blotchy and her eyes looked bruised.

"Blythe is on the phone, breathing fire," Helen said. "She wants to speak to you."

"Oh, please," Solange groaned. Helen noticed her usually flawless manicure was chipped. "I don't need to deal with her today. I have another meeting with Mr. Ironton. What's Blythe complaining about now?"

"She claims the locker room restroom was closed for repairs for an hour yesterday and she couldn't use it," Helen said. "I've checked the repair reports. There was nothing noted on the list."

That was true.

"Has anyone else complained?" Solange said. "Sometimes the repair crews forget to write down emergencies."

"No, Blythe is the only one," Helen said. Also true. "She says she tried to complain to customer care, but no one was on duty in our office at eleven yesterday morning."

"That's ridiculous," Solange said. "We had a full staff here."

"I told her that," Helen said.

Solange gave a put-upon sigh. "OK. I'll deal with Blythe. I'll also note this in her file. Really, that woman is unstable."

Helen didn't feel guilty for *Gaslighting* Blythe. The golfer was growing more demanding by the day, and she had an ugly temper. But was Blythe crazy enough to club two people to death?

I hope so, Helen thought. If Brenda's nasty golf partner turned out to be the killer, it would make our lives much easier. We could settle down at work. Now we're jumpy, nervous and watching one another. We feel guilty and uneasy. None of us liked Brenda. We're all glad she's dead. But every one of us is wondering: Did someone in this office kill her?

Everyone, that is, except the killer.

Helen polished off her third coffee of the morning, and knew her jitters weren't due to caffeine overdrive.

The strain showed on the staff in different ways. Solange looked ragged. Kitty was weepy. Xaviera snapped at people. Cam sucked on his puffer. Jessica was pale and drawn. Jackie retreated into herself. She sat scrunched up at her desk, as if she was making herself smaller.

"Can someone here help me?" a woman at the counter said.

Helen jumped. That was the other problem. Every time a club member came through the door, Helen wondered if she was waiting on Brenda's killer.

This member looked mild enough. She had shiny blond hair, a soft, round face and thirty extra pounds. She wore pretty peach linen and carried a dainty Prada purse, a trifle that would cost Helen a month's salary.

"I'm Gillian Aciphen," the woman said. "I can't use my card in the club restaurant. There must be something wrong with it." Gillian had the smile of a woman who knew the world did what she wanted.

"I'll check for you," Helen said. "Sometimes the strip on the card gets demagnetized."

Helen looked up Gillian's photo in the computer, to make sure the card wasn't stolen. Nope, Gillian Aciphen's photo matched the woman at the counter—if you padded her with those extra pounds. Mrs. Aciphen was pretty in person, but she'd been drop-dead gorgeous when the photo was taken four years ago.

Helen checked the Aciphen account on her computer.

Uh-oh. Here was the problem in big red numbers. The account was one hundred twenty days in arrears. It had been frozen. That's why Gillian couldn't charge anything. Overdue notices had been sent to Harold Aciphen's office. He'd ignored them.

"Let's go in here where we can talk," Helen said, ushering Gillian into Kitty's empty office for privacy.

"Is something wrong?" Gillian's blue eyes were wide and trusting. Her lightly freckled nose was small and pert.

"I'm very sorry, but your account is three months in arrears."

Gillian looked confused. "There must be some mistake. My husband pays the bills every month. Harold told me he paid this one. Something is wrong with your computer."

"No, ma'am," Helen said. "We've sent three overdue notices."

"I didn't see any of them," Gillian said.

"They were sent to your husband's office," Helen said.

Mrs. A turned white as typing paper. "That can't be," she said. "I know Harold—" Then she stopped abruptly. The light seemed to go out of her eyes. Her shoulders slumped. She gripped her pretty purse and said, "Thank you. I'll look into this."

Helen watched her leave, a beaten woman. Gillian knows what's wrong, Helen thought. Something made her stop in midsentence. Helen wondered what she'd remembered: an odd phone call, lipstick on a collar, a husband who suddenly started working late?

Whatever it was, Gillian Aciphen had just realized her comfortable life was coming to an end. She would never again smile in that same confident way.

Maybe Harold was having problems with his business and was afraid to tell his wife he was in financial trouble. Gillian liked expensive things.

Maybe Harold was paying the bills for a new love, and Mrs. Aciphen was about to be slapped with a divorce.

Judging by the changes in the photo, Helen thought it might be the latter. Get yourself a good divorce lawyer, Gillian, she wanted to say. That's where I went wrong.

"Why are you staring into space in my office, sweetpea?" Kitty said.

Helen looked at her Kewpie-doll boss. Kitty's dark curls were flat and her big brown eyes were red-rimmed. Her face was freshly powdered. Helen wondered if she'd been covering up tear tracks.

"I had to break some bad news to Mrs. Aciphen," Helen said. "She just found out her club account is three months in arrears. Her husband told her he'd paid it."

"Harold told her a lot of things that weren't true," Kitty said.

"He's cheating on her, isn't he?" Helen said.

"Everyone knows it but Gillian," Kitty said. "It's the old story. The blind, stupid, trusting wife is always the last to know." Kitty threw her notebook so hard on her desk, the teddy bear bounced off and fell on the floor.

Helen picked up the bounced bear. "Are you OK?"

"I'm fine," Kitty said. "As soon as I can find five thousand dollars for my kids' tuition, I'll be better. If you could catch Brenda's killer before my next meeting with Mr. Ironton, I'd be just ducky. He seems to hold me personally responsible for her death."

Her boss seemed so small and hurt, Helen was tempted to hug her.

Kitty daubed her damp eyes with a tissue, careful to avoid smearing her makeup. "I'm sorry, sweetie. I shouldn't go on like this. It's unprofessional. Run along and answer the phones. I hear them ringing. Solange is on a rampage, and the phones will set her off."

Helen worked the phones, managing to avoid the notorious complainers. Solange returned from her meeting with Mr. Ironton looking like a bomb-blast survivor. Her red hair hung in lank hunks like cheap yarn and she had a run in her stocking.

"Ladies and Cam," she said, standing in the middle of the room. "Get off the phones now. I need to speak with you."

Jessica was taking guest pass information. Solange glared at her until she hung up.

"I said get off the phone immediately," Solange said. "I meant it, Jessica."

"But the club member wanted—" Jessica began.

"I don't care," Solange snapped. "When I talk, you should have the courtesy to listen."

Everyone in the office kept silent, even Xaviera. Solange was usually too lazy to get this angry. The customer care phones rang and rang, but no one answered them. Helen knew the club members would be furious. For once, they had a good reason.

"I want that Winderstine file. Now," Solange said. "Cam, you're going to reorganize the file room until it's found."

"Me?" Cam said. "Why me?"

"Because I said so." Solange's voice was dangerous.

"I have allergies," Cam said. "It's dusty in there. I'll have an asthma attack."

"Take your inhaler," Solange said. "The faster you find that missing file, the quicker you can leave the file room."

"But it will take months to go through all those files," Cam said.

"Then you'd better get started."

Solange turned on her heel and shut her office door. Cam left gripping his puffer and his bottle of hand sanitizer, muttering to himself. The big pudgy man shambled away like an angry bear.

Xaviera raised her eyebrows, but still didn't dare speak.

Helen started retrieving missed messages and soothing irate club members. The next time she checked the clock, it was after noon. Enough time on other people's problems, Helen decided. Time to help myself. I promised Phil I'd look into Dr. Dell's affairs, pardon the pun.

She checked the dead doctor's file, looking for the woman who got the day of relaxation that led to the surgeon's eternal rest.

The doctor's staffer was named Mandy. According to the customer profile she filled out, she lived in Pembroke Pines, had "raven" hair with no split ends and fair skin with a "T-zone problem." Mandy was five-feet-six, weighed ninety-seven pounds and was twenty-three years old.

Shame on your hairy hide, Dr. Dell, Helen thought, chasing a woman thirty-five years younger.

Helen called the doctor's office and asked to speak to Mandy.

"I'm sorry," the receptionist said. "Mandy's not here."

Must be in mourning for the late doctor, Helen thought.

"I'm sorry. I shouldn't have bothered her," Helen said. "I know you've had a death in your office. When Mandy returns, could you have her call me? I have a refund check. She overpaid her bill by a hundred dollars."

"Mandy's not coming back," the receptionist said. "She's on her honeymoon."

"She's married?" Helen tried to keep the surprise out of her voice.

"And on the *Queen Mary 2*. How cool is that? The cruise must be a gift from her parents, because Dave's a hottie, but he doesn't have two nickels. Oops. My bad. Do I sound jealous? Guess I am. Some girls get all the luck and all the men. And now you want to give her money, too."

Helen looked at Mandy's address in the club files. "So are they going to live at her place in Pembroke Pines?" she asked.

"No, they're moving into Dave's home in Hollywood. I think her townhouse in Pembroke is cuter, but Dave owns the house off Johnson Street."

"I'll send the check there," Helen said.

So much for Mandy in mourning, Helen thought as she hung up the phone. The doctor wasn't in the ground before she married a hot younger man.

"Ta-da!" a loud voice announced.

Helen looked up. Cam was triumphantly bearing a fat file through the office. Solange came running out.

"I found it," Cam said. "I have the missing Winderstine file." He held it over his head like a trophy. Helen saw the coffee ring on the file folder, in the same place as the file that had been hidden in Brenda's desk.

"Where was it?" Solange said.

"On the bottom of the file drawer," Cam said. "It had slipped under the other files, so you couldn't see it. Do I get a reward?"

"You certainly do," Solange said. "You're the only one in this office smart enough to find that file. How would you like to take your girlfriend out to dinner?"

"Can I take my mom instead?" Cam asked.

Xaviera rolled her eyes.

"You can take whomever you want," Solange said. "I have a gift certificate to Ruth's Chris Steak House."

"That's funny," Jessica whispered to Helen. "I checked that file drawer when I searched the room, and looked under the other files. I know I did. The Winderstine file wasn't there."

Helen knew she did, too. That coffee-ringed file had been on Brenda's desk, then disappeared after her murder. Now Cam found it. How did it get back in the file room?

Was it really there? What if Cam had hidden it somewhere in the building and produced it now? His timely discovery saved him from months in a dusty file room.

Cam had recently bought an expensive condo—way too expensive for an eleven-dollar-an-hour clerk. Where did he get the money? Was he selling club information to Rob?

What if Brenda had discovered the missing file in Cam's desk on one of her snooping missions? Cam was the only person in the office with a locked drawer. But supervisors had keys to all the locks.

Cam could have come in early and killed Brenda. He'd been making up the time he'd taken off for his condo closing in the mornings.

Cam knew the club, its back roads and passages. He'd worked a variety of scut jobs before he'd landed a cushy place in customer care. He could find ways in—and out—of the club that weren't under the watchful eye of the employee gate camera.

Cam hated Brenda. He'd wanted to dance on her grave.

Did he kill her? He had a good reason. Brenda would have ruined his career at the club with that file. She loved destroying people.

But why would he kill Rob, the source of his money?

"People, listen up, since I have you all here together," Solange said. "We're getting new uniforms in customer care."

"What color?" Xaviera asked.

"Black pants and jackets with white T-shirts," Solange said.

"Boring," Xaviera said. "This is South Florida. Haven't they ever heard of tropical colors?"

Solange ignored her. "The good news is the T-shirts won't need to be starched and ironed. You can wash them at home. You won't be at the mercy of the employee laundry for your shirts anymore."

The staff cheered at that news.

"However," Solange quieted the cheers with a glare, "the uniforms still have to be dry-cleaned. Please make your appointment for a uniform fitting today. The new uniforms will be ready in two weeks. In order to receive them, you must turn in your old uniform, including your five shirts or blouses. If we do not have your complete uniform, you will be charged for the missing pieces."

"What?" Jessica said.

"That's not fair," Cam said. "The employee laundry lost one of my uniform shirts."

"I'm missing a blouse," Jessica said. "I'm not paying thirty bucks to replace it. I didn't lose it."

"I have one gone, too," Jackie said. "I can't afford that kind of money."

"I didn't make the rules." Solange waved their protests away like annoying flies. "Deal with it, people. I need a manicure. If there's a crisis, call me on my cell."

The grumbling continued long after she left. Cam pouted and refused to answer his phone. Even laid-back Jessica slammed papers around on her desk. Two angry red spots stood out on her pale cheeks.

"I can't believe this," Jessica said. "Everyone knows the employee laundry is hopeless. They lose our things all the time. Now we'll have to pay for their mistakes."

"Do you still have your laundry ticket? Maybe you can prove the blouse is lost," Helen said.

"Maybe," Jessica said. "But don't bet on it."

"They took my laundry ticket when they looked for my missing shirt. They lost that, too," Cam said. "I can't even prove I took the shirt to the laundry."

"Inexcusable," Jackie said.

"Criminally careless," Jessica said.

Careless, definitely. The employee laundry was notoriously bad.

Criminal? That was another question.

Helen definitely thought this lost shirt was a crime.

But was it lost in the laundry? Or did Cam throw it away because it was covered with Brenda's blood?

CHAPTER 21

Helen's last call of the day was the worst. Phil phoned her at the Superior Club, something he rarely did. As soon as she heard his voice, she knew the news was bad.

"What's wrong?" Helen said.

"The body on the beach wasn't Rob's," Phil said. "The dental records didn't match. I thought you'd want to know."

"Who was the dead man?" Helen asked.

"Nobody knows," Phil said. "His description doesn't match any other missing person. He could be an illegal immigrant, a drifter or homeless. He could be some tourist down here alone. The body was so battered by the waves it's hard to tell much, and he wasn't wearing any clothes or jewelry. They don't even know how he died."

"No clothes, no name and no identity," Helen said. "What a lonely death."

"They may still find out who he is," Phil said. "Someone who knew him could come forward. How are you feeling? I know this isn't the news you wanted to hear."

"Relieved and disappointed at the same time," Helen said. "I want it to be over. I want to be rid of Marcella. Now I have to call her and tell her the news."

"Margery will call for you," Phil said.

"And the Black Widow will tell Margery to call me. Margery isn't my errand girl. I'll make my own calls."

"I'm here if you need me," Phil said. "I know you don't want to hear this, but I'm glad the dead man wasn't Rob. You don't need the police interested in you right now."

"Or any other time," Helen said. "Thanks. I'll call Marcella."

Helen didn't feel nearly as brave once she hung up the phone. She didn't want to call Marcella and be drawn once more into her lonely world of power and money.

Might as well get it over with, she thought. My phone won't dial itself. She took a deep breath and called Marcella.

"I have news," Helen said.

"The dead man on the beach wasn't Rob," Marcella said.

"Then you already know," Helen said. Good, she thought. Now I won't have to meet with her.

"I still want to meet with you," Marcella said.

Damn.

"I get off work in fifteen minutes," Helen said. "I'll stop by the yacht club on my way home."

"Do that," Marcella said, and hung up.

Helen put her head down on her desk. Her heart was beating wildly and her hands were shaking. She had to get away from the Black Widow. The woman had said three sentences and Helen felt ice forming on her bones. Helen had convinced herself Marcella was evil, and she couldn't shake that feeling.

"Are you OK?" Jessica asked. They were the last two people working in the customer care office at this hour.

"It's been a rough day," Helen said. And I have to meet with a serial husband killer, she thought.

"Tell me about it," Jessica said. She sipped her tea and made a face. "Yuck. It's cold." She dropped the tea bag in the trash, then emptied the dregs in the waste can, something else Brenda never permitted.

Helen watched, fascinated by the quick, efficient movements of the actress's thin fingers. Jessica's smallest gesture was photogenic.

"I keep looking at all the club members and wondering which one is the killer," Jessica said. "I rush up front when I see them at the counter. I don't want them angry at me."

"Do you really think the killer is a club member?" Helen said.

"Of course," Jessica said. "Who else could it be?"

Helen said nothing.

"You think it's one of us?" Jessica said. "After all the time you've spent in this office? Thanks a lot, Helen."

"I don't think it's you, Jessica."

Jessica flung her arms wide, to take in the whole office. "Then who? Jackie?" She laughed theatrically.

"Xaviera?" She pointed an accusing finger at Xaviera's empty desk. "If Brenda had been stabbed with a rhinestone-tipped fingernail, I'd say Xaviera was the killer."

She waved her hand at Kitty's empty office. "How about her? Our boss is really dangerous. She might drown them in tears."

"I think it's Cameron," Helen said.

"Cam? You're joking. That big mama's boy? He'd never kill anyone. Dead people have too many germs. Besides, haven't you figured out by now how lazy he is? Brenda was beaten more than fifty times. That's too much work for Cam."

"He started doing the worst jobs at the club," Helen said. "He was a porter. He lugged garbage and took out used cooking oil. He scrubbed pots in the club kitchen. Those are hard, dirty jobs. He finally worked his way up to a nice desk in customer care, and Brenda tried to get him fired. She wrote a memo to Mr. Ironton ratting out Cam for buying his condo on company time."

"Brenda lied," Jessica said. "Solange won't do anything, but Kitty will fix it. She'll tell Mr. Ironton the truth."

"Some of that accusation will stick. It always does. Cam was furious. He'd kill Brenda to save his easy job."

"Stop this," Jessica said. "Stop it, right now. We have to work together. It's us against the members. We need one another to survive this awful job. I'm sick of the fighting. I'm tired of being broke. I hate it. I hate it. I hate it!"

Jessica slammed her teacup down on her desk so hard, it cracked. She threw it in the trash, picked up her purse, and walked out without another word.

The silence that followed was like the quiet after a disaster—unnatural, uneasy. Helen had no idea laid-back Jessica had so much fury in her. But she'd been under terrible pressure at work and at home. Helen remembered the stack of past-due bills and Jessica's hissed arguments with her husband. And that list of agents who never called her for acting jobs.

Actresses were good at manufacturing fake feelings and hiding real ones.

So who was the real Jessica: the raging woman who smashed crockery? Or the easygoing actress?

Helen brooded as she closed the customer care office for the night. It was dark when she left the club, and the path to the Superior yacht basin was crossed with wind-shifting shadows. The Black Widow's yacht loomed over the dock, white as bleached bones. The windows were black and shiny as a new hearse.

Helen boarded the *Brandy Alexander,* her thoughts heavy with dread. Bruce materialized at the ramp to greet her. She could see the shape of his skull under his shaved head. Helen heard ghostly laughter coming from the back of the yacht. She'd heard it before, the night Margery had introduced the Black Widow to Rob.

Marcella was being courted by a new man. Rob was definitely dead to the Black Widow. She was looking for his replacement.

The new husband candidate was sitting in one of the white chairs on deck, relaxed and easy. He was about forty, with thick brown hair and a nicely weathered face. He nodded to Helen, kissed Marcella's hand, and wished her good evening. Marcella didn't introduce him to Helen.

The man seemed vaguely familiar, but Helen couldn't place him. She thought he was a good choice, though—handsome, tall, but not so young he made Marcella look ridiculous.

In this light, Marcella could almost be the same age as her new man. She seemed younger and slimmer. Her makeup was softer and her hair color not so harsh.

The Black Widow needed men, Helen thought. She fed off their admiration and absorbed their vitality.

"May I offer you a drink?" Marcella was sipping a frosty margarita from a salt-rimmed glass. She must save the martinis for when she wanted to pound down the booze. Helen realized she'd never seen Marcella eat so much as a peanut. She wondered if the Black Widow was like one of those demons who couldn't touch human food.

"Just water," Helen said. "I have a long drive home."

"Bruce will bring it. Let's get down to business. Anything more on the dead man they found on the beach?"

"Nothing. They still don't know who he is."

"Too bad it wasn't Rob," Marcella said. "I'd love to see him dead."

We have something else in common, Helen thought. She said, "I'm sure you have a good prenup. It won't cost you much to get rid of him."

"It's already cost me. He stole my jewelry."

Helen knew Rob was a con artist, a sponger and a womanizer. Now he was a common thief. "Are you sure?"

"Of course I'm sure." Marcella tossed back the rest of her margarita. The silent Bruce replaced it with a fresh drink, and put a crystal glass of water in front of Helen along with a plate of thin lemon slices.

"When did you find out your jewelry was missing?" Helen asked.

"It's not missing," Marcella said, and sparks snapped in her dark eyes. "It was taken deliberately. Rob and I are the only ones with the combination to the safe on board the yacht."

"When's the last time you saw it?" Helen said. "The night of the Clapton concert?"

Helen had seen enough guests at the gate to know the concert was a glittering event. Safe deposit boxes had been raided from New York to Miami for the Clapton party.

"I didn't open the safe that night," Marcella said. "I keep my everyday diamonds in a smaller safe in my dressing room. This safe is hidden in the master bedroom. Rob took two or three expensive pieces, the kind I wear once or twice a year. He replaced them with junk jewelry, so the boxes had some heft. I wouldn't have known they were missing for months if I hadn't sent my ruby necklace for cleaning. The jeweler called and said the piece I'd sent him was a fake, bought at a shopping mall. A mall! I was humiliated."

Rage ate away at her newfound youth. The Black Widow looked old and scary. Her tiny, pointed teeth were bared in a frightening snarl.

Helen gulped her water.

"I'm still going through all my things, but he's made off with more than two million dollars' worth of jewelry."

"Ohmigod. Did you report this to the police?"

"I don't want the police in my life," Marcella said.

Helen had a sudden inspiration. Phil was looking for Elsie's missing ring as a favor to Margery. Maybe she could get him some money for his good deed. "I know a detective working on another jewelry job now, checking the pawnshops and outlets for a stolen ring," she said. "I can put him on your case, too."

"No detectives," Marcella said. "I told you. I don't want that kind of attention."

"This isn't an ordinary detective," Helen said. "Ask Margery."

"I will," the Black Widow said. "Wait here while I make the call."

Marcella disappeared inside the huge yacht. Helen wondered if she'd ever see more than the bathroom. Maybe you couldn't walk inside until you knew all the right names for the boat parts.

Helen stared into the soft darkness. She could hear laughter and the clink of glasses on another yacht and the sound of slow, sweet jazz. The water lapped at the sides of the boat. There was a plopping sound and a big fish jumped up in the water.

Marcella was back. "Look at that," Helen said. "Is that a dolphin?"

"Barracuda," Marcella said.

Naturally, they'd congregate here.

"Margery says this Phil is OK," the Black Widow said. "Tell him

I'll pay his regular fee plus a bonus if he finds the jewelry, but I don't want any written reports or billing statements."

"Do you have photos of the missing pieces?" Helen asked.

"They're in a safe deposit box in New York. I'll have them faxed here and delivered to Margery."

"Do you have a fax machine on board?" Helen asked.

"Of course." Marcella sounded insulted, as if Helen had asked if she had indoor plumbing. "I have a state-of-the-art satellite phone setup with Internet access. The fax has a phone number and works just like it does on land. That's how we get our weather updates. The only problem is when it's really overcast or there's a heavy storm. Then our reception may be disrupted. That's when we need it most. So much for satellite technology."

She sighed, as if no one could understand the special burden of being rich.

"May I ask you a question?" Helen said.

The Black Widow shrugged.

"Why do you call your boat the *Brandy Alexander*? I've never seen you drink one."

"Lost my taste for them after my second husband died," Marcella said.

Helen held her breath, afraid to say more. She'd stumbled onto a dangerous subject.

"His name was Alexander," Marcella said. "I called him Alex. Brandy Alexanders were our special drink. Ever have one?"

"It's sort of an alcoholic ice cream sundae," Helen said.

"A brandy Alexander looks innocent, but it's destructive. It's loaded with fat, calories and liquor. One was enough to knock me out. I kept the name. It's bad luck to rename a yacht. Besides, it was a reminder."

Helen didn't have the nerve to ask, "Of what?" The Black Widow answered the unspoken question.

"Treachery," she said, "can seem so sweet. So can revenge."

CHAPTER 22

"The curse is broken," Margery said, lifting her wineglass high. By the glow of the tiki lights, she looked like an ancient priestess at an arcane ceremony.

"It's official," Margery said. "Apartment 2C is no longer a crook magnet. My nice normal couple, George and Nancy, are leaving at the proper time."

"For 2C? That would be midnight, right?" Helen said.

Margery ignored her. "Their checks didn't bounce and the cops didn't bust them," she said.

"You still have a day or two. The police could come through the gate yet, yelling 'Freeze!'" Phil said.

He grinned at Margery, but that was no joke. Several 2C renters had been hauled off in handcuffs. They were still guests of the government.

"I hope you counted the towels," Peggy said.

"And everything else that isn't nailed down," Helen said. "Remember the crooks who took your shell mirror and the teakettle?"

"Awk!" Pete said.

"I got them back," Margery said, stiffly. "I'm so happy to have a normal couple, I'm giving George and Nancy a good-bye party."

The umbrella table was covered with trays of party treats: raw vegetables, Doritos, dips and desserts. Pete eyed the bowl of cashews until Peggy moved away from temptation and gave him a celery stalk. The little green parrot gnawed it morosely.

Margery uncorked a bottle of Fat Bastard, another sign the celebration was serious.

"Usually when a renter leaves, you drink box wine and we try to cheer you up," Helen said. "Of course, those renters take off in the middle of the night."

"Shush," Margery said. "George and Nancy's door just opened. The guests of honor are on their way."

The tiki lights' smoky flames cast a romantic glow on the turquoise pool and the purple bougainvillea. The old palm trees rustled and whispered in the dark. The partygoers wore Florida casual: shorts and sandals. Peggy's red hair turned to fire in the torchlight. Pete perched on her shoulder like a small green demon.

Phil looked muscular and primitive in the flames. We're not going to waste this night eating Doritos by the pool, Helen decided.

"Hey, hey," said George. "It's party time." Nancy waved and smiled.

George dropped a six-pack of Grolsch beer in the cooler, opened one, and headed for the Doritos and dip like they were long-lost relatives. "I should be drinking the wine," he said. "Fat Bastard. That's me." He patted his office pudge proudly.

"Where's your colorful friend, Elsie?" George asked Helen. "She wanted financial advice at the last party, but I wasn't much help."

"She's OK," Helen said. "But I don't think she feels like celebrating right now." Elsie was worried sick about her lost ring. Helen hoped Phil could find it.

Nancy picked up a pretzel and dredged it through the dip. "Is Elsie getting a little funny?" she asked.

"No," Helen said. "She's a free spirit. Elsie is smart, but she's not logical. It can make her seem ditzy."

"Mom kept her marbles to the end," Nancy said. "We were lucky."

"Margery says you've wrapped up your mother's affairs here," Helen said.

"It's over," Nancy said. "Her condo was sold to a nice gay couple who adored Mom's fifties furniture. They called it 'retro' and bought it all. It would make her happy to know that her years of lemon waxing were appreciated.

"I gave her clothes to charity, kept her china and photos, and sent some keepsakes to her friends and family members. We finished packing today. I'm ready to go home. I'd like to sleep in my own bed again."

"Too bad you're going home in January. It's cold in Ohio," Helen said.

"Not at my office," George said. "Things are way too hot. I wanted a few days on the beach, but now I have to hurry back."

"What's wrong?" Helen said.

"I'm on the company search committee," George said. "We're looking for a new CFO. Our top candidate turned out to be a loose cannon. He told us he'd left his previous company for a better offer."

"And he didn't?" Helen asked.

"He got fired. Our boy threw a stapler at his secretary when she made a mistake in a letter. Clipped her on the shoulder."

"You're looking at lawsuit city," Helen said. "Especially if he loses his temper again."

"We can't have someone unstable in an executive position," George said. "It's too dangerous. You're right. We could get sued. Now we have to start the executive search all over again."

"How did you find out?" Helen asked. She'd been in human resources. She couldn't even legally say that a former employee had had a sex change operation.

"A little bird sent us copies of the secretary's complaint," George said. "She got an out-of-court settlement to keep her mouth shut. The incident was hushed up and he got another job."

A little bird, Helen thought, or a big vulture?

"Would you excuse us?" Phil said.

"Certainly, certainly. Didn't mean to monopolize the pretty lady," George said. He went back to monopolizing the Doritos. Helen suspected they were George's real love.

"Thanks for getting me the Black Widow as a client," Phil said. "She can afford to pay for me traipsing all over South Florida."

"Any luck on Elsie's missing ring?"

"None. But I may have a lead. I'm driving to Palm Beach County tomorrow. I'll be gone until late."

"Palm Beach must be prime territory for pawning dubious rocks," Helen said.

"I hope so," Phil said. "I'll have my cell phone off, but don't worry about me. I won't be back until late tomorrow."

"How about dinner at my place when you get back?" Helen said. "I'll whip up some scrambled eggs."

Actually, it was the only thing Helen knew how to make. Phil didn't find her other culinary specialty—tuna out of the can—as exciting as Thumbs did.

"It's a deal," Phil said, and kissed her. "Mmmm. That was nice. Want to come over to my apartment and look at my . . ."

"Etchings?" Helen said.

"Faxes," Phil said.

"I don't think anyone will miss us," Helen said. They ran hand in hand through the flickering shadows to Phil's place.

Phil had a guy apartment, with black leather, chrome and a plasma TV. A CD tower held his Clapton collection. He brought out a bottle of merlot and a can of Planters peanuts. Helen picked up the faxes of Marcella's missing jewelry from the black-and-chrome coffee table.

"Wow. I've never seen jewelry like this outside a museum," Helen said. "These rocks are so big, they look fake."

"Marcella likes gaudy stuff," Phil said. He popped a handful of peanuts in his mouth and sipped the wine. "I'm guessing these pieces will be broken up and the stones sold in New York."

Helen studied a pair of delicate, dime-sized earrings. They were the only things she'd wear from the Black Widow's treasure trove, even if she could afford them.

"It's a shame if those ruby-and-diamond earrings are broken up," Helen said. "They're really lovely."

"I'm hoping those will be sold intact," Phil said. "There's a good chance. They haven't been reported as stolen, though the provenance is dubious. The jewelry is our only lead. There's still no sign of Rob, and no activity on his credit cards or bank account."

"Maybe he took the jewelry to New York," Helen said.

"How?" Phil said. "Unless he has a passport and a driver's license under another name, he can't rent a car or buy a plane ticket."

"He could talk some woman into driving him," Helen said.

"It's possible," Phil said.

"Maybe," Helen said. "But I still think he's dead."

Phil reached for his wineglass again, and the fax cover sheet slipped off the table and across the floor. Marcella's fax and phone numbers were written on it.

"Look at her fax number," Helen said. "It has four sevens."

"What did you expect?" Phil said.

"Three sixes would be more like it," Helen said. "The mark of the beast."

"Marcella really spooks you," Phil said.

"Yes, she does. But I wonder how much is my imagination."

"Well, there are those dead husbands," Phil said. "You didn't imagine them."

"Yes, but Marcella has never done anything violent around me. Except when she snapped a champagne goblet and cut her hand. The blood ran down her fingers and she didn't notice. She didn't seem to feel anything. That gave me the shivers. Also, I've never seen her eat."

"And that proves?" Phil said.

"She's not human, Phil. She doesn't react like other people. She lost two million dollars in jewelry and she acted like she'd misplaced her sunglasses. She said she'd wished Rob was dead, but she was so cool about it. No, she was cold. She didn't scream, or rant or throw things."

Helen stopped dead. "Rob," she said. "Throw things."

"What?" Phil said.

"Tonight, I was talking to George, Margery's renter. He said they were going to have to find a new candidate for CFO at his company, because the man they originally wanted threw a stapler at his secretary. Someone slipped them confidential information about the guy. They changed their minds about hiring him."

"What's that got to do with Rob?" Phil said.

"I think that's what Rob did. He sold confidential information to corporations about potential hires or promotions. That's safer than selling club information to art thieves and housebreakers. Companies like to know if candidates for executive positions have misbehaved.

"The Superior Club files are loaded with high-powered names and bad behavior. They're a gold mine. All Rob would need was a little bribe money and a contact in customer care.

"Malpractice lawyers would be thrilled to learn that Doctor X was so drunk he drove his SUV into the club fountain. They could prove he had an alcohol problem and that's why he botched the gallbladder operation.

"We have every human frailty in the club files: drug overdoses, assaults, adultery. Recently, some big executive shoplifted six golf shirts. He didn't realize that he'd committed grand larceny. The shirts cost two hundred fifty dollars each, and the club will prosecute him. The one thing they won't tolerate is theft—from them.

"Marcella thought no one would care that Sawyer Winderstine was sixty days behind in his club bills. But what if he was up for, say, treasurer at his company? The fact that he couldn't manage his own finances would be a career killer."

"Would Rob be smart enough to do something like that?" Phil asked.

"Never underestimate Rob's sneakiness," Helen said. "You told me that."

"Right. When he traced you down to Florida," Phil said.

"Rob would be perfect," Helen said. "He'd be discreet. He'd work for cash only, so there would be no awkward bills or visits from scruffy detectives."

"Hey, watch it," Phil said.

"I didn't mean you," Helen said. "Although you can look pretty scruffy when you want to. Remember when you dressed up like a biker?"

"I am a man of many talents," Phil said.

"You've proved that," Helen said, and kissed him. "Rob operated in the Superior Club world. He knew how to dress and how to act. He could pass for one of them. A potential buyer could meet him for cocktails in the club bar. Rob could pass the information and collect his money, and no one would be the wiser."

"The question is," Phil said, "what did Rob uncover in those files that got two people killed? And where is he now?"

"I think the Black Widow killed him when she found out her jewelry was missing," Helen said.

"We're back to her again," Phil said. "You don't have to be afraid of her."

"Yes, I do," Helen said.

"Not now." He pulled Helen down on the couch and kissed her. His lips were soft and warm and tasted of red wine. "You're safe with me," he said.

"You don't feel safe," she said, and gave him a long, lingering kiss.

"Good," he said.

CHAPTER 23

"This is Noah Plavin. I want a guest pass. My friends will be at the club gate in ten minutes. Don't keep them waiting."

Noah did not speak to inferiors. He commanded them.

Helen tried to remain polite. "Mr. Plavin, we've explained the system before. It takes half an hour to issue a guest pass. I have to fax you the paperwork, you sign it and send it back, then we type it up."

"Any dummy can do that in five minutes," Noah Plavin said.

"I'll try to get it done for you in time, Mr. Plavin. What's your member number?"

"Look it up," he said, and slammed down the phone.

"Who was that?" Jessica asked. The actress had forgotten her blowup yesterday. Jessica's dramatic defense of her co-workers now seemed like a scene from a play.

"Noah Plavin," Helen said. "He wants a guest pass in ten minutes. How many times do we have to tell him? He's as bad as Mrs. Buchmann, who always calls for a pass two minutes before we close."

"He won't get it today," Jessica said. "The fax machine is broken."

"Again?" Helen said.

"Jammed," Jessica said. "I've called the service department."

"I'll hike over to the main office to fax this," Helen said. "Mr. Plavin's guests will have to wait. Maybe this will teach him."

Helen filled out the fax cover sheet and guest pass form.

"You left his member-number space blank," Jessica said.

"Let him look it up," Helen said.

I'm getting as nasty as the members, she thought. All the tender feelings from her night with Phil were gone. An hour at the Superior Club had wrecked her good mood.

You're in South Florida in January, she told herself. The rest of the country is under a foot of snow. Relax. Enjoy. This day is a gift.

Helen felt the warm sun on her back and breathed in something sweet on the soft air. Well-bred gardenias bloomed along the sidewalk. Red impatiens rioted in the planters. Everything is beautiful here, she thought. Except the members.

The club lobby looked denuded without its thronelike chairs and ancient wrought-iron chandelier, like a forest whose old-growth trees had been chopped down.

Helen crossed the marble floor to the club concierge's desk and stopped dead in surprise. She knew this man. He'd been drinking margaritas on Marcella's yacht. He was even better-looking in daylight. Nice crinkly lines around the eyes. Thick wavy hair. Bit of a tan and a devilish smile. Marcella had chosen well. Helen wondered if he was husband number seven.

His name tag said MICHAEL. He gave no hint that he'd seen Helen aboard the *Brandy Alexander*. Michael was discreet.

"May I help you?" Michael asked, and smiled that smile.

"I'm Helen in customer care. Our fax is broken. May I use yours?"

"Of course," Michael said. "I'll fax it for you. Do you want a transmission receipt?"

"No, thanks," Helen said. "I have to wait here for a return fax."

Helen paced the lobby until Michael returned with a fax signed by Noah Plavin. She took the scenic way back to the office, a path that wound under a banyan tree with a fantastic twisted trunk. White orchids bloomed in its branches. A yellow bird darted through the thick green leaves.

This is paradise, she thought. How could the members be so miserable? They had money, freedom and beauty. They had to work hard to be so unhappy. Was this how God felt when She looked at Her wrecked world?

Helen heard a car honking impatiently at the main gate, and wondered if it was Plavin's guests, demanding their passes. Back at the customer care office, she typed up the passes and sent them to the gate computer.

The repair person was working on the fax-copier machine. Angie was small, stocky and efficient. Helen loved her Brooklyn accent.

"Can I use the fax now?" Cam asked Angie.

"Not yet, sweets." Angie pressed a button and the machine belched out a long list of phone numbers, times and dates.

Cam tapped his foot impatiently. "I have to send a fax," he said.

"Not from this machine," Angie said. "It's DOA." The fax machine's guts were strewn across the floor.

"It's a terrific day for a walk to the main office," Helen said. "They'll fax it for you."

"My allergies are acting up. I don't want to go outside," Cam said.

Angie rolled her eyes, just like Xaviera.

"What's that?" Helen asked, pointing to the newly belched list.

"A printout of the faxes sent from this office machine," Angie said. "I wanted to see if a particular phone number triggered the problem."

"That's an incredible number of calls," Helen said. "I had no idea we faxed this much."

"You need a bigger machine," Angie said. "This one is overworked."

"So are we," Helen said.

"Sorry about that," Angie said, "but it makes sure I have plenty of work to do. I need the money."

"Any chance that fax machine will be ready soon?" Jessica asked. She was as insistent as Cam, but more polite. "I have to fax some guest passes."

"People, please. Give me another ten minutes," Angie said. "I'm pedaling as fast as I can."

"Can I look at this list of faxes?" Helen asked Angie.

"Keep it," the repairwoman said. "And if you three eager beavers will give me some air, I'll fix this faster."

Cam, Jessica and Jackie backed away a few feet, but they wouldn't let Angie out of their sight.

Helen unrolled the list of fax numbers on the front counter and studied them. She recognized the area codes for New York, Los Angeles and San Francisco, and the country codes for France, Germany, Britain and Brazil. The club members were a far-flung lot.

One number looked familiar. The fax number had four sevens. It was the Black Widow's. The number was repeated more than a dozen times on the list.

Helen waited until her break, then went into the club bathroom, locked the stall, took out her cell phone and called Marcella. The Black Widow answered her own cell phone.

"Did Rob get faxes on your yacht?" Helen said. Her voice echoed off the bathroom marble.

"All the time," Marcella said. "He said it was business. He refused to go anywhere unless he received that fax. Such a bore."

"Ever see the faxes?"

"Of course not," Marcella said. "I couldn't be bothered with his petty business."

Too bad, Helen thought. You wouldn't be in this fix if you'd paid attention to your husband's crooked little deals.

"Did he receive the faxes on any particular day?" Helen could check the dates on the calls and figure out who was working in the office.

"Saturday mornings," Marcella said. "Always on Saturday."

Saturday morning was the club's busiest day. Helen worked Saturdays. So did Jessica, Jackie, Xaviera—and Cam.

Cam had to be the killer, Helen thought. He was familiar with the back ways into the club. He'd lost a uniform shirt, the one he wore when he killed Brenda. He needed money for his high-priced condo.

He knew Brenda kept those golf clubs in her office. He came into the office early.

Motive, means, opportunity: the deadly trifecta.

Helen flushed the toilet and unlocked the stall. She thought she heard a door shut softly, and hoped it wasn't Blythe St. Ives. The bad-tempered golfer would report Helen for making personal calls on club property.

When she returned, the fax machine was working. Cam had commandeered it.

Solange came in with an announcement. "Girls and Cameron, we're adding a new membership exercise program—pole dancing."

"Classy," Jessica said. "That should really please the Old Guard."

"Where are you teaching it, at the strip club on Dixie Highway?" Xaviera said.

"Why do we need a class?" Helen whispered to Jessica. "Most of the club's trophy wives got their husbands by pole dancing."

"But it was only a six-inch pole," Jessica said, and Xaviera cracked up.

"What's so funny, girls?" Solange's face was nearly as red as her hair.

"I didn't realize Lilly Pulitzer made pole-dancing togs," Helen said, naming the club members' favorite casual-wear designer.

"Go ahead and laugh," Solange said. "You're showing your ignorance. Pole dancing is the current hot fad. Our members requested it."

Helen tried to imagine the skinny, horse-faced club women with their legs wrapped around a metal pole—or anything else.

"Maybe their husbands will consider pole dancing a job skill when they dump their current wives for someone younger," Xaviera said. "Less alimony."

"Are we having lap-dancing classes, too?" Jessica said.

"That's enough!" Solange sounded like an outraged schoolmarm. "Back to work, everyone."

The rest of the afternoon passed in a flurry of phone calls and paperwork. It was nearly five o'clock when Xaviera said, "Look at the rain. It's a tropical downpour. We'll all get drenched walking to our cars."

"Not me," Helen said. "I'm working alone here until six. The rain will stop by then."

"Helen has to prepare Mrs. Buchmann's guest pass when she calls at five fifty-eight," Jessica teased.

Jackie fretted over the drenching rain. "I walked to work," she said, wringing her hands. "It was supposed to be nice all day. My uniform will be soaked. Does anyone have an extra umbrella?" She looked shrunken and worried, older than her years.

"I need mine," Cam said. "I get sinusitis if I get wet."

"There's an umbrella in the lost and found," Jessica said. "Use that. I'll drive you home so you don't have to walk in the rain."

"But I live by the main gate," Jackie said. "We have to leave by the employee entrance at the back of the club. Taking me home will put you miles out of your way."

"I'll take the member gate," Jessica said. "The arm and camera are still broken."

Helen stared at her.

"It doesn't work half the time," Jessica said. "I use it when I'm running late. Saves me ten minutes."

"Don't do that," Jackie said, worry lines creasing her pale forehead. "What if Mr. Ironton catches you? It's a firing offense. He uses that gate."

"Mr. Ironton doesn't know me from Adam," Jessica said. "Quit fussing, Jackie, and let me help you. Bye, Helen. Hope the rain drives away any members who want something."

Her co-workers left in a chattering crowd. Jessica's wish came true: The rain did silence the members' demands. Nobody wanted to go to the beach or dinner at the club in a monsoon. Helen had an hour to search Cam's desk, if the phones didn't ring. She wasn't looking forward to this duty. He'd have to be confronted with his crime. Helen felt sorry for him. He'd thrown away his young life for a few thousand dollars.

Helen had borrowed a skeleton key from Margery. She waited five precious minutes, in case any staffers returned to the office. Then she opened Cam's locked drawer. The key didn't quite fit and she had to wrestle with it, but the drawer finally opened.

Inside, Helen found a folder with photocopied pages of Brenda's calendar: the dates when she'd gone to the doctor on company time. Cam had been fighting back. Under the folder was a letter on scented blue stationery. Did Cam have a girlfriend?

Helen opened it without a qualm.

The letter was from Cam's mother in Wisconsin:

> Your father and I believe you are doing the right thing buying a condo now when prices are low. You are our only son, and we brought you up to be financially responsible. Rather than wait until we are dead, we'd like you to enjoy our money now. We are sending you enough for the down payment, plus a little for furniture. We expect you to fix up the guest room first, so your father and I can visit when the weather turns bad in Wisconsin. We're glad your condo allows pets under thirty pounds, so Misty can come, too.

Misty had to be the little dog in the photo on Cam's desk.

Cam, careful as ever, had made a copy of the cashier's check. It was for two hundred sixty thousand dollars. Thanks to Mom and Dad, he'd only have to take out a loan for about forty thousand dollars. He could afford that, even on his salary.

The weather was bad in Wisconsin now, and had been for months. Helen looked at the postmark on the letter. Last March. Long before Rob met Marcella. Helen's ex had never been to the club then.

Cam wasn't the killer. He didn't need to sell club information. His money came from Mom and Dad.

But Helen had seen the numbers on that printout. The killer had to be someone who sent faxes from the customer care office. Helen remembered the conversation as the staff left for the day. Jessica had offered Jackie a ride home. A shortcut. Because Jessica knew a back way in and out of the club. One that wouldn't show up on the cameras.

No, please. Not Jessica, Helen thought. Not my good friend.

But now too many puzzle pieces were fitting together.

Jessica also hated Brenda.

Jessica had a missing shirt. Jessica needed money. Jessica had a stack of overdue bills. The contractors made her crazy. So did the members. She'd been tightly wound for weeks. She was an actress. She could kill someone and pretend it never happened.

Please, no, Helen thought. No, no, no.

But all the evidence said yes.

Helen shut her eyes, hoping she could wish this away. She wanted Cam to be the killer. She didn't like him. But Jessica was right: Cam was too lazy to kill anyone. Besides, he didn't have to. He was blessed with indulgent parents.

Jessica was not.

Helen was too heartsick to work. She sat at her desk, grateful for the silent phone. She wanted to go home and hide from her terrible knowledge.

Jessica made the job at the Superior Club bearable. She was funny. She was talented. She worked hard, much harder than Cam the hypochondriac. Jessica worked so hard, she'd cracked right down the middle.

Why, oh, why couldn't Cam be the killer?

I can't confront Jessica alone, like some dippy woman in a slasher movie, Helen thought. I need to be sure. I need to be careful. I'll talk to Phil tonight at dinner. We'll work out a plan. Maybe he'll tell me I'm wrong.

But I don't think so.

CHAPTER 24

Helen was alone in the Superior Club office as night crept around the old building. She could swear Brenda was there, an angry, angular presence. The room seemed to vibrate with her malign energy. Maybe Brenda would rest easier, once her killer was caught.

Maybe I'll quit jumping at shadows and imagining things, Helen thought.

She took a last bite of her apple and buried the core in the wastebasket.

Why am I being so careful? she wondered. Brenda won't be going through the trash, looking for evidence of illegal eating. Not anymore.

She gave Brenda's door a guilty glance. Her office was still sealed. Helen didn't even like to pass it.

Helen checked the clock. Five twenty-five. Two eons ago it had been five twenty-three. It was never going to be six o'clock. Tonight, she'd even welcome a call from Blythe St. Ives. Anything to break the dark, heavy silence. It seemed to weigh down the air in the room and press Helen into her chair.

Move, she told herself. Do some work. Quit moping. You'll feel better.

She couldn't feel worse. Not since she'd figured out Jessica was the killer. Helen didn't want it to be true. But what did she really know about her office friend? Nothing. She'd never even been to Jessica's house, never met her husband. She only knew Allan through whispered arguments on the telephone.

Helen's mind was running in circles, like a toy train around a Christmas tree. Any more speculation was useless. She needed to discuss the facts with Phil, then make some serious decisions.

Might as well clean up the office early, while the phone stayed silent. Mrs. Buchmann would call for another guest pass at five fifty-eight. She always did.

Helen turned off the photo-card machine, closed the curtains, and locked the back door.

She tidied the pens and papers that littered her desk and uploaded the day's data to the main computer. She dropped her cell phone into her pocket and her sunglasses into her purse. She wouldn't need them now. It was depressingly dark at six p.m.

There. She was ready to leave. Mrs. Buchmann could call and Helen would still clock out on time. She caught a glint of something shiny on the carpet and stooped to pick it up.

Helen was on the floor, picking up paper clips, when she heard the customer care door open. It was five forty-seven. Helen prayed it wasn't Mr. Casabella's blond bimbo Designated User, needing a new club-card photo. Helen would need ten minutes to restart the machine.

She was relieved to see Jackie clutching a pink ruffled basket, a leftover from her glory days when she could afford charming trifles. As her co-worker stood in the shadows, Helen caught a glimpse of the glamorous socialite Jackie used to be. Then she moved into the light, and Helen saw the strain lines around her mouth and eyes.

"Couldn't stay away from work?" Helen said. "You missed me that much?"

"I left some papers in my desk," Jackie said. "I was so upset about the rain when I left, I forgot them. The rain cleared up, so I walked back to get them. It's a nice night."

Jackie hesitated, but Helen heard the rest of the sentence. "I can't stand to be home alone." Before Phil, Helen had had nights when the walls of her tiny apartment closed in on her. She must have walked over half of Fort Lauderdale.

"I knew you'd be working by yourself. I brought you a treat," Jackie said. "A friend sent me the most delicious chocolates and cinnamon tea."

"That's so generous," Helen said. Jackie had so little, she thought, but she was still willing to share. She didn't deserve her life.

Jackie pulled a pink thermos out of the pretty basket and poured Helen a drink in a dainty cup. "Try it," she said. "And have a chocolate."

Helen took a sip of the tea. There was a slight bitterness under the cinnamon flavor. A chocolate might take away the taste. She reached for a square one that looked like a caramel.

"Try the one with the pink rose on top," Jackie said. "It's exquisite."

"This caramel is really good," Helen said.

"I know you can't resist good chocolates," Jackie said.

"You got that right," Helen said. "That pink one doesn't have a jelly center, does it? I'm not a big fan of jelly."

"Absolutely not. I promise you've never had anything like it," Jackie said. "It's the loveliest strawberry creme."

Ick. A creme center. That was almost as bad as jelly.

"Delicious," Helen lied. She faked a bite and let the creme–center chocolate slip under her desk. She'd throw it out later.

"How was your date?" Helen said, hoping to distract Jackie while she pretended to chew the nonexistent chocolate.

"My date?" Jackie looked blank. She was sitting at her desk, fiddling with a pencil. Helen could hardly bear to look at her gnawed fingernails.

"Didn't you have a lunch date with someone you knew from . . . before?" Before your divorce. Before your life imploded.

"Oh, I almost forgot about that," Jackie said.

"No wonder," Helen said. "You were going out before Brenda died. That must seem like another lifetime."

"It does," Jackie said. "I'm afraid the date with Alvin was a disappointment. We went to lunch at a lovely restaurant where I used to go . . . before. I thought we had a lot in common. I'd seen Alvin at charity events back when I could support them. He had the same interests in good causes that I did. He'd been divorced for years. Alvin is an older man of means, about seventy. That's why his behavior was so shocking."

"What did he do, Jackie?" Helen asked.

"We went to a restaurant where many of our friends lunch. I wore my pink Chanel. It's not new, but Chanel never goes out of style. Alvin was nicely dressed, too. The waitress took our order. He had a steak. I had a salad. The waitress had barely left the table when he said, 'I have to tell you, I'm interested in lots of sex. If you're not, then consider this a lovely lunch.'"

"That's disgusting," Helen said. "What did you do?"

"I said, 'What about making love?'

"He said, 'That comes later. Maybe.'

"Alvin was wrong. It wasn't a lovely lunch. But I was too embarrassed to walk out because too many people there knew me. I didn't want a scene."

"I'm sorry," Helen said. "I can't believe a seventy-year-old man wanted to jump your bones like a horny teenager. He has no class."

"I'm through with dating. I'd rather live alone."

"I don't blame you," Helen said.

Jackie switched the subject. Helen figured she was embarrassed by the memory of her awful date. "You seemed startled when Jessica said she came in the member gate. You didn't know she did that?"

"I never guessed," Helen said. "It seems risky. Mr. Ironton is always raving that if the staff uses that gate, it's a firing offense." She took a sip of cinnamon tea. Then she took a big drink. It was good.

"I think risk taking is part of the thrill," Jackie said. "Jessica dislikes this job. Subconsciously, I think she wants to be fired."

"But she's worried about paying her bills." Helen drank more tea. It was tasting much better. She'd misjudged it.

"Aren't we all?" Jackie said, and snapped the pencil in two. She didn't seem to notice. Helen saw how strong her hands were. Jackie looked fragile, but she'd played golf and tennis for years . . . before.

"We're all trapped," Jackie said. "We can't even afford to look for something better. There are higher-paying jobs in Fort Lauderdale, but I can't buy the gas to drive there, and I'm too tired to look for work even if I could. This place wears me out. Jessica's in the same situation."

Helen decided to tell her about Jessica's deal with Rob, without mentioning names. Jackie was smart. Maybe she could help Helen. Maybe she even knew what Jessica was doing.

"Let's say an interested outsider gave a customer care staffer a chance to earn several thousand dollars," Helen said. "This outsider offered her an incentive to mine some of the damaging information in the files. Information about people who abused her daily. People who deserved whatever happened to them if their peccadillos were made public."

"I don't have any money," Jackie said.

"What?" Helen said.

"I don't have any money. Brenda wanted money, too, when she found out what I was doing. I told her I was broke, but she wouldn't listen."

Helen choked on her tea. Jackie's conversations raced through her mind. Jackie needed money. Jackie walked to the club, so there would be no record of her entering the employee gate. Jackie was missing a blouse. Jackie hated Brenda, who tormented her every chance she got.

Brenda loved to search customer care desks. She'd found the missing file—in Jackie's desk. Jackie came back to retrieve it, just like she came back now to get some papers. Incriminating papers that Helen had overlooked.

Because she was too busy trying to put the blame on Cam and Jessica. Her good friend, Jessica.

"It's you," Helen said. She felt sick. She thought she might pass out.

"I'm really sorry," Jackie said. "But I knew the minute you saw that fax-number list you'd figured it out. I followed you into the bathroom and heard you talking to Marcella. You asked if Rob ever received any faxes on the yacht. When I heard that, I had no choice. I'm so sorry. You're nicer than Brenda. I don't want to kill you."

You don't have to, Helen wanted to say. But the words wouldn't come out.

She could hear the phone ringing, far away. It's Mrs. Buchmann, calling for a guest pass, Helen thought. I'm going to die at exactly five fifty-eight.

Helen saw the darkness gathering at the edge of her vision. Then it closed over her.

CHAPTER 25

I'm dead, Helen thought. I'm dead and buried in a coffin.
I must be decaying pretty fast. I smell awful.

Wait. I'm breathing. I'm not dead. I'm buried alive.

Helen tried to scream, but panic strangled the sound, and it died on her dry lips. The hot, dark air was thick as felt. She was smothering. She tried to move her hands but they were bound in front of her.

Did undertakers tie dead people's hands in coffins?

Wait. There was something thick and sticky around her wrists. Duct tape. Her hands were bound with duct tape. Undertakers didn't use duct tape. She tried to kick out with her feet, but she couldn't. Her legs were bound at the ankles.

Helen was buried, but not in a graveyard. Sweat trickled into her hair. She tried to calm herself, to remember what had happened. Her head ached. She'd thrown up and the sour smell turned her stomach. Her head felt stuffed with Styrofoam.

She tried to piece her scattered thoughts together, but they slid away in the panicked darkness. She wanted to claw, kick and scream. She knew she had to think.

Jessica. I thought Jessica was the killer. Helen imagined her actress friend at her desk, laughing and talking on the phone.

And Cam. I blamed Cam, too.

Then Jackie had stopped by the office just before closing. Jackie with her little pink basket, tempting me with pretty poison like a witch in a fairy tale. Jackie wanted me to eat a chocolate with a pink icing rose. "I promise you've never had anything like it," she'd said.

She was right, Helen thought. I'd never had poisoned chocolate before. If I didn't hate creme centers, I'd really be in a coffin. She gave me tea, too. Tea with a bitter taste. Tea that made me black out. Jackie drugged me and tried to kill me.

Helen was gasping for breath, sweat running in streams down her body. The swampy darkness seemed to suck the air out of her.

Jackie should have killed me, Helen thought. Dying slowly in a dark box is worse than a quick death. What if I never see Phil again? Who's going to feed Thumbs? Margery hates cats. What if—?

What if I quit whining. I'm not dead. I don't know why, but I'm alive. I'm going to get out of here. The first step is to find out where I am.

Her head was clearing a little. Helen could move her elbows slightly from side to side in the narrow space. She hit the left side with her funny bone, and shrieked in pain. But over the stinging, searing hurt, she felt something. The left side of the box was definitely wood. Thick wood. She moved her right elbow carefully and struck cardboard. Boxes. She was shoved in with stacks of cardboard boxes. She heard the tinkle of little bells. Christmas ornaments.

Of course, Helen thought. Jackie couldn't carry me out past the valet stand, no matter how strong she was. Someone would notice. Instead, she dragged me across the office carpet and into the back hall. Helen hoped her uniform had protected her from rug burns.

Jackie shoved me into the long, narrow supply cabinet. It was big enough to hold me. She must have rolled me into the bottom shelf. She'd already bound my feet and hands with duct tape, so I'd be easier to drag. Clever Jackie gave me handles, like a suitcase.

She didn't wait around to make sure I was dead. She knew she couldn't keep the office lights on or the door open after six p.m. That would make security suspicious. Jackie waited until I passed out and then left. Good thing she didn't put duct tape over my mouth, or I would have choked to death when I threw up.

"Help! Someone help me!" Helen screamed.

She knew it was useless to yell. No one could hear her in the deserted building. Jackie had closed the office for the night. Helen was stuck in the cabinet until morning. How far away was that: One hour? Eight hours? Twelve?

Helen wasn't sure she could survive that long without fresh, cool air. The cabinet was a hotbox.

By the time the staff comes in at eight tomorrow morning, I'll have used up all the air, she thought. I'll be dead, or too weak to call for help. There's no guarantee they'll find me in the morning. This cabinet is filled with holiday decorations. They might not find my body till they put up the plastic shamrocks for St. Patrick's Day.

Helen slid her bound hands sideways and pounded awkwardly on the cabinet door. It wouldn't budge. It was locked—or jammed. Helen stopped, exhausted and panting. Her mood wavered between terror and defiance.

Think, she commanded her foggy brain. This is a wooden cabinet, not a bank vault. You need something to cut that tape.

The cardboard boxes were too flimsy. Brenda had been so proud when she'd packed the decorations away and labeled the boxes with her prissy lettering. She'd made us stop everything to admire her work.

Brenda. Mousy little Jackie had beaten Brenda bloody with a golf club, then whacked Dr. Dell.

Helen couldn't believe it. But she remembered the strength in Jackie's hands. And her habit of snapping pencils when she was upset.

Something had finally snapped for Jackie.

She'd lost everything: her husband, her money, her friends. She wound up working at the club where she used to be an honored member, suffering sly humiliations from her ex-friends and abuse from Brenda.

Jackie, the former jet-set beauty, was hoarding stocking coupons and lunching on boiled eggs.

That disastrous date with Alvin was her last chance to return to club society. Jackie probably never had a chance with Alvin, but that date had given her hope. She was still glamorous and thirty years younger than Alvin. But he had treated Jackie like a cheap whore.

He'd killed her last hope.

Then Brenda had found out that Jackie had been selling club information. She'd demanded money Jackie didn't have and threatened to fire her. Jackie would lose her little apartment in Golden Palms. She'd clung to that address in the town where she'd lived all her life. It was the only thing she had.

Brenda wanted to take it away.

It was too much. Jackie had murdered Brenda, then killed Dr. Dell when he walked in at the wrong time.

It seemed so obvious now. I've been a fool, Helen thought, blundering around in the dark, suspecting innocent people based on my half-wit conclusions. I should have told the police what I knew about Rob, and damn the Black Widow. But I had to play amateur detective. Look where it got me.

"Help!" Helen screamed again. She pounded on the door until her hands were scraped and bloody. The adrenaline rush made her feel better, but she knew it wouldn't last. Soon she'd wear herself out, and she would be too tired to struggle. She turned her face closer to the door hinge, hoping for cool air.

Helen moved her bound hands up to the lock, feeling for some way to open it. She couldn't work it. But she discovered the lock had a sharp edge. She ran her taped hands across it once. Then twice. Then again and again. The lock made a small tear in the duct tape. She tore long scratches in her wrists and hands, but Helen was beyond feeling that kind of pain. Concentrating on cutting the tape calmed her. Her breathing grew more even.

After what seemed hours, she managed to free her hands and pull the tape off.

She still couldn't open the cabinet. She pounded the wooden door until her hands bled and her shoulder hurt. She scooted forward to try a different angle of attack and felt something hard in her pocket.

Her cell phone.

Why didn't I think of that sooner? Helen thought.

Because I am the last woman in America to get a cell phone.

She managed to pry it open and power it up. At last, she saw a welcome light. She was no longer in the dark. The time glowed: eleven seventeen p.m. She'd been locked inside the cabinet more than five hours. She could see by the comforting light of her phone. She'd guessed correctly. She was up against boxes marked "Christmas tree stand" and "ornaments."

She dialed club security and heard a man's voice, "Hello. This is Steven."

"Xaviera's Steven? This is Helen. Help me." That's what she wanted to say. But her voice was a hoarse croak and her words rushed out in a jumble.

"Helen, what's wrong? Where are you? You don't sound like yourself."

"I was attacked," she said. "Someone tried to kill me."

"Ohmigod. Are you hurt?"

"I'm OK. I'm trapped in the customer care office. In the supply closet in the back hall. I need to get out of here. I'm running out of air."

"I'll get help. No, I'm coming right over. Stay there."

"I can't go anywhere," Helen said.

"I meant, stay on the phone," Steven said, and promptly disconnected her.

Helen thought that was funny, now that help was on the way. She called Margery next and said, "I can't stay on the line. I'm OK, but I don't think I can drive home. Can you pick me up at the club?"

"What the hell happened now?" Margery roared. "Why do you sound like something in a tomb?"

Helen thought she could see her landlady's cigarette smoke coming through the phone. "It'll take too long to explain," Helen said. "But I'm in a tomb, sort of, and they're getting me out. Just get here, please. Come to the front gate. Ask for Steven in security."

"Don't do this to me, Helen," Margery said. "What tomb? What's going on?"

"I'm fine," Helen said, and hung up. She had to. She heard Steven calling her name.

"Here," she shouted and pounded on the cabinet door.

"Hold on, Helen," Steven said. "The door's jammed. I'm opening it now. I'll have you out in a moment. Just stay calm."

It was Steven who sounded nervous. The metal catch rattled and she felt someone slamming the door from the other side.

"Am I hurting you?" Steven asked, as he kept hitting the door.

"No. Just open the door," Helen said.

And then he did.

Helen rolled out of the cabinet into the cool office. She landed on her back, gasping like a beached fish. Helen lay on the worn tile filling her lungs with delicious fresh air.

"Look at your hands," Steven said. "You're bleeding. The club doctor is on his way. So are Detective O'Shaughnessy and Marshall Noote, the head of security."

Helen groaned.

"Hang on," he said. "You'll be fine."

Not if the police and Marshall Noote show up, she thought.

"Can I get you water? Some coffee? Tea?"

"No tea," Helen said. "Water. Water's fine."

Steven found a cold bottle in the department fridge. "Tiny sips," he said. "We don't want you drinking too much and getting sick."

Water had never tasted so refreshing. Helen pressed the cold bottle against her forehead, then took another sip. "Thanks. This is delicious."

So was Xaviera's surfer boyfriend. Helen, on the other hand, was rancid. She had vomit on her shirt and in her hair. Her uniform looked trampled and the sleeve was ripped.

Steven didn't seem to notice the vile smell. He took out his pocket-knife and began cutting the tape off Helen's ankles.

He was nearly done when the club doctor came running in with his black bag. He wrinkled his nose in disgust when he bent down to examine Helen. He spent his days in a perfumed office on South Beach, installing fake boobs in fake blondes. The club waived his monthly dues to keep him on call, but he mainly handled sunburns and poolside slip-and-falls. The doctor probably hadn't worked a messy emergency in years.

"Let's get her in a chair," the doctor said.

Helen didn't know if this was out of concern for her or his suit. He didn't bother introducing himself, and Helen couldn't find his name in her useless brain. The doctor poked and prodded. By that time, Detective O'Shaughnessy, Marshall Noote and enough security to staff a rap concert were crowded into the office.

Once again, Helen was struck by the father-son resemblance between O'Shaughnessy and Noote: same thick neck, thick fingers and short hair. Same cop eyes. They stayed trained on her while she told her story.

O'Shaughnessy seemed to believe her. She suspected Noote did not.

Things seemed to happen very fast now, in little jagged scenes. The medics arrived. The police collected a sample of her vomit. They searched for Jackie's pink basket, the cup and the thermos, but those were gone. So was the petty cash—the five hundred dollars that Solange kept in her upper drawer. The drawer was open.

"Everyone in the office knew Solange kept the key under the plant on her desk," Helen said.

Jackie had taken the money and run. The incriminating fax numbers that Helen had on her desk were gone, too. Jackie's desk was empty.

The petty cash drawer was fingerprinted. The tape from Helen's wrists and feet was collected to be checked for fingerprints.

A police officer was dispatched to Jackie's apartment. The officer knocked on the door and no one responded. A neighbor said that Jackie had thrown some suitcases into her car and left about six thirty that evening. The same neighbor also said that Jackie had brought her tea earlier that afternoon. Now the neighbor couldn't find her phenobarbital. She didn't want to accuse anyone, especially sweet little Jackie, but she was the only visitor in days.

The neighbor kept her medicine in plain sight on the kitchen counter. She needed phenobarb for her seizures. Maybe Jackie took it by accident. Could the nice officer ask Jackie about it, please, when they found her?

When they found her. Now there was the question.

"We have a BOLO for her car," Detective O'Shaughnessy said. "She's wanted for assault, theft and double homicide."

The words made Helen feel even more unreal. Quiet little Jackie had racked up an impressive list of crimes.

"She drives an old silver Geo," Helen said. "I don't think it goes very fast."

"Doesn't have to," O'Shaughnessy said. "It's twelve thirty in the morning. She's had a six-hour start. We'd like to get a search warrant for the suspect's apartment."

"She tried to kill me. Can't you just break down the door?" Helen asked.

"Doesn't work that way," O'Shaughnessy said. "Unless the person who has the privacy rights associated with the property has knowingly and voluntarily waived those rights, a search warrant is always needed if any evidence obtained is to be admitted in court."

I'm still woozy, Helen thought. But I think he's saying that he needs Jackie's consent for a search.

"To obtain a search warrant," O'Shaughnessy said, "one needs probable cause to believe that whatever is the object of the search is in or on the property sought to be searched."

"Huh?" Helen said. Now she was totally lost.

"The tea," he said. "Do you have reason to believe that she made this tea at home? What about the chocolates? Did she bring them from home? Your statement will help us get a warrant."

"Definitely," Helen said. "She said she got the tea as a gift. She brought it from home in a thermos. The chocolates, too. Except they didn't come in a thermos. They were in a basket."

The police found the chocolate Helen had dropped under her desk. It was taken for analysis.

The club doctor told her she was lucky she'd only pretended to eat it. "That's a needle mark on the bottom," he said. "That chocolate has been injected with something. I suspect there were sleeping pills in that tea. You were supposed to eat the chocolate, drink the tea, pass out and die. You're lucky you didn't aspirate your own vomit and choke."

Now Helen felt really sick.

"You need to go to the hospital and have your stomach pumped," the doctor said.

"No, I don't," Helen said. "I didn't eat the chocolate. I just drank some tea and threw up. I'm fine."

"Then you'll have to sign a paper that you're refusing treatment."

The great healer is afraid I might sue, she thought.

"Thank you for caring," Helen said.

"We prefer you go to the ER, Miss Hawthorne," Detective O'Shaughnessy said. "We don't know for sure what you've consumed or if anything is still in your system. It's for your own safety. Also, we'll need the hospital staff to collect urine and blood samples for testing. We need proof of what you were given to bring your assailant to justice."

"OK, you can take me," Helen said to the medics. "Do I have to go on that stretcher?"

"Regulations," said a strapping young man in a blue uniform. He was too big to argue with.

As they were wheeling her away, Helen said, "Steven, my landlady's coming to the club. Will you direct her to the hospital?"

"No problem," Steven said.

Marshall Noote trotted alongside her, like a big friendly dog. He patted her hand, as if he really cared. Helen knew better.

"You don't fool me," he whispered in her ear. "I know you staged that poisoning attempt. Gave yourself just enough to get a little sick. You framed poor Jackie. She got scared and ran. She's no killer. I knew her from the old days. Sweetest woman I ever met. She wouldn't hurt a fly."

"She tried to kill me," Helen said. "What do I have to do to convince you—die?"

"That might work," Noote said.

CHAPTER 26

"You want tea with your toast?" Margery asked.

"You're joking, right?" Helen said. "I never want tea as long as I live."

"You could just say, 'No, thank you,'" Margery said. "Phil's gone out for coffee. I thought you wouldn't want to wait for some hot caffeine."

She glared at Helen. So did her cigarette. Helen found all those red eyes unnerving.

It was now four in the morning, with a cold clammy mist drifting on the ground. Helen sat snug in Margery's purple recliner with a plate of warm buttered toast in her lap.

She stank like a Dumpster. She'd changed her smelly shirt and torn uniform, but she couldn't shower or wash her hair yet. Helen's damaged hands were wrapped in gauze mittens. She had to keep the salve on a little longer. Her arm had an ugly green bruise where the techs had drawn blood for the police.

"Do you know what you put me through?" Margery said.

For once, Helen's landlady looked every day of her seventy-six years. Her wrinkles plowed furrows into her face. Her purple T-shirt was on inside out, tag in front. She must have dressed in a hurry when Helen called for help.

"First you call me up at eleven at night, croaking like a raven," Margery said. "Then you tell me you're buried in a tomb."

"I said 'sort of,'" Helen said.

"That was real cute," Margery said. "Especially after you hung up without explaining."

"I didn't hang up. Help had arrived."

"Why didn't you say so, instead of making me wonder what happened? I didn't know if you were dead or alive. Phil drove me down to Golden Palms, racing in and out of traffic at a hundred miles an hour. I'm surprised we didn't wipe out on the highway—or wind up in jail."

"Not on I-95," Helen said. "Everyone drives like that."

"You're being cute again." Margery's eyes blazed with anger. "You don't care what you put us through. When we finally got to the Superior Club, that Steven bird said you were in the hospital. That message took another ten years off my life. Didn't make Phil feel too good, either. You're lucky we didn't let you hitchhike home."

"I'm sorry," Helen said. "The police wanted my blood."

"So do I," Margery said. "What were you doing, drinking poison with a killer?"

Helen wasn't sure if the smoke in the room was from her furious landlady or her cigarette. "I didn't know she was a killer."

"That's the problem, isn't it?" Margery said. "Why don't you leave the murder investigations to the police?"

"That's what I thought I was doing," Helen said.

"You borrowed my skeleton key to go snooping through that guy's desk," Margery said.

"And I found information that proved Cam couldn't be the killer."

"So you turned around and blamed that poor actress," Margery said.

"I never said anything to Jessica."

"You didn't get a chance to," Margery said. "Instead you sat down to tea with a serial killer."

"Jackie's not really a serial killer," Helen said. "She only killed two people."

"Only!" Margery howled. "Gee, let's have her over for a barbecue."

"I mean, she's not Jack the Ripper," Helen said. "She just lashed out when she was cornered."

"She beat that woman's head in," Margery said, "then killed another man and tried to kill you. I'd say she's pretty violent."

Helen couldn't argue with that. "At least I figured out the killer worked in the club office. The police were still interviewing the doctor's old girlfriends. That would have kept them busy for the next decade."

"Maybe if you'd told them the truth, the cops wouldn't have wasted their time," Margery said.

Helen winced. That hit home. "Well, at least they're looking for the right suspect now. They think Jackie killed Brenda because she tormented her, which is true enough." Helen still hadn't told the police about the club information Jackie had sold Rob. She was more scared of the Black Widow than the police.

"Humph," Margery said, and breathed out a huge cloud of smoke.

"And the police couldn't have gotten the search warrant without me," Helen said.

"I bet they could have figured out something to tell the judge."

Margery wouldn't give an inch. She ground out her cigarette and lit another. Helen quietly munched her toast. Slowly, the anger seeped out of the room. Margery had said what she needed to say.

Half a cigarette later, Margery broke the silence. "Did the police find anything to connect Jackie to the murder?"

"A few things. At least from what I overheard last night," Helen said. She was grateful for a peaceful conversation. "The police got their warrant and Jackie's landlord unlocked her apartment. The place looked like it had been ransacked. They found her closets open and her clothes flung everywhere. Her car was gone. The police think Jackie did a hasty packing job and fled.

"They found two things to back up my story: The neighbor's bottle of phenobarbital was sitting on Jackie's kitchen counter, with about half missing. They also found ant killer that contained arsenic."

"Arsenic! Where did she get that?" Margery said.

"Wal-Mart. You only need a twentieth of a teaspoon to kill someone."

"Good lord," Margery said.

"That's why drawing my blood and getting a urine sample was so important. If the tests find phenobarb, they've got Jackie for attempted murder. Ditto for the arsenic in the chocolate. There was cinnamon tea in the kitchen cabinet, so they can tie that to Jackie. But they couldn't find the pink thermos or the cup. The chocolates were missing, too. And there's no sign of the bloody shirt or the papers Jackie stole from my desk at the club."

"I bet they're long gone," Margery said.

"Maybe, but I'm here," Phil said. He bent down and kissed Helen. "How are you feeling?" he asked.

"Better than she deserves," Margery said.

Helen felt another stab of guilt. Phil looked tired and worn. His silver hair straggled down his neck, his skin was oily, and there were deep bags under his dark blue eyes.

Margery sniffed the air. "You've changed your aftershave," she said. "But I like it."

"Hot coffee and warm Krispy Kremes," Phil said. "The way to a woman's heart."

"Definitely the way to mine," Helen said. "I'm ready for a sugar rush. Mmm. Sweet creamed coffee and warm glazed doughnuts."

There was a respectful silence while they ate and drank. Two doughnuts later, Helen said, "You listened to me on the ride home from the club. But I never heard about your trip to Palm Beach, Phil. What happened with your trip today?"

"I thought you'd never ask," Phil said. "I'd spent days tracking down rumors of a jeweler who sold expensive items to 'special customers.' The shop carried new and antique jewelry—and according to the rumors, some pretty shady goods. I finally found it on the northern edge of Palm Beach County."

More guilt, Helen thought. Phil had driven more than two hundred miles today, if you counted the trips from Palm Beach to Miami and back. No wonder he looked exhausted.

"I thought I was going to have the big news tonight." Phil took out a blue velvet box, got down on his knees in front of Helen and opened it. Inside was a sparkling diamond ring.

"Oh, Phil, you shouldn't have," Helen said. She felt confusion, surprise and what she least expected—happiness.

"Of course I should," he said.

Helen threw her arms around Phil and kissed him. He smelled of hot coffee, Krispy Kremes and slightly sweaty man. They should bottle this, she thought. There's nothing sexier.

"I can't believe you did this," she said. "I never expected it."

"Hey, I promised Elsie I'd get her diamond ring back and I did," Phil said.

Helen pulled herself away and tried to hide her disappointment in a third doughnut.

"Right," she said. "Elsie's ring. I'm so happy. For her, I mean."

"I can tell," Margery said. Her sarcasm went right by Phil, but Helen knew her landlady had seen everything, including Helen's disappointment that the diamond ring wasn't for her.

"The dumb bastard had it on display in his store," Phil said. "Can you believe that?"

"Dumb," Helen echoed weakly. Margery knew she wasn't talking about the ring.

"He was unbelievably arrogant," Phil said.

"Arrogant," Helen repeated.

"When you're overconfident, you let yourself in for some nasty surprises," Margery said, twisting the knife.

"Not only was Elsie's ring on display," Phil said, "so were Marcella's ruby-and-diamond earrings. They were out there as appetizers, to lure in customers to buy the whole set. I asked to see the earrings. I said I was looking for a present for my fiancée. I hope you don't mind, Helen. I needed a pretext."

"Pretext," Helen said.

"That's her," Margery said, malice lighting her old eyes.

"The shop owner said, 'Excellent choice, sir. Would you be interested in a larger piece? I have something in the back you may want to see. We're getting ready to ship it to New York.'

"As soon as I saw the necklace," Phil said, "I knew it was Marcella's, and this guy had been dealing with crooks. The rumors were true.

"He's slippery. He won't take goods that the police list as stolen. But he knows there are gray areas, where the owners hesitate to call in the law: A child hooked on coke steals his mother's diamonds and hocks them. A boy toy takes his lover's Rolex. A fiancé runs off with the silver. The owners are too embarrassed to report the thefts."

"So what did you do?" Helen said. She was surprised she sounded so normal.

"The shop owner said the jewelry hadn't been reported as stolen. But he didn't have any provenance on those pieces. He knew the kid who brought in Elsie's antique diamond couldn't afford a ring like that. I showed him the insurance photo of Elsie's missing ring and he gave it back to me."

"Just like that?" Helen said. "He just turned over a diamond ring?"

"I told him I'd have Elsie report it as stolen and the police would come down on him so fast he wouldn't know what hit him. I said I'd call the media and the TV trucks would be waiting outside his shop. He doesn't want any attention. He gave that ring up way too quick—the sign of a guilty man."

"And what about Marcella's jewelry?" Margery asked.

"In exchange for me not saying anything, he promised to return it, no questions asked. He says the seller has more pieces. He's going to get him into the shop tomorrow to deliver them. Then I'll leave him and his store alone."

"Is Rob the seller?" Helen asked. "Is he alive?"

"I'm not sure. It was a pretty generic description. He said the seller was wearing a ball cap and sunglasses. I thought you'd want to go with me. Now I guess you're too sick."

"I'm going," Helen said. "I'd rise from the dead to be there."

"Let's see if Rob does," Phil said.

CHAPTER 27

Helen put on a black Escada top that clung to her curves. It was sexy but not slutty.

Short black skirt.

Sky-high heels.

She dressed with extra care for the maybe meeting with her ex. She wanted to remind Rob what he'd lost. He'd married an older woman for her money. Let him see what money couldn't buy.

Helen washed her hair and tamed it into lush waves with a blow-dryer. She wore it longer since their divorce, almost to her shoulders.

She couldn't do much about her battered hands. They looked like they'd been run through a shredder. But Rob's eyes would probably never travel past her legs—they were long, lean and tanned.

Phil whistled when Helen stalked out of her apartment in her killer clothes. "Wow! I need to take you to Palm Beach more often. Is that new?"

"I bought myself some treats when I got the Superior Club job," Helen said. Her new credit cards were already in meltdown, but she'd worry about paying them later.

"Wish I had a limo instead of a Jeep," Phil said.

He opened the door to his dusty vehicle and admired her legs while she slid into the seat. Phil didn't know this show was for another man.

Phil had slept off his exhaustion. This morning he looked alert and rested and way too handsome to be cooped up in a car on a sunny day. The drive up I-95 seemed endless. Conversations started and stopped.

"Do you really think Rob is dead?" Helen said.

"Don't know," Phil said.

"None of Marcella's husbands has escaped before," Helen said. "Why would she show mercy to a cheat and a thief like Rob?"

"Murder gets riskier every time you try it," Phil said. "Marcella is smart enough to know she'll get caught eventually, no matter how many lawyers she can buy."

"I wonder why Margery hangs around with a notorious killer like the Black Widow?" Helen asked.

"No one ever saw Marcella kill anyone. She's never been arrested. Ever wonder what happened to Margery's husband?" Phil asked.

"I assume she divorced him."

"He disappeared after Hurricane Andrew," Phil said. "He's presumed dead, but there's no body. Maybe Margery and Marcella have more in common than you think."

They rode in silence for a good ten miles after that. Phil was marshaling his thoughts for the confrontation with Rob. Helen reviewed what Phil had told her before about Marcella's marital history.

At twenty, Marcella had married her first husband. She was a stunning natural beauty, with long wavy hair and a lush body. Her husband had his own shipping company. He was lonely, fabulously wealthy, and fifty years older than Marcella. There was even some evidence that she loved the man. He died of a heart attack ten years later. Marcella inherited half a billion dollars, four houses, a yacht and a teak sailboat. She was thirty. She wore black for six months, then married a twenty-three-year-old Chippendale.

Her second husband had a great body and all the right moves except one: Chip swung both ways. Marcella caught Chip with his boyfriend and made a terrible scene. It was the talk of the seaport bars. Shortly after that, Marcella and Chip went on a sailboat trip to the Bahamas. She told the police that her second husband had had a lot of wine that evening and must have fallen off the boat during the night. A fisherman found the body two days later.

The coroner ruled the death accidental. Chip's boyfriend was never seen again. No one went looking for him. He was a drunk and a drifter.

Husband number three was a member of the yacht crew, another empty-headed stud fifteen years younger than Marcella. Gossip said she caught this one with an island hottie, but nobody would say anything on the record.

Two days after Marcella supposedly caught her third husband in bed with another woman, he ate some bad seafood and died in agony. The island police didn't investigate his death too carefully. He was seen eating three lobsters that night in a restaurant in the capital of Georgetown. Two other lobster-lovers at the restaurant were also sick, but they survived. Marcella ate steak, the most expensive thing on any island menu. She was once more a widow. After the inquest, she buried her handsome young husband at sea.

Marcella was fifty-two when she met her fourth husband at a bar in the Caymans. That wedding nearly equaled Madonna's extravaganza with Sean Penn, according to *People* magazine. The million-dollar wedding was in a pavilion by the sea, decorated with ten thousand pink roses.

Two years later, the groom drowned in a diving accident. Marcella's fourth husband was only thirty. The police investigation found nothing unusual and Marcella seemed to have no known reason to kill him.

The fifth husband died in the Bahamas, again on that fatal sailboat. He was a bodybuilder who cheated on Marcella with a sixteen-year-old Nassau girl. He told the girl the rich old bag he married was so grateful, he could do anything. The young woman got pregnant and her mother told Marcella.

Marcella had a very public reconciliation with her husband on Bay Street. It was so touching, tourists and locals alike applauded them.

The couple sailed for a second honeymoon on that teak boat. Marcella wanted to picnic on a remote island, just the two of them.

The cook packed a basket with caviar, lobster and champagne. Her fifth husband was an inexperienced sailor. The sailboat hit a sudden squall, the boom swung wildly in the wind, and he was cracked on the head. He died before Marcella could get him to a hospital.

The coroner ruled the head wound was consistent with injuries sustained by a blow from the boom. Marcella had the bodybuilder cremated.

Rob was husband number six. He cheated on the Black Widow and stole her jewelry.

Helen kept asking herself how she could be so wrong about everyone—Rob, Jackie, Cam, Jessica, maybe even Margery. She didn't trust herself to judge bananas at the supermarket anymore.

She was relieved when they reached the jewelry store, a marble cube in a shopping strip between a Botox specialist and a pricey pet store.

NEW AND PRE-OWNED ELEGANCE, the jewelry shop window proclaimed in scrolly gold letters. Inside, the shop went for the discount Versailles look: gold-framed mirrors, fake Louis XVI chairs and crystal chandeliers. The counters had stubby gold legs. The white carpet was thick and soft. Walking on it was like wading through a warm snowstorm.

The shop owner oozed around the counter, also on stubby legs. Fine tailoring couldn't mask his rotund figure. Helen suspected even if he wore sunglasses, his eyes would still look shifty. He clasped his soft white hands, as if trying to keep from grabbing the jewelry off his customers. His wide oily smile straggled away when he recognized Phil.

"This is Mr. Harpet," Phil said.

Helen barely rated a nod.

"The client is due in less than ten minutes," Mr. Harpet said. "The best observation post is through a two-way mirror in the back room."

"Just like at the police station," Helen said.

Mr. Harpet's look said she was not the better class of client.

"There's a speaker in the room," he said. "You'll be able to hear everything the same as I do." Mr. Harpet ushered them into a dingy back room. The hidden mirror let them see the whole store from behind the main counter. It was as if they were standing behind him.

"Best seats in the house," Phil said.

He and Helen sat on two crippled gold chairs and waited impatiently. Phil got up and paced. Helen shifted in her chair and wondered if her slippery former spouse would show. He seemed to have a sixth sense when things weren't going his way.

"What if it is Rob?" Helen said.

"We let him complete the deal. I want the whole thing on tape," Phil said. "Then we grab him and the jewelry."

Helen heard a bell. The shop door opened. She saw a man silhouetted in the sunlit doorway, but he was too far away to see his face. He was about Rob's height. He wore new jeans, a baseball cap, and judging by the drape, an expensive shirt.

As he walked toward the counter and the hidden mirror, Helen finally made out his face.

"That's him!" she said.

"It sure is," Phil said.

Helen wanted to leap through the glass and strangle him. After what he'd put her through, Rob strolled in to boldly sell his wife's jewelry. Incredible.

Phil squeezed her hand in a gesture of affection and warning. "Easy," he said. "I know you're angry. Sit tight and we'll nail him."

Helen watched Rob shake hands with Mr. Harpet. She was fascinated by their body language—two liars talking to each other. Mr. Harpet slathered on his charm like cheap suntan oil. Rob did his good ol' boy routine, which was hard to carry off in Gucci loafers. She almost believed him, even after all these years.

Mr. Harpet sat down at a spindly gold desk. Rob pulled up a gold silk chair and took a black velvet bag out of his pocket. He spilled the contents on a velvet pad on the desk. Even across the room, Helen could see the green and white fire of diamonds and emeralds.

Mr. Harpet pulled out a jeweler's loupe and moaned in pleasure. Helen blushed, as if she were eavesdropping on an intimate moment.

Rob started bargaining for the best price on his wife's stolen jewelry. Mr. Harpet offered him ten cents on the dollar, then let Rob bargain him up to nearly full price. Why not? He was never going to pay the money.

"Then it's a deal," Mr. Harpet said, with a Judas smile.

Those words were the signal.

Phil opened the door and stepped into the plush front of the store. Helen followed. She saw Rob turn nearly as white as the corpse he was supposed to be.

"Welcome back from the dead, Rob," Phil said. "It's business as usual, I see. We've got your transaction on tape. I'm sure the police will be interested."

"The necklace was a present from my wife," Rob said. Except for the color change, he was cool. Helen had to give him that.

"That's not what Marcella told me," Phil said. "She paid me to track you down. She doesn't want you. The Black Widow has her next husband picked out. But she'd like her jewelry back."

"You must be the famous Phil," Rob said. "No wonder you're here. I heard you liked used goods."

Helen grabbed Phil's arm, before he punched Rob. "Don't let him bait you," she said. "He's not worth the skin off your knuckles."

"You're pussy-whipped, man," Rob said. Without warning, he picked up the gold silk chair and swung it at Phil's leg. Helen heard a crack, then a crash of glass.

"My mirrors! My display case!" shrieked Mr. Harpet.

"My leg," Phil said.

Rob streaked out the door, the bell jangling merrily.

"He's got the jewelry," Phil said, rubbing his leg in a welter of glass. "Helen, go get him."

"What about you?"

"I'm fine. Don't let him get away."

"No chance," Helen said. "He hunted me for years. This is payback time."

She started to run and nearly tripped on her spike heels. She kicked the shoes off, but grabbed one as a weapon. Then she took off barefoot down the street, her skirt hiked so she could run faster.

Her feet pounded the warm sidewalk. A woman walking a Yorkie picked up her little pet and held him protectively. Rob was running across the parking lot.

"Stop, thief!" Helen cried. She could see Rob dodging an SUV. He turned down a quiet street. Helen followed, determined to catch him.

Rob bolted across a yard and leaped a fence. Helen hitched up her skirt almost to her waist and jumped, too. Her new skirt ripped on the chain link. Now she was beyond mad. The skirt wasn't paid for yet and it was ruined.

They were tearing through a weird park with flowers, stuffed animals, and balloons on sticks in the grass. No, wait. This wasn't a park. It was a cemetery. With rows of flat gray granite stones.

She could see Rob jumping over the headstones. Helen followed him, running past the rows of graves. She was closing the gap. She could see the names on the stones that nearly grazed her feet: MUFFIN. COOKIE. DUMPLING.

Bizarre. Why would someone put food on a tombstone? Then she passed a tombstone shaped like a bone and knew where she was: a pet cemetery. Those were the names of much-loved dogs and cats.

Rob was slowing down, getting winded. Helen ran faster, powered by fury. Her ex wasn't getting away. Not this time. She'd follow him into hell.

She only had to follow him another row and a half. Rob dodged left, tripped over a stone, and fell facedown in the stringy grass. The fall knocked the breath out of him. Helen landed on his back.

"Uhf!" Rob said, panting like an old dog. "You've put on weight since we were married."

Helen hit him with her high heel.

"Dammit," Rob said. "That hurt."

"It was supposed to," she said. Then she started laughing.

"What's so funny?" Rob asked, between gasps.

"I just noticed the tombstone you fell over. It says, 'Beloved Rover. Faithful Unto Death.' That would definitely trip you up."

Rob said nothing. He was still trying to catch his breath. Phil's Jeep roared onto the cemetery road. Phil stopped at their row, left the engine running, and limped across the grass.

"You got him," he said to Helen. "Good work. I knew you were smarter than he was. I didn't know you were faster and stronger."

Phil bent back Rob's hands and cuffed him. Rob struggled, but Helen stuck her knee in his back, where it would hurt the most. Rob yelped like a stepped-on poodle.

Phil extracted the velvet bag from Rob's pocket. That's when Rob really howled. "Hey! You can't do that."

Helen kicked him in the gut. It felt good. His belly was soft. He'd been lifting beer and bags of nachos since he'd died.

"Shut up or she'll kick you again," Phil said. "She wants to hurt you even more than I do."

"Are you OK?" Helen asked Phil. "You're limping. Should you be walking?"

"I'm fine now that you caught this idiot. I don't think my leg's broken. I'm well enough to kick him all the way back to Miami."

"I'm not talking," Rob said.

"Fine." Phil powered up his cell phone. "You can talk to the police. Just remember, you're a dead man."

"Wait. I can explain," Rob said.

Rob could always explain, Helen thought. Her ex-husband believed he could talk his way out of anything. Usually, he could.

"Let's get him out of here," Phil said. "I don't want him attracting more attention."

Phil and Helen frog-marched the handcuffed Rob across the cemetery and shoved him in the cramped back of the Jeep.

"Can't you cuff me in front?" Rob whined. "I'm wedged in here. This hurts."

"Good," Helen said. Phil backed out of the cemetery and swung the Jeep toward the highway.

"You move pretty fast for a dead man," Helen said. "Police in three counties have been looking for you. The cops thought I killed you. Why did you put Marcella and me through this?"

"I told you," Rob said. "But you didn't listen. You never do. I wanted to get away from her. I needed money to leave her."

"So you stole from your own wife," Helen said. "Just when I thought you couldn't go any lower."

"She never wore that crap. She wouldn't have missed it, if she hadn't sent those rubies to be cleaned. I was desperate." Rob pleaded with hurt-puppy eyes. "You don't know what it's like to be that desperate."

"Sure I do," Helen said. "I was married to you."

"She's tired of me," Rob said. "She wants to kill me. She'll get away with it, too. She's the Black Widow. I had to save myself. I wanted everyone to think I was dead. It was the only way to survive. The cops would suspect she killed me, but they'd never prove it."

"So why drag me into this?" Helen said.

"I thought it would be better if I had two murder suspects."

Phil grabbed Helen's blouse before she went over the back of the seat after Rob. "He's not worth it, remember?" he whispered in her outraged ear.

Helen took a deep breath to calm down. Phil was right. She wouldn't take the bait. "You provoked that fight with me at the club," she said. "You wanted me to hit you. That would mark me as a suspect."

"You enjoyed it," Rob said. "You've wanted to pop me for years."

"What about that blood in the parking lot?" Helen said. "How'd you fake that?"

Rob shook his head so his hair flopped to the side. Helen could see deep scabbed cuts at the edge of his hairline. "I cut my forehead with a razor blade. See? It's an old wrestler's trick. Bleeds like a son of a bitch, but doesn't hurt much. I could hide the cuts with my hair. I made another cut in my arm, sucked the blood up with a syringe and then squirted it over the Dumpster so it looked like arterial blood spray."

"How'd you know to do that?" Helen said.

"It's all on the Internet if you read the forensic Web sites. I knew I couldn't stockpile my blood, like they did in that TV show."

"*Desperate Housewives,*" Helen said.

"Right. That trick doesn't work. Blood clots pretty quickly. But if I took it out with a syringe and squirted it right away, I'd have a decent blood spatter pattern." Rob was puffed with pride over his plan. "I got kind of queasy. I tried not to think this was my own blood. It worked. At least, it fooled the cops. I hated to lose the shirt, though. It was a favorite."

Helen made a low growl, like an angry dog, but she stayed in her seat. Phil patted her knee.

"It was worth the sacrifice. I knew Marcella would lawyer up," Rob said. "But you couldn't afford a good lawyer. The cops would keep after you."

Phil gently rubbed Helen's back, another reminder not to respond. He didn't have to worry. Helen couldn't say anything. She couldn't find the words to answer Rob.

The Jeep turned off I-95 onto the road to Golden Palms. The ordeal was almost over.

"You know, Rob," Phil said. "I was going to call the police and let them know you were alive and well and selling stolen jewelry in Palm Beach County. But your wife doesn't want the publicity. I doubt she'll press charges. I hate wasting police time. They don't like it, either. Instead, I'm taking you home to your wife. That way Marcella can decide if she wants to be a widow again."

"No!" Rob's smirk vanished. Helen could see real fear in his eyes. "No, please. Call the police."

"Nope," Phil said. "You've bothered the police enough. Helen, we're five minutes from the Superior Club. Call Marcella on my phone and tell her she has a visitor."

"I'll scream when we get to the club gates," Rob said. "Security will come running. They know me. You won't get away with this."

Phil pulled the Jeep behind the pumps at a deserted gas station. He turned around and said, "Sure I will." Phil slammed Rob in the jaw. His eyes rolled back and he slumped back unconscious.

"I've wanted to do that for a long time," Phil said, as he put the Jeep in gear. "Helen, please call Marcella. Let her know her visitor is a little under the weather. I'll deliver him and her jewelry momentarily."

Helen gave the message to the skin-domed majordomo, Bruce.

"Certainly," Bruce said. "Someone will be on the dock to help the gentleman aboard. Marcella thinks a short sea voyage is just what he needs."

Helen shivered when she hung up the phone. Men didn't return when they sailed with Marcella.

Michael, the devilishly handsome club concierge, was waiting on the dock with a wheelchair. The *Brandy Alexander* loomed over him, its black windows like eyeless sockets. Michael eased the handcuffed Rob out of the car and into the wheelchair with practiced moves. Club members regularly drank themselves into a stupor and the concierge tactfully wheeled them to their rides. The club could maintain the fiction that these members weren't drunk, just a little under the weather.

Rob was still unconscious. His head lolled to one side and his mouth was open. The concierge tucked a blanket around Marcella's unfaithful spouse to conceal his handcuffs, then wheeled the chair up the ramp. Rob never stirred.

Phil handed the velvet bag of jewelry to Bruce. Bruce handed Phil a check. Marcella did not come out to thank Phil or Helen.

Helen and Phil watched the white-uniformed crew cast off. The club concierge stayed on board. Helen wondered if the new husband would dispose of the old one.

Helen and Phil watched the Black Widow's ghost-white yacht sail away. This time, Helen did not run screaming along the docks to save her ex.

She held Phil's hand and said nothing.

CHAPTER 28

"Bye, George. Good luck back at your office," Helen said.

"Thanks." George shoved a fat flowered suitcase into his car trunk and mopped his forehead with a handkerchief. "I'll need it. I don't want to go home. It's four below in Ohio."

George had been hauling boxes and suitcases out of apartment 2C for the last hour. The *bump, bump, bump* of luggage down the stairs woke Helen at seven thirty in the morning. It was her day off, but she didn't mind. She'd been trying to ignore her cat, Thumbs, since six. He'd been walking on her head, meowing for breakfast.

Helen finally gave up, got up and fed the big-pawed cat. She made herself some coffee, then slipped outside to enjoy the glorious morning.

Helen sipped her coffee by the pool and felt sorry for George and Nancy, with the easy pity Floridians saved for the unfortunates who lived in the gray frozen north. Phil sat beside her, barefoot and in jeans, deliciously shirtless. He was taking the day off, celebrating his fat check from Marcella.

It was eighty degrees on a sunny-bright morning. The white

curves of the Coronado glowed in the soft light. The air was sweet with flowers. Margery looked like an exotic plant in lavender clamdiggers and a gauzy purple shirt. She was skimming bougainvillea blossoms out of the pool. Helen wished her landlady would let them float on the water.

Nancy came out on the upstairs walkway dragging a heavy dark wool coat. She handed it to George and called down, "Want to do the final walk-through, Margery? We're about finished here."

"Sure." Margery left her skimmer by the pool.

Helen looked at Phil. They nodded in silent agreement, and trailed up the stairs behind Margery. George stowed Nancy's coat in the car and stayed by the pool. "I want to enjoy the sun," he said. "I'll be freezing in Ohio soon enough."

Apartment 2C had one bedroom, a tiny bath, a decent kitchen and a comfortable living room, furnished in the same fifties furniture as Helen's place. The turquoise couch was slightly butt-sprung and there was a cigarette burn on the coffee table. But the place was clean. Operating room clean. Helen was nearly overcome by the lemon wax and ammonia fumes.

"How did you get those crusty old windows to shine?" Margery asked.

"Scrubbed them with crumpled newspapers," Nancy said. "My mother used to do that."

"It works," Margery said. "This old stove is a wonder. What did you use on that?"

"Elbow grease," Nancy said.

The old furniture gleamed with fresh polish. The porcelain kitchen sink was bleached white again. The bathroom shelves were stacked with clean towels and bed linens. The shell mirror was dusted.

"How'd you get the dust out of all those curvy shells?" Helen asked.

"Q-tips," Nancy said.

There were vacuum trails across the rugs. The brass teakettle was polished to a high shine. Even the flamingo salt and pepper shakers had been washed.

"It's perfect. Ready to rent," Margery said. "No one's ever left it this clean."

"And she's been cleaned out by a lot of tenants," Helen said.

Margery glared at her.

"May I ask a favor?" Nancy said. "Could you refund our deposit before we go?"

"Might as well," Margery said. "Save me a stamp."

She sat down at the kitchen table, which had been polished to a soft glow, and wrote a check for the first and last months' security deposit.

"It's been a pleasure," Margery said. "Come back. And tell your friends up north."

"Nancy, time to saddle up and ride," George called from downstairs. "You need help carrying anything out?"

"Just the two suitcases by the door," Nancy said. "I can handle them. Everything else is in the car."

She handed Margery the apartment keys. "I'd like to use the little girl's room before we start the long drive. Last chance for a clean restroom before Ohio."

"Be my guest," Margery said. "Pull the front door shut behind you."

Helen and Phil followed her outside. While they waited for Nancy, George folded his trip maps and fretted. "I've been married thirty-six years and I've never figured out why women take so long in the bathroom. What do they do in there?"

"You don't want to know, George," Phil said. "Some things should remain a mystery to man."

"Let Nancy enjoy her privacy," Margery said. "The restrooms along the road are nasty."

The door to 2C finally opened, and Nancy struggled out with a fat leather purse and two suitcases. Phil gallantly leaped up the steps and took the luggage from her.

"Look at those things," George said, as Phil manhandled the suitcases down the stairs. "She wore shorts and golf shirts the whole time we were here. I got my clothes in a gym bag. How does she fill two suitcases the size of Subarus?"

Phil looked a little winded as he wrestled the heavy suitcases to the couple's car. George opened the trunk. Phil rearranged the other luggage to fit in one big suitcase. The other monster went on the backseat.

"It's been a pleasure," George said, and shook hands all around.

"This was a tough time, but you made it bearable," Nancy said. She gave Margery and Helen a hug and kissed Phil chastely on the cheek.

"Have a safe trip home," Helen said, as they waved good-bye to the Ohio couple.

When they were out of sight, Phil said, "I checked the trunk when I fitted in that big suitcase. There was nothing in the car that belonged to you."

"I told you," Margery said. "The curse of 2C is broken. Did you see how they cleaned the place? They left it better than when they moved in. It's ready to rent. Except I want to paint that bathroom. It's looking a little shabby."

"Let me fix myself some breakfast and I'll help you," Helen said. "It's my day off."

"Deal," Margery said. "Come over to my place. I'll nuke some brownies."

"Can I help?" Phil said.

"There's not room in that bathroom for three people," Margery said.

"I mean, can I help eat the brownies?" Phil said.

They followed Margery into her warm kitchen. "What can I do to help?" Helen said.

"Pour yourself a cup of coffee and go sit in the living room out of my way. You want fresh orange juice?"

"It seems right, since you confiscated that juicer from a crooked tenant. We can toast the end of the curse," Helen said.

Helen and Phil filled their cups and retreated to Margery's living room. The roar of the juicer, as it ground up orange innards, covered their conversation.

"How are you this morning?" Phil asked.

"Fine," Helen said, kissing his warm lips. "Better now."

"No worries about Rob? No bad dreams?"

"No, he gave me enough nightmares while he was . . ." Helen started to say "alive" and changed it to "here."

"Are you worried what Marcella will do to him?" Phil asked.

"No," she said. "That was last time, before he came back into my life and tried to frame me for murder. He's no good, Phil. I hope he's far away."

Something hard and hurting covered her heart, a little tumor of pain and betrayal that she didn't want to think about and didn't want to remove. Rob had made her a fool once more. She'd thought he couldn't hurt her anymore, but she was wrong. Again.

Margery came in balancing a plate of warm brownies and three glasses of orange juice. "Drink this first," she said, "or your brownies will taste off."

They clinked glasses and toasted. "To the end of the curse on 2C," Helen said.

"To no more crooks in that apartment," Phil said.

"Amen," Margery said.

They talked and ate for almost an hour. Then Helen changed into her paint clothes. Phil helped carry the paint, brushes, rollers and drop cloths up the stairs.

Margery unlocked the door to 2C. Once again, Helen was nearly knocked down by the odor of ammonia and lemon polish. The smell was the same, but the apartment seemed different. There was an empty double hook on the wall in the little entranceway.

"Did you take down your shell mirror so we could paint?" Helen said.

"Hell, no," Margery said. "They took my mirror." She ran to the bathroom and stared at the empty shelves in the linen closet. "My new towels are gone. The sheets, too. No wonder Nancy washed everything."

Helen checked out the bare kitchen. "She took the shiny copper teakettle."

"And the salt and pepper shakers," Phil said.

"She cleaned me out. She even got my new purple bedspread and the throw pillows on my couch," Margery said.

"She left the ashtray, but it's chipped," Phil said.

"But we saw all your things here when you did the final walk-through," Helen said.

"The suitcases," Margery said. "Those two big suitcases by the door were empty. Nancy went back after I gave her the refund check and stuffed everything in them. No wonder she was struggling to carry them."

"Phil helped her," Helen said. She started laughing. "And George distracted us with folksy conversation. Your nice normal couple from Ohio were crooks after all."

"Not even interesting ones," Margery said. "Plain old tourist towel thieves."

"You want me to go after them?" Phil said. "They've had about an hour's start. I could probably track them down."

"Not worth your time or gas money," Margery said. "I got the towels on sale at Target and the shell mirror at a garage sale. Damn, I liked it, though. That's the last time I have anyone ordinary here."

"Yoo-hoo! Anyone home?" a voice called from the Coronado courtyard.

"I think you got your wish," Helen said, looking out the door. "It's Elsie."

"She told me she was coming over to pick up her ring," Margery said. "I'll go get it." She ran to her apartment.

Elsie was standing by the pool, waving frantically. She was dressed in black leather pants, black satin bustier and biker boots. The outfit was studded with metal rings, loops and chains. Lumps of white flesh popped out of various gaps, like gophers from their holes.

"Incredible," Phil said.

"I knew you'd like it." Elsie beamed. Her dyed blond hair was streaked cherry red. It matched her lipstick, which crept into the cracks in her lips. Clumps of black mascara colored her light eyelashes. She batted them at Phil.

"I have a present for you." Elsie handed Phil a foil-wrapped package.

He tore off the gold paper and said, "Glenlivet scotch." Phil kissed Elsie's brightly painted cheek. "My favorite."

"I can't thank you enough," Elsie said. "You were so nice when I was foolish. My son would have locked me away for sure. You saved me from living in a managed care facility."

Margery came out carrying the velvet ring box. She handed it to Phil, and he gave it to Elsie. She opened the box with trembling fingers. "That's it." Elsie's smile was brighter than the diamond. "That's my mother's ring. I never thought I'd see it again."

She unleashed another flirtatious smile for Phil. "I never thought I'd be getting a diamond ring from such a handsome young man."

"You aren't the only one who was surprised," Margery said.

Helen glared at her landlady.

CHAPTER 29

"Helen, did you hear the news?" Xaviera asked.

"Did they find Jackie?" Helen asked.

"Not yet," Xaviera said. "She's over the wind."

"In the wind," Helen corrected.

"Do you want to teach English or hear my juicy gossip?" Xaviera tossed her long dark hair. "You've had two days off. You don't know what you've missed."

"It must be good," Helen said. "I just walked in the door on a Monday morning. I didn't even get to my desk yet. Sounds like I need to be sitting down to hear this momentous news." She grinned at Xaviera.

"Well, don't stand there. Hurry up." Xaviera drummed her long fingernails on the desk. They were ten works of art. Each nail was painted yellow with an orange sun, blue water and a tiny palm tree.

"Wicked nails," Helen said, as she passed Xaviera's desk.

"And completely against the dress code," Cam said.

Xaviera swiped her painted nails at his face like a cat. Cam held up his bottle of hand sanitizer for a shield. "Keep those things away from me. They're crawling with germs."

"They'll crawl all over your face if you make trouble for me," Xaviera said.

Helen was grateful for the distraction. It helped get her past the ugly landmarks in the customer care office. She still shuddered when she passed Brenda's sealed door. Jackie's denuded desk, with the drawers askew, haunted her. She still couldn't believe her colleague had tried to poison her. Jackie seemed so quiet. Of course, Helen had read that phrase in a thousand newspaper interviews with a killer's neighbors.

Helen dropped her purse in her drawer and plopped down in her parrot-print chair. Her eyes caught something outside her window. A long yacht was blocking her view of the water, a white ghost ship with cruel black windows, like a drug dealer's limousine.

Helen thought she was hallucinating, but she could see the boat's name.

"The *Brandy Alexander*," she said softly.

"You heard," Xaviera said. She sounded disappointed.

"Heard what?" Helen said.

"Michael, the club concierge, has given notice. He's going to marry the Black Widow tonight."

"What?" Helen sat up so fast, the old chair squeaked in protest.

"Why couldn't she marry me?" Cam moaned. "I'm younger and better-looking."

"And she has enough money to pay your doctor bills," Xaviera said.

"Marrying that woman is bad for your health, Cam," Jessica said. "She's been widowed at least five times."

Helen finally recovered enough to say something. "The Black Widow can't marry the concierge. She already has a husband."

"No, she doesn't," Xaviera said.

"She got her marriage to Rob annulled this fast?"

"Didn't need to be annulled. It never took place," Xaviera said.

"But I saw—" Helen started to say she saw Rob and Marcella getting married aboard the yacht. But she hadn't seen them actually standing before a preacher. And she didn't want her co-workers to know about that embarrassing episode, when she ran screaming down the Seventeenth Street Causeway.

"—where Marcella called herself Rob's wife," Helen finished. It sounded lame.

"And how many women who live with men say that?" Xaviera said.

"I hear it all the time," Jessica added. "The designated users come in here and say 'my husband' this and 'my husband' that and the couple has never tied the knot."

Helen knew that was true. Many women called themselves "wives" because they didn't care to explain their marital status.

But Margery had said that Marcella was old-fashioned. Like Elizabeth Taylor, she always married the men she slept with. "I'm sure she's married," Helen insisted.

"Oh, no," Xaviera said. "She has a paper saying all her husbands are deceased and she never married that Rob guy. My boyfriend, Steven, saw it. Michael the concierge has a copy."

"Ex-concierge," Jessica said.

"Was that paper prepared by Marcella's lawyer, Gabe Accomac?" Helen asked.

"How did you know?" Xaviera said.

"Just a hunch," Helen said. Just a hunch that a lot of money had changed hands and a marriage had been erased.

"I thought that Rob guy was dead," Cam said.

"He turned up alive," Xaviera said. "Steven says he went on a bender and disappeared for several days. Had no idea where he was. Woke up beat-up and hungover in a motel near Miami. Dumb move. While he was gone, his rich girlfriend found herself another man. She dumped that Rob, and I don't blame her."

So that was the story, Helen thought. She had to admit it sounded plausible.

"Are you and Steven invited to the wedding?" Jessica asked.

"No. Michael says the ceremony is private. The Black Widow probably doesn't want any younger women there for comparison," Xaviera said, and wiggled her hips.

Ringing phones put an end to the good-natured whistles and cat-calls.

Helen picked up her line and was surprised to find Marcella calling. "I hear congratulations are in order," Helen managed.

"I wanted to give you the news before it got out," Marcella said. "I see I'm too late. Would you join me for lunch?"

"I'm not hungry," Helen said.

"Then meet me for a drink."

Helen thought of the Black Widow's spinning champagne goblets and her stomach twisted. She'd hoped she would never have to meet with Marcella again. She'd also hoped Rob would disappear, but that wasn't going to happen. If Helen wanted to know what was going on with her ex, she'd have to swallow her pride and her disappointment. Also Marcella's bottled water.

"I can get away for half an hour at one o'clock," Helen said. "But I thought you were getting married tonight. Don't you have things to do?"

"Bruce takes care of that," Marcella said.

Helen wondered why Marcella didn't marry Bruce, the one man who seemed faithful to her. It wasn't a question she could ask.

Helen spent the rest of the morning writing guest passes and dealing with club members.

At one p.m., Helen clocked out and walked up the path to the yacht club. On the way over, Helen decided she'd pretend she didn't know the marriage to Rob supposedly never took place. A florist van was parked by the docks, and two men were carrying vases of opulent white orchids up the ramp to the *Brandy Alexander.*

Bruce met her on the yacht. His bald dome seemed polished and his white uniform was extra crisp. Once again, he took Helen to the back deck. A striped sunshade flapped in the afternoon breeze. A glass of water with a lemon slice was waiting beside an empty chair. Marcella was drinking white wine. Helen wondered if she saved the heavy drinking for her manless nights.

Marcella wore a black pantsuit and bloodred lipstick—a Black Widow indeed. She looked ageless. It was not a good look. She did not belong to any time or place. Marcella was a lost soul.

"Congratulations," Helen said. "I've worked with Michael at the club. I'm impressed."

Marcella shrugged. She didn't care what Helen thought.

"You've known Margery since you were young secretaries, right?"

"Yes," Marcella said.

"Why do you stay friends with her? You're rich and she's—"

"Still my best friend," Marcella interrupted. "Do you know how broke I used to be? I lived on tomato soup and canned tuna. Margery let me borrow her black Victor Costa cocktail dress that I wore on my first date. She also paid for my beauty salon appointment. That snagged me my first husband—and a fortune. Margery's never asked me for anything, and I know she's been through some hard times. She's the only person I can count on to tell me the truth. Yes, I can buy and sell her, but Margery doesn't give a damn. She's her own woman."

Helen thought it was sad that Marcella didn't trust any of the men in her life. Bruce was a servant and her many husbands were dead, except for Rob, the thief and liar. Helen didn't envy Marcella her money. It bought her a lonely life.

"How did you get a divorce so fast?" Helen said. "It took me way too long to get rid of Rob."

"I didn't need one," Marcella said. "There was no marriage."

"Marcella, you can tell that to your new husband. But I saw you and Rob on your wedding day on this boat."

"You saw us in white suits with a lot of flowers. Did you see us getting married?"

"No."

"Did you see any documentation?" Marcella said.

"There was a marriage," Helen said. "I can't prove it, but I know it. I'm going to sketch out a scenario. You can nod yes or no. You owe me that much after what I did.

"I'm guessing the minister who married you and Rob has been paid to forget the ceremony. Either he didn't file the paperwork properly, or some money changed hands with a clerk or two and it vanished. Computers make it easy to lose records, especially in Florida. I suspect your wedding was conducted by someone who was a bit borderline in the first place—not affiliated with any established church. Possibly even a mail-order minister. You or your attorney, or whoever chose the minister, deliberately built a trapdoor in the marriage from the beginning, in case you wanted to bail out.

"I'm thinking the witnesses won't be a problem. They probably came from some cruise ship or hotel and they're long gone. And with no paperwork, there's no way to track down their names."

Helen watched Marcella. She thought she saw a nod. Or maybe the boat just rocked a little.

"The minister—I'm going to guess he's no longer in Fort Lauderdale. He's suddenly come into enough money to realize his dream and open a wedding chapel in Reno."

"Las Vegas," Marcella said. "We're honeymooning in Las Vegas."

"Going to be hard to take the boat there," Helen said.

"We'll fly," Marcella said. "The sea doesn't always have happy associations for me."

"Why aren't you a widow?" Helen asked.

"Widowhood was getting tiresome," Marcella said. "And Rob was seen in Palm Beach County. He nearly destroyed that jewelry shop."

"Oh," Helen said. "I forgot about that."

Marcella was too smart to let herself be blackmailed by that greedy little store owner. Simpler to pay off a slightly sleazy minister and a couple of clerks. They'd have more to lose if word got out.

"If Rob's body didn't show up for some reason, it would take ages to get him declared dead. I wanted to marry again. I gave Rob some money to go away."

"Where?"

"I didn't ask," Marcella said. "He signed all the papers my lawyer needed and took off as soon as the check cleared."

"How much did he get?" Helen said.

"Only a million." She waved her hand as if the money was unimportant. "My jewelry was returned. Rob agreed to clear out and not contest anything."

"You rewarded his treachery with a million dollars?" Helen could not believe how her ex skated through every disaster.

"It won't be a reward," Marcella said. "He went for a cruise with me and got a little taste of what will happen if he doesn't keep his agreement. He promised never to come near me again. Besides, a million isn't much. Not after what he's used to. He'll go through the money in no time and be even more desperate."

"Then he'll come after me," Helen said. "He can do that. If you and Rob were never married, then he'll try to collect the money the court says I owed him. I thought I was rid of him when he met you. Now I'm back where I started."

"That's your problem," Marcella said. "You had two chances to kill him."

CHAPTER 30

"This isn't a good picture of me," Jake Dourwich said.

This was the fourth time Jake nixed his club card photo. The man was worse than an aging Hollywood actor. Helen was stuck in the hot little photo booth, snapping photos he refused to approve.

"It looks just like you, Jakie," cooed his wife, Tiffany.

It did. That made it one scary photo. Jake Dourwich looked like a snake with a suntan.

"It sucks. I don't like my eyes," Jake said.

Helen didn't, either. Jake's eyes were flat, black and merciless. A predator's eyes, watching a yummy little bunny. Helen could take fifty photos of Jake, but nothing would make his eyes look human.

"Take another," Jake ordered Helen.

"I want to go to lunch," whined his wife. Tiffany was a skinny blonde whose tiny white halter dress showed off enormous boobs and a little potbelly. Tiffany was pouting, unless her lips had overdosed on collagen.

"Shut up," Jake said.

"You shut up," Tiffany said.

Their daughter, a sweet chubby child with newly budded breasts, slipped behind a file cabinet, trying to make herself disappear. Helen felt sorry for the girl. She deserved better parents.

Helen pressed the button for the fifth photo while Jake hissed insults at his wife. Then she showed him the latest picture on the computer monitor.

"This sucks, too," Jake said. "What's wrong with you? These photos are shit."

I only photograph what's standing there, Helen wanted to say. But she remembered her enormous credit card bill and even bigger car repair bills. "The lighting seems to cast some shadows, sir," she lied tactfully. "I can't adjust it. Maybe if you wore your sunglasses."

"Yeah, Jakie," his wife said. "Wear your Gucci glasses."

Jake slipped on his shades with the gold logo. Now he looked like a drug dealer, but at least that was halfway human. Helen pressed the button again, and the new photo appeared on the computer screen. Jake looked better with those scary eyes covered.

"I like it," Jake said, and gave Helen a thumbs-up.

Helen ushered Jake and his family out of the customer care office with their new member cards. She returned to find Xaviera arguing with a man who looked like sculpted lard.

"Whaddya mean, I blew six hundred bucks at the bar? I didn't drink that much." Mr. Lard loomed over Xaviera, his face red and greasy with rage. His thick New York accent made his words more threatening.

Xaviera didn't back away. "These receipts have your signature, sir." She handed him a fat file.

He flipped through the receipts, then slammed them on the desk and snarled, "Why don't you speak American? I'm sick of you people."

Helen had seen this reaction before. When faced with an ugly truth, the club members insulted the messenger.

"Why don't you?" Xaviera said. "Your accent is worse than mine."

The man grabbed the receipts and stomped out.

"That son of a pig," Xaviera said, when he slammed the door.

"Please," Jessica said. "That's unfair. Pigs are intelligent."

Xaviera and Jessica burst into giggles. Helen tried to laugh along with them, but she was losing her sense of humor. She didn't like the club members—and she didn't like herself.

Helen had spent part of last night cursing her luck. Her ex had married a serial husband killer and slithered away with his life and a million dollars. She spent the rest of the night wondering what kind of woman she was: She'd wanted her ex-husband murdered.

A woman with plenty of company, she decided. Many women wanted their ex-husbands six feet under. But none came as close as I did.

At least the *Brandy Alexander* was gone. The Black Widow's white yacht no longer haunted her. It had sailed after the sunset wedding last evening. Helen had no idea if Marcella was really going to Vegas with her new husband. All she knew was the view out her office window was once again a postcard with pretty palm trees and blue water.

The view inside had improved, too. Brenda's office was finally opened, repainted and redecorated. The blood-soaked carpet and desk had been replaced. But no one staked a claim on Brenda's empty room, even though it was prime private space. Cam walked past the door holding his bottle of hand sanitizer like a cross before a vampire.

Jackie's desk was still empty. One drawer stuck out like an accusing finger. No matter how many times Helen closed it, she'd find it open again.

It was a little after eleven o'clock when Xaviera's phone rang. Helen could tell by the way she covered the receiver that Xaviera was talking to her blond boyfriend, Steven. Suddenly, she stood up and shrieked.

"It's either a proposal of marriage or major news," Jessica said.

"I have major news," Xaviera shouted.

"Are you OK?" Kitty, their little brunette boss, came running out of her office, looking worried.

Solange, her red hair artfully tangled, stood in her doorway. She was dressed in a casually expensive green linen pantsuit. "What is that noise, girls? I expect professional behavior in this office."

"They found Jackie," Xaviera said.

"When?" Solange asked, her lecture on professionalism abandoned.

"Yesterday," Xaviera said.

"Where?" Jessica asked.

"Working in the café at the Down and Dirty Discount store in Ocala."

"Yuck," Helen said. "I won't shop at Down and Dirty. There's one chain that lives up to its name."

"Makes Wal-Mart look like Nieman Marcus," Jessica said.

"My boyfriend, Steven, says Jackie was in bad shape. She'd lost weight and stank like old hot dogs and greasy popcorn. She had blisters on her hands from the fry cooker."

"Elegant Jackie was covered with grease?" Helen almost forgave the woman.

"Steven said she gave up when the officers came to her counter. 'Take me to prison,' she said. 'It can't be any worse than this.' "

"She's got that right," Helen said. She knew from personal experience that a bad job was a prison sentence. She'd worked as a telemarketer, selling septic tank cleaner. Six weeks into that job, Helen understood why companies hired prisoners for telephone work. If she went to hell, she'd be a telemarketer.

"What a sad end for a woman who used to be a social leader at this club," Kitty said. Her brown eyes were brimming with tears. "I liked Jackie. I'm sorry she's come to this."

"Why are the police keeping it quiet?" Cam said. "You'd think Golden Palms would tell the world they caught a double killer."

"Right," Jessica said. "They really want the networks camping out in the city, asking some of the richest people in Florida rude questions."

"And branding Golden Palms as the home of a double murderer," Xaviera said. "Jackie had a Golden Palms address. She used to belong to this club and she killed a member. What's that going to do to property values?"

"It's best we keep that information quiet," Solange said. "Back to work, people. We've wasted enough time gossiping." She shooed them back to their desks.

Despite Solange's command, the staff did little work. FedEx packages didn't go out. Member requests were ignored. Ringing phones went unanswered, except for Xaviera's. Her Steven supplied hourly updates.

At noon, Xaviera reported, "Jackie has a public defender."

"She's screwed," Cam said. "She's probably got some kid fresh out of college."

"No," Xaviera said. "There was some kind of conflict with the PD's office and her ex-husband. She's getting an attorney from a top private firm as her public defender."

"Good," Helen said, then wondered why she was rooting for the woman who'd tried to kill her.

Because I've been in her shoes, she thought. Or close enough. In her mind, Helen had murdered her tormentor, Rob, so many times, she should be arrested.

"Twelve thirty," Cam said. "It's Helen's turn for lunch."

"I don't want to miss the next update," Helen said.

"I'll fill you in," Jessica promised.

Helen rushed through lunch in the staff cafeteria, not sure if she ate a hamburger or a ham sandwich. She was back at her desk by one o'clock.

At one-oh-seven, Xaviera reported, "Steven says they're trying to work out a plea."

"Think she'll confess to killing Brenda and Dr. Dell?" Jessica asked.

"And me," Helen said. "She tried to kill me."

"She'll have to, won't she?" Xaviera said.

"Aren't they moving awfully fast?" Cam said.

"Steven says Golden Palms doesn't want a murder trial splashing the city's name all over the media," Xaviera said. "They want to expedite this, so Jackie goes away quietly."

Good, Helen thought. She didn't want her name all over the news, either.

A little before two o'clock, Xaviera had another bulletin: "They think

Jackie is going to confess to both murders. She says she's sorry about you, Helen. Her court-appointed lawyer is still trying to work out a plea."

"Jackie should get a medal," Cam said. "I mean, not for trying to kill you, Helen. For getting rid of Brenda."

"Cam is a big 'no man is an island' fan," Jessica said.

"I didn't see that movie," Cam said.

Jessica and Helen burst out laughing.

"I can't help it if you guys are old," Cam said. He stuck out his lower lip like a giant baby.

At three o'clock, Steven called again. "Wait till you hear this." Xaviera nearly levitated in her excitement. Kitty and Solange came out of their offices, drawn by the promise of fresh, hot news.

"Jackie was selling club information from the customer care files," Xaviera said.

"That's outrageous," Kitty said.

Solange moaned and pulled at her already tangled red hair. Her look was sliding from casual to crazed. A button dangled loose on her jacket and her linen suit had more wrinkles than a Shar-Pei puppy.

"Who bought the information?" Jessica said.

"That Rob guy, the one who didn't marry the Black Widow," Xaviera said. "He was selling it to other club members, mostly."

Solange gave a graveyard groan and twisted the fiery strands around her fingers.

"What kind of information?" Jessica asked.

"The only one Jackie mentioned was a sale to a divorce lawyer," Xaviera said. "The lawyer bought information that a husband had his club bills mailed to a PO box. The husband didn't want his wife to know he was taking his cookie to lunch here. The lawyer also found the husband had a separate bank account in the Bahamas. The husband had kept that asset well hidden."

"I hope the lawyer nailed the bastard," Kitty said.

"Kitty!" Solange said, her voice shrill with fear. "If word gets out, we're all in trouble. We better pray Jackie takes that plea. Otherwise, we could lose our jobs."

Not we, Helen thought. You. It happened on your watch.

"Xaviera, what else do you know?" Solange sounded desperate for good news.

"Jackie said she faxed Rob seven club members' files. She made about seven thousand dollars and used it for her rent and car payments. She was months behind. Then Brenda discovered the missing Winderstine file in Jackie's desk during one of her compulsive cleaning attacks."

"Winderstine!" Solange said. "Why would anyone want his file?"

"He was going to be a CFO, until his company found out he was sixty days behind in his club bills. They decided if he couldn't handle his finances, he couldn't handle theirs."

Solange looked like she was going to faint. She clutched the counter to steady herself and said, "If Winderstine finds out, he'll sue."

"You shouldn't have made such a fuss over that file." Xaviera must be feeling feisty, dishing important information she got from Steven.

"Jackie came in early to sneak the Winderstine file back in the cabinet," Xaviera said. "That's when Brenda confronted her. She'd come in early, too. Brenda guessed Jackie was selling information. She wanted the cash that Jackie had been getting—all of it. Jackie said the money was gone, and she still owed thousands. Brenda gave Jackie a week to come up with the money or she was fired.

"Jackie actually got down on her knees and pleaded with that heartless witch," Xaviera said. "She said this would ruin her. She promised to give Brenda her future earnings.

"Brenda said, 'You're going to do that anyway. You deserve to be fired. I'm trying to help. Do it my way and you keep your job. Otherwise, you're on the street, and nobody will hire you, loser.'

"Jackie finally had enough. 'I'm the loser?' she said. 'You play golf with Blythe St. Ives, the club member no one else will play with—and you *have* to lose. How pathetic is that? You couldn't even afford your own breast surgery. You had to sleep with Doctor Dell, a man who looks like an ape. You got fake boobs for fake sex. I've had my problems, but I've always had my pride.'

"Brenda went ballistic. The insults must have hit home. She picked up one of her golf clubs. Jackie was sure Brenda was going to hit her.

She wrenched the club away and hit Brenda. Jackie said she couldn't stop beating her. That's when Dr. Dell walked in, hoping to pay his bill. He said, 'What's going on here?'

"'You're another one,' Jackie said. 'You cheated on your sweet wife and misled that poor girl in your office.' Then she clubbed him, too."

There was a sad, shocked silence when Xaviera finished.

Jessica was the first to break it. "I didn't know the poor little mouse had it in her."

"Even a mouse will fight when cornered," Helen said.

"Jackie had luck on her side, if you want to call it that," Xaviera said. "She'd walked to the club, so she avoided the gate cameras. She tried to make the murders look like Brenda had been caught by a jealous lover. That's why she cut off Brenda's golf shirt and took it with her. Jackie had carried her blazer when she walked to work, so she wouldn't get it sweaty. She put it back on over her bloody shirt, walked home, showered and changed. She threw her bloody shirt and the golf top in the Dumpster at her apartment. Then Jackie went back to work. Except this time, she came in by the employee gate."

"I guess the thirty-five hundred dollars cash she took from Dr. Dell financed her escape," Helen said.

"That's the funny thing," Xaviera said. "Jackie insists she didn't take the doctor's money. She says she would not rob a dead man."

"Weird," Jessica said. "She'll admit to a double murder, but not to stealing."

They were still discussing this news when Steven called with another bulletin at four o'clock. They gathered around Xaviera's desk.

"Big problem," Xaviera announced.

Solange wrung her hands and pulled her hair. Her makeup had worn off, and she looked pale and frightened. "What now?"

"The whole deal may go south," Xaviera said. "Jackie still refuses to admit she stole the doctor's cash."

"That makes no sense," Cam said.

But something nagged at Helen. Some fragment she couldn't quite retrieve. She tried to remember her conversations with Jackie, hoping to find it.

The office settled into a strange limbo. No one wanted to work, but the staff didn't want to leave until they knew Jackie's fate. Their jobs were riding on her decision.

It was four thirty when Steven called again. "Jackie confessed to taking the money," Xaviera said. "The deal's on." Solange looked sick with relief. Cam and Jessica cheered.

"It's over," Kitty said. She looked sad.

"There's still a lot to do," Xaviera said. "There's the presentence investigations—PSI—and the victim impact statements. A lot depends on them."

"But you're sure the deal will go through?" Solange said, her eyes big with fear.

"Pretty sure," Xaviera said.

"I guess Dr. Dell's wife will make sure they throw the book at Jackie," Jessica said.

"Demi?" Xaviera said. "She'd thank Jackie, if she could. She's rid of the philandering doctor and she gets to keep his money. She's a rich widow."

"What about Brenda's family?" Jessica asked.

"What family?" Xaviera said. "Her parents are dead. No brothers or sisters."

I'm the only victim left, Helen thought. I won't make trouble. I want this to go away, too.

"Steven said Jackie said odd things. She wanted to know if she would get more time if she confessed to taking the money and if she had to be paroled."

Had to be paroled? Helen wondered if that's what Jackie said, or if it was filtered through Xaviera's slightly warped English.

"They said if Jackie pleaded guilty, she'd probably get twenty years to life, pending the results of the PSI and the victim impact statements. Then she asked something really strange: Could they make sure she didn't get paroled?"

"She didn't do it," Helen said.

"Of course she did," Xaviera said.

"Jackie killed Brenda and the doctor," Helen said. "She tried to kill me. But she didn't take the doctor's money. She wants three meals a day, medical care and no rent. If she goes to prison, she'll spend the rest of her life being cared for."

"That's ridiculous," Cam said.

"You've never had to worry about your next meal," Helen said, staring pointedly at Cam's inflated midsection. Xaviera giggled. Cam's ears turned red.

"You don't have to worry about your rent, your credit card bills, or your car payment," Helen said.

"Hey," Cam said, "nobody's rich in this office."

"Yes, but you're lucky, Cam. Jackie didn't have a doting mommy hand her two hundred sixty thousand dollars."

"You were in my desk drawer," Cam said. "That's private. I'm filing a complaint with HR."

Helen crossed to Cam's desk and lowered her voice so only he could hear. "Really? Done any 'relaxing' lately?"

Cam swallowed hard.

"Remember," Helen said. "They give random drug tests at the club. It takes three days to get pot out of your system. Now, if you'll excuse me, I have to make a phone call."

"You're calling HR!" Cam looked panicked.

"I'm going to catch a thief," Helen said.

CHAPTER 31

"How'd you manage to shut Cam up?" Jessica whispered. "That's a trick I'd like to know."

"I reminded him the club does random drug testing," Helen said. "He's shaking in his shoes, afraid I'll call human resources."

"I hope you do. I'd love to get rid of that lazy creep," Jessica said.

"Sorry. I'm after bigger game," Helen said. "Jackie didn't take Dr. Dell's cash. But I think I know who did."

"Why are you saving the woman who wanted to kill you?" Jessica said.

"Because one day I snapped, just like she did. Only I was lucky. I beat up an SUV instead of my ex."

"You weren't lucky," Jessica said. "You're a better person than you give yourself credit for. Jackie plotted to kill you to save her own skin. She didn't try to murder you in the heat of the moment."

"I'm still here," Helen said.

She couldn't find it in her heart to condemn Jackie. Like her, Helen had fallen from a great height. Except Helen had had a softer landing—and better friends. She'd learned a bitter lesson after her divorce: You never knew who'd stand by you. Even Helen's mother had abandoned her. Well, she wouldn't brood about that.

Helen picked up the phone on her desk and called the offices of the late Dr. Dell. The line was busy. It took three tries to get through. The doctor's practice seemed to be thriving without him.

She got the same chatty receptionist.

"Hi," Helen said. "I'm a friend of Mandy's. Is she back from her cruise yet?"

"Yes, she's at home," the receptionist chirped.

"And living in her husband's house off Johnson Street, right? Except it's her house now, too."

"That's the place. I hear she misses her pretty little Pembroke townhouse. No pool where she's at now." Helen heard it. That note of malice said this woman would dish with a little encouragement.

Helen summoned her courage to ask the next question. It was a wild guess. "So when's the baby due? I wanted to send a gift."

"Mandy's almost six months," the receptionist said.

Bingo! Helen thought. My hunch was right. She wasn't fat. She was pregnant.

"Looks like she shoplifted a beach ball. She's going to be big as a house." The receptionist couldn't hide her glee.

"I bet the baby will have Mom's hair," Helen said.

"If it's smart, it will. Dad has dark hair, too. I'd say the chances it will be a brunette are good, unless someone's been playing around."

It was hard to keep a secret in a doctor's office, Helen thought. "I want to send Mandy a gift, but I think I wrote down her address wrong," Helen said. "I have it as five four eight three Taney."

"I think you sort of reversed the numbers," the receptionist said. "It's eight five three six. Stop by and see her. Mandy might like some company. I hear her handyman husband's working overtime these days, trying to make enough money for the baby." Once again, Helen heard the smug satisfaction in the receptionist's voice.

Helen hung up the phone, sweating with relief. She'd guessed right. Mandy was pregnant. She'd bet her next paycheck the doctor was the father. Helen suspected Mandy had tried to blackmail the doctor with the baby.

Helen hoped the poor child didn't look like Dr. Dell. She wondered if they made infant depilatories. Any baby sired by the doc would look like an orangutan.

Helen kept checking her watch. She hadn't done any work all day, but she was exhausted. Solange, Cam, Xaviera and Jessica left the office at five. Kitty and Helen stayed until six. After what happened to Helen, Kitty decreed none of her staff would work alone in the office.

Finally, it was five fifty-six. Helen uploaded the day's computer data and cleaned off her desk. "You clock out, sweetpea," Kitty said. "I'll close up."

Helen crawled through the highway traffic in the belching Toad, trailed by thick black smoke. She was glad Phil worked late tonight. She wanted to ask Margery for help, but she didn't want Phil around. Her man was too straitlaced for this project.

Helen found her landlady out by the pool, hosing off the warm concrete. Margery worked with brisk, efficient movements, using the water to push leaves and dirt into the grass.

"I need you," Helen said.

"Nobody's said that to me in a long time," Margery said. She grinned at Helen.

"Look, you got me into this mess, manipulating Rob to marry Marcella, and then getting Marcella to pay for my lawyer when he disappeared."

"I saved your sorry ass," Margery said. "You aren't the least bit grateful."

"You got me in deep and now you're going to get me out."

"By doing what?" Margery looked at her suspiciously. "Something you can't ask true-blue Phil?"

"He won't steal a pregnant woman's purse."

"I might. But I need a good reason before I stoop that low," Margery said. She lit a cigarette and said, "Spill."

So Helen told her about Mandy and Dr. Dell. "I think the doctor's pregnant receptionist extorted money out of him, maybe for an abortion.

I'm guessing she wanted lots more—either money or marriage. Either way, she followed the doctor to the club on the morning of his death, hoping to make an embarrassing scene."

"How'd she get in?" Margery asked. Her cigarette winked at Helen.

"She stole the wife's club card. When Demi got home from her retaliatory shopping spree in New York, she called the club and said her card was missing. She thought she'd left it on her dresser at home, but she couldn't find it. I think Dr. Dell gave himself a little extra thrill by boinking his girlfriend in his wife's bed. That's when Mandy stole the card."

"Men like that deserve to die." Margery's face looked hard in the waning light, and Helen wondered if she was talking about the not-so-good doctor.

"I gave Demi a new club card," Helen said. "I'm an expert on adultery after working at the club. Guys who cheat often pick women who look like their wives. Mandy has dark hair. The club card picture is the size of a thumbprint. The doctor's girlfriend could pass as his wife if anyone questioned her. But the day Mandy went to the club, the member gate was broken. She didn't need the card.

"Here's what I think happened: Mandy followed the doc to the customer care office. He'd just discovered Brenda's body. He was in shock. He blurted something nasty to Jackie, who whacked him with a golf club. Mandy saw his murder, hid until Jackie fled, then robbed the dead doctor."

"Nice people," Margery said. "How are you going to prove it? Are you going to the police?"

"They won't believe me at this point. I need more," Helen said. "Besides, Jackie has already confessed to the theft."

"So why are we stealing a pregnant woman's purse?"

"To get Demi's club card."

"Which will prove nothing," Margery said.

"Except Mandy has been in the doc's house," Helen said. "And could get into the Superior Club with the card. If I can pinpoint the time, the police can do a search. She may turn up on a surveillance tape somewhere, if they know when to look for her. Or she could have left hair and fibers in the customer care office."

"Why would she keep the card?" Margery asked.

"People don't let go of a Superior Club card. Besides, Mandy might need to get back in the club. Margery, I am not confronting her alone, even if she is pregnant. A woman who'd rob her dead lover is too scary. You need to go with me."

"It's almost seven," Margery said. "What if Mandy's husband is home? The guy works with hammers and chain saws."

"He's working late these days to make extra money for the baby."

"That might not be his. The poor dumb bastard. All right," Margery said. "I'll pretend to be an old biddy signing up new mothers for baby gifts. Give me a few minutes to change."

Helen's jaw dropped when Margery came out of her apartment ten minutes later. She was wearing the most conservative outfit Helen had ever seen her in: a lavender shirtwaist dress, pearls and chunky purple heels.

"June Cleaver lives," Helen said.

"I'm trying to look the part," Margery said. "I'll drive my car. Yours is a little run-down."

"Mine is going to be shut down by the EPA," Helen said. "It's belching black smoke."

"That's what I mean," Margery said. "We need to stop at a drugstore."

"What for?" Helen said.

"Diapers," Margery said. "They'll get us in the door."

They bought disposable diapers, a rattle, some baby wipes and a pink-and-blue gift bag. "That should do it," Margery said. "No new parent can resist freebies."

All the way to Hollywood, Helen kept staring at Margery's Junior League getup.

"What are you looking at?" her landlady finally said.

"I can't get over you in that outfit. You look so . . . trustworthy."

"I am," Margery said. "You can trust me to help bury the body if you ever murder Rob."

"He's gone," Helen said. "Turn left here."

"You really believe that?" Margery said.

"I really believe that's Mandy's house on the right," Helen said.

Mandy's neighborhood was a comedown for a woman who'd dreamed of a doctor's seaside mansion in Golden Palms. She lived in a dusty concrete-block box, with faded mustard paint and rust trails dripping down the walls from the window bars. The lawn had dead brown patches, like an old dog with mange. A skinny palm tree struggled to survive near the front door. Helen wanted to put it out of its misery.

Margery parked and ground out her cigarette. "Can't smoke around the baby," she said.

"If Mandy's husband is a handyman, he's sure not doing any home improvement," Helen said.

"Tearing it down is the only way to improve this home," Margery said.

The dying yard was surrounded by a chain-link fence that made it look more like a detention center than a home.

"If the husband's there, we'll say we have the wrong address," Margery said.

She knocked on the door five or six times. Finally, an impatient voice shouted, "I said I'm coming. Hold your horses, willya?"

The door slammed open and there stood a very pregnant Mandy. Her belly was swollen and so were her ankles. Her dark hair straggled down her neck. She wore an oversized red T-shirt, an unfortunate color that emphasized her blotchy complexion. Pregnancy had not been kind to her voluptuous body. It certainly didn't improve her temper.

"I'm not buying anything." Mandy started to slam the door.

"I'm giving away free diapers and baby gifts," Margery said, and managed a grandmotherly smile. She held out the gift bag.

Mandy opened the door.

There was hardly room for the three of them in the living room. Most of the space was taken up with a huge brown plush sofa. A cigarette-scarred coffee table was piled with bags of Cheetos, Doritos and Oreos—all the food groups ending in O.

The baby wasn't the only cause of Mandy's dramatic swelling, Helen thought.

Mandy sat down wearily and put her swollen feet on the coffee table. Margery plopped down on the edge of the couch, effectively blocking her exit.

"We have so many wonderful things for new parents," Margery began. Mandy kept eyeing the gift bag, but Margery kept it out of reach.

Helen spotted a brown purse by the couch. It looked like it was pregnant, too.

"Excuse me," Helen said. "May I use your bathroom?"

"Down the hall," Mandy said, never letting the gift bag out of her sight. If she watched her baby half as well, she'd make a heck of a mom.

Margery handed over the gift bag, while Helen slipped into the tiny bathroom to examine the purloined purse. There was barely room for both of them. Helen winced when she turned on the light. Shower mold and yellow flowered linoleum were not a pretty combination.

Helen pawed through the purse and found Demi Dell's Superior Club card in a zippered side pocket. She used a tissue to pull it out. She didn't want to mess up any fingerprints.

"But only if you sign up today," Margery was saying when Helen returned.

Helen gave her a nod, then held up the stolen club card. "Look familiar, Mandy?"

"What's that?" Mandy asked.

"You know what it is," Helen said. "A Superior Club card belonging to Demi Dell, your dead boss's wife. I found it in your purse."

"What are you doing in my purse, bitch?" Mandy asked.

"Looking for stolen goods. Would you like to explain this to Demi?"

"You put it there," Mandy said.

She was a cool customer, Helen thought. "Nope," Helen said. "I handled it very carefully. The police will only find your prints."

"The police? I didn't run up any club charges on Demi's card. I don't have to talk to you," Mandy said. But she didn't sound quite so confident now.

"No, you don't. And I don't have to tell your husband why he needs a DNA test for that baby—not if you tell me what happened to the doctor's thirty-five hundred dollars."

This time, Mandy didn't try to pretend she didn't know what Helen was talking about. "I stole it," she said. "So what?"

"That's not all you stole," Helen said.

"I took everything I was entitled to," Mandy said.

"Everything you *thought* you were entitled to," Helen said. "That's not quite the same. You followed Dr. Dell into the club. You knew he played golf that morning. You were going to confront him with your pregnancy."

"Wrong-o. He already knew," Mandy said. "I'd told him two days before that."

"He wouldn't marry you, would he?" Helen said. "That's why you settled for a handyman husband and a house in Hollywood. The doctor wanted you to get an abortion."

"Worse," Mandy said. Her face turned hard. "I told him our baby was a girl and I needed money for her. He said, 'I already spent three thousand dollars on you.'

"I said, 'For clothes I can't wear now that I'm pregnant. You said you were tired of your wife. You promised to marry me.'

"'You must have misunderstood,' he said. 'I'd never leave Demi. I made one mistake. I won't pay for two.' He stuck his finger in my gut and said, 'Get rid of it. The world doesn't need another flat-chested slut.'"

Helen gasped at the cruelty. Even Margery raised an eyebrow.

"I spent two days crying," Mandy said. "Then I decided my baby was going to get what she deserved. I was going to embarrass the doctor into supporting her. I knew he played golf early in the morning. I followed him to the club. He never noticed my car. He stopped at the customer care office. I figured he was probably going to pay that three-thousand-dollar club bill before his wife saw it. It was a good place to confront him—plenty of people around, so he'd be embarrassed.

"He must have walked in right after that Brenda lady got killed. He was standing over her body. I slipped behind those heavy window curtains by the door.

"At first, I thought he'd killed her. He was in a daze, calling her name: 'Brenda.' Even I could see she was dead—and I'm not a doctor. There was another woman in the room. She was about forty-five, skinny, with dark hair. Dr. Dell was yelling at her, 'She was my finest work. Look at those tits. Perfect. I created them and you destroyed them.'

" 'You're another one,' the brunette said. 'You cheated on your sweet wife and misled that poor girl in your office.' She whacked him twice with the golf club. I think she wanted to hit him more, but she heard a noise. It turned out to be the trash truck at the loading dock. She wiped her fingerprints off the club, cleaned out some money in a desk drawer and left. She never saw me."

"And you didn't go to the police?" Margery said. "You witnessed a murder."

"Why should I? That woman was the only person who felt sorry for me. The girls at work all knew I'd been knocked up by the doctor. They laughed at me. I wasn't going to turn in the one person who'd said something nice. She did me a favor. I knew the doctor carried a lot of cash. He had thirty-five hundred dollars on him that day. I took it all."

"You could get money from Dr. Dell's estate for your child," Helen said.

"No, I couldn't. Demi and her lawyers will fight me until the kid's in an old folks' home. Besides, my husband thinks the kid is his. Maybe it is. I'm not upsetting my meal ticket. The baby needs a father and Dave's a decent guy and a hard worker."

Now there was true love, Helen thought. The only thing worse than being trapped in this house with the plush sofa and the shower mold would be living in Mandy's head.

Mandy picked up a bag of Cheetos the size of a couch pillow. "Get out of here," she said. "Dave's due home and I don't want him running into you. If you tell the cops what I said, they won't believe you."

"Yes, they will," Helen said. "Demi's club card will get the cops interested in you. It shows you were in the doctor's house. It has your fingerprints on it. I'm sure there's hair and fiber evidence to prove you were in the club that morning. If you confess to taking the money, Jackie could get a lighter sentence."

Mandy gave a hard, harsh laugh. "She doesn't want it. Trust me. I know the assholes she had to deal with at that club. Jackie's where she wants to be, in prison with three squares a day—just like me. We both wanted something better, but we settled for what we could get. Anyway, Dr. Dell owed me a lot more than thirty-five hundred bucks. I didn't do anything wrong."

"You robbed a dead man," Helen said.

"He wasn't going to use it," Mandy said.

CHAPTER 32

The slammed door seemed to reverberate through the night. Mandy had shut Helen and Margery out of her house and her life.

"She's right, you know," Margery said, as they walked back to her car. "Jackie's not going to recant her confession. She'll go to her grave swearing she stole that money. And you'll never nail that tough little cookie, Mandy."

"I still want to ask Jackie," Helen said.

"Ask her what?" Margery said.

"If she wants to say she stole the doctor's money when I've found the real thief."

"What else do you want to ask her?" Margery said.

"I don't know what you mean," Helen said.

"Sure you do." Margery lit a cigarette, then put the big white Lincoln Town Car in gear and pulled away from Mandy's self-made prison.

"Mandy is serving a life sentence of motherhood," Margery said. "Heaven help that poor baby. She's going to take the blame for her mother's failed ambition. That poor sap Mandy just married has my sympathy, too. She'll remind him every day that she settled for second best. I wouldn't want to be trapped behind that chain-link fence with those three.

"Jackie put herself in prison. You can talk to her about the doctor's money, but that's not what you really want to ask Jackie. You want to know why she tried to kill you. You want to know if you're capable of killing someone, too. Jackie can't answer either of those questions."

Helen didn't appreciate Margery's instant psychoanalysis, but she didn't want to argue. She rolled down her window and breathed in the cool night air, tangy with ocean salt. She closed her eyes and pretended sleep. Soon she drifted off and didn't have to pretend anymore.

Early the next morning, Helen called the sheriff office's jail information line. Jackie was being held at the Palmheart Women's Detention Facility, awaiting the final outcome of her plea. A recording said prisoners could have visitors once a week, and this was Jackie's visiting day. Helen didn't want to wait another seven days. She called her boss, Kitty. "I'm having car trouble," Helen said. "I'm really sorry. It will take another hour or two to fix the car."

"Don't worry, sweetpea. Come in when you can," Kitty said.

Helen felt like a rat, lying to someone as nice as Kitty. But she had to see Jackie today.

Palmheart was a dusty little town near the Everglades. The jail looked like a high school. It was a grim beige building with slits for windows. Helen waited in line for the metal detector, behind a plus-sized woman in hospital scrubs, a sad old man with a bowed gray head, and a busty Latina in a see-through blouse and a sliver of skirt. That outfit was against the dress code, but the guard waved her through. Helen showed her fake driver's license and hoped she didn't look guilty. Then she realized everyone here looked guilty. She fit right in.

Helen wondered if Jackie would even see her. Prisoners had the right to refuse visitors. But there she was behind the Plexiglas shield, in a beige jumpsuit that looked oddly like another uniform. Her dark hair was pulled back in her usual chignon, but Jackie wore no makeup. She looked pale but younger and her nails were no longer bitten to the quick.

Jackie picked up her phone and said, "Helen, it's so good of you to see me. I didn't expect this."

"How are you?" Helen asked. It felt strange talking to Jackie on a phone, when she was sitting across from her. But the Plexiglas barrier made talking easier.

"Fine," Jackie said, as if they were sitting at lunch at work. "I'm rested for the first time in ages. I know you're not supposed to be able to sleep in jail, but the noise doesn't bother me. My apartment was by the Dixie Highway and the railroad tracks. I learned to shut out noise. How's everyone at the office? Is Xaviera engaged yet?"

"No, she's waiting for Steven to get a promotion."

"I hope it comes soon," Jackie said. "Xaviera's not getting any younger and she wants children. Is Kitty still getting a divorce?"

Helen filled Jackie in on the office gossip. They both ignored the black hole opening between them until Helen was afraid it would swallow them. Finally, Jackie tiptoed to the edge of the abyss.

"How are you, Helen?" She stopped. "Did you suffer any ill effects from—" Jackie still couldn't say that she'd tried to kill Helen.

"I'm OK," Helen said. "I didn't eat the chocolate. I don't like creme centers."

"I don't know what came over me," Jackie said. "After Brenda died—" She stopped again, unable to admit how Brenda died. "I felt like I was in a bad dream and couldn't wake up. That's no excuse, Helen. But I'm glad it didn't work."

"Me, too." Helen figured that was as close as she'd get to an apology.

"Jackie, I know you didn't take the doctor's cash," Helen said. "Mandy, his assistant, sneaked into the customer care office and stole it."

"Is that the poor girl he got pregnant?" Jackie said.

"Yes. Listen, I think I can prove Mandy was the thief. I can go to the police."

"No, don't!" Jackie said. "I know it sounds strange, but I like it here."

"Don't you miss your freedom?" Helen asked.

"What freedom?" Jackie said. "I got up at six and worked until dark. I was so exhausted I slept most weekends. The only places I could afford to go were the library and church. Occasionally, a friend would take me out for a pity lunch, or give me last year's suit, like some charity case.

"My life here is much easier. The food's not very good, but I've lived on boiled eggs for so long, I don't really care what I eat. I haven't much appetite anymore.

"The other inmates have their problems, but they're not as nasty as the club members. If they act out or scream at me, they get punished. I never have to worry about my rent or my car payment. I can take college courses. I've always wanted to go back to school. Now I have the time.

"You know the best part?" Jackie said. "Nobody in here ever says, 'Do you know who I am?'

"We all know who we are. That's Denise on my right." Jackie nodded toward a large, doughy woman with stringy blond hair, talking on a phone. "Denise is in here for setting her boyfriend on fire. She got tired of him coming home drunk and beating her up.

"That's Gemelle on the left. She's in for armed robbery." Gemelle, a small, cinnamon-skinned woman with brown braids, looked dangerous as a new puppy.

"And everyone knows who I am, because I did what every woman in here wants to do: I killed my vicious boss. Then I killed an unfaithful husband.

"Do you know who I am, Helen? I'm a hero."

Helen left the jail feeling oddly disconnected. She'd fallen through the looking glass, but instead of seeing Jackie's life, she saw her own. Was Jackie's old life really so harsh she preferred prison? Helen pondered that question all the way back to the club.

She slid into her desk in customer care at eleven thirty. Cam was cleaning his phone with alcohol spray. Xaviera was on the phone trying to explain a sixty-dollar lunch charge. "Yes, ma'am, I understand that you were in New York on the twenty-first," Xaviera said. "But someone used your card for lunch. I'm sorry, but if you lend your card to your pool boy, you're responsible for the charges he makes, even if you didn't approve them."

Jessica was trying to calm a club member about a bill. She nodded at Helen and kept saying, "I'm sorry, ma'am."

Helen's phone rang. She picked it up on the first ring. She recognized that buzz-saw whine immediately.

"No one is answering the customer care phone," Blythe St. Ives said. "It rang and rang. I had to call back." She made it sound as if she'd had to walk barefoot to Palm Beach in the sweltering heat.

"I'm sorry, ma'am, but we're shorthanded."

"Do you know who I am?" Blythe said.

"Yes, ma'am," Helen said. "You're rich, rude and unhappy for no reason I can understand, and I'm tired of dealing with you."

There was a gasp. "I'll have your job!" Blythe shrieked.

"I hope you get it," Helen said. "You deserve it."

She hung up the phone. Next to her, Jessica finished her call and said into the dead phone, "Bitch."

"I hate you, too," Xaviera muttered, as she slammed down the phone.

"No, I can't have it ready in half an hour. You'll have to wait," Cam said to someone on his phone.

Helen listened to the chorus of curses and insults for a moment, then stood up and said, "I quit."

"Another one bites the dust," Cam said.

"Maybe you'd like to take a short vacation," Jessica said.

"Or a long one," Xaviera said.

Kitty came out of her office, wringing her hands. "Helen, please don't go," she said. "We love you."

Helen looked into Kitty's sad brown eyes. "I can't do it anymore," she said. "I can't take the meanness."

"I'll handle the mean ones," Kitty said. "Send them to me."

"I meant the meanness in me," Helen said. "I spend my days taking petty revenge on people I don't like, until I'm as nasty as they are. I don't want to be like that. I don't want to hear 'I'm a doctor' or 'Do you know who I am?' one more time. I started asking myself, 'Do you know who I am?' I didn't like the answer."

"The abuse gets to all of us," Jessica said. "But we get over it."

"No," Helen said. "We pretend to get over it. But it still hurts. Jessica, you're a great actress. I'm not. I'm sorry."

Helen walked out the door and away from the best-paying job she was likely to find in South Florida. She was jobless, without a decent reference and deep in debt. But she knew who she was. And she was tired of dealing with nasty people.

She fought the bucking, belching Toad all the way home on the highway. She pulled into the parking lot at the Coronado and noticed a trail of drips behind the car. Water? Oil? Transmission fluid? She was afraid to find out.

Margery was raking dead palm fronds in the yard. "What are you doing home in the middle of the day?" She looked at Helen's face and said, "You've quit, haven't you?"

"Yep," Helen said. "I heard that question once too often: Do you know who I am?

"I was losing sight of who I was—a woman who'd learned how to enjoy life. For years, I slaved away at my job in St. Louis, hating it, but making so much money I couldn't quit. I put myself in golden handcuffs. Then I lost my job and my life and wound up here in Florida.

"I learned to enjoy life. I toasted the sunset with cheap wine and good friends. I found the man I love. I worked a lot of jobs I didn't care about, and I had the luxury of walking away when I wanted. I was off the books and under the radar.

"Then I got that job at the Superior Club and everything changed. I had credit card debt, a cell phone bill and car repairs."

"You made double the money at that job," Margery said.

"And got triple the misery. It's not worth the price I had to pay. Jackie taught me one thing: You put yourself in prison. Well, I'm breaking out."

"Last time I checked, you didn't win the lottery," Margery said. "And you've run up big car repair and credit card bills. How are you going to pay them?"

"I'm going to sell my car," Helen said, "and go back to taking the bus. I'll give up my cell phone. Take back the new clothes I bought, if I can. Then get a real dead-end job, with nice people and no pressure."

Margery snorted. "You're living in a fairy tale."

"It's my story," Helen said, "and I'm going to live happily ever after."

EPILOGUE

Helen came back to the Superior Club for the last time one month later.

Kitty had asked her to reconsider her resignation. "Wait thirty days, sweetpea," she'd said. "You'll feel different about the job."

Helen didn't. Today she was going to turn in her office key and her employee card and pick up her last check. Her uniform was neatly folded in a bag on the seat of the Toad.

There was a traffic jam at Ives Dairy Road again, and the Toad bucked as Helen slowed it down. The junker made an ominous grinding sound, and Helen hoped the worthless hunk of iron would get her to the club and back home.

She'd already canceled her cell phone. She couldn't call for help if the Toad died.

The traffic jam broke up and the Toad quit bucking. At high speeds, its ride was almost smooth. Helen sighed with relief. She was going to make it. Phil had found a buyer for the Toad. A car collector offered seven hundred dollars for the steaming heap. The man planned to use it for spare parts. The money he offered would nearly cover the cost of the car repairs. Helen was going to deliver the Toad to the slaughter-house tomorrow, provided it made this trip.

She'd almost returned to her old life. She was able to take back about half the clothes she'd bought in her spending spree. The rest she had to pay for, including the skirt she'd destroyed capturing Rob.

She'd nearly emptied the stash she kept in her stuffed bear, Choco-late. But it was worth it. When she made the last payment, Helen cut up her credit card. She was once again a free woman.

Now she was looking for another dead-end job. She hadn't found anything yet, but she was choosing carefully. She figured her stashed money should hold out for another month.

The Toad belched stinking smoke into the rarefied air of Golden Palms. A woman walking her Pomeranian glared at the smelly rolling wreck. Her little dog yapped.

Helen waved to the guard at the Superior Club gate and drove to the employee lot, the place where she'd punched Rob in the face a life-time ago. I paid a high price for that moment of satisfaction, she thought. If I'd kept my temper, would any of this have happened?

It was another question Helen couldn't answer. But she knew she was happier now that she wasn't working at the club.

Helen walked into the Superior Club office. It was as if she'd never left. Cam was scrubbing down his desk with alcohol spray. Xaviera was giggling into her phone, and Helen could tell by the pretty flush on her cheeks that she was talking to her boyfriend, Steven. Jessica was placat-ing someone on her phone: "I'm sorry you're not happy, ma'am."

"May I help you?" A fortyish blonde was sitting in Jackie's old desk. Jackie's replacement seemed polite and efficient.

She thinks I'm a member, Helen thought. I don't know whether to be insulted or pleased.

"Helen!" squealed Jessica. She put down her phone and ran up to the front counter. "Give me a hug. I've missed you. We have so much to tell you."

"Yes, we do," Xaviera said, and presented her left hand. A diamond sparkled on her fourth finger.

"Congratulations," Helen said.

"Steven got the job with the Lauderdale police," Xaviera said. "We're getting married in June."

"And I've given notice," Jessica said. "I have a part in a new cop show set in Miami. I play the hero's boss. I'm a lieutenant." Her pale skin glowed like fine ivory.

"We call her the Loot," Xaviera said.

"Speaking of the Loot, where's Kitty?" Helen said. "I don't see her in her office."

"Oh, you don't know," Jessica said. Her eyes grew wide—a storyteller primed to begin a fantastic tale.

Xaviera giggled.

"What's so funny?" Helen said.

"Solange was fired when Mr. Ironton found out that the club files had been sold to Rob," Jessica said.

"He'd been looking for an excuse for months," Xaviera said.

"I guess you never see Solange," Helen said.

"Oh, no," Jessica said. "She's in here all the time. She's Mr. Casabella's new DU."

Helen's jaw dropped. "Solange has taken up with a gangster?"

"We think she's going to be wife number four," Jessica said.

"I thought he only liked blondes," Helen said. "Solange is a redhead."

"Was," Jessica said. "She dyed her hair for the part."

"Which part is that?" Xaviera said, trying to look innocent.

"You're disgusting," Cam said. He waved his bottle of hand sanitizer as if their dirty laughter were full of germs.

"And you heard about Jackie? She got life without possibility of parole," Xaviera said.

"That's what she wanted," Helen said.

Kitty came out of Solange's office, looking happier than she'd been in months. There were no tear trails on her cheeks. Her skin glowed. She was wearing her wedding ring again. She was back with her husband.

"I wondered what caused the commotion," Kitty said, and smiled. "Are you coming back to us?"

"I can't," Helen said.

Kitty's face clouded.

"You're one of the nicest bosses I've ever had," Helen said. "But this isn't a good place for me. It's not your fault. It's mine." She turned in her employee card, her office key and her uniform.

Kitty gave Helen her final paycheck. "Come back to us if things change, sweetpea. You're welcome anytime."

Helen hugged everyone, except the germ-phobic Cam. She left in a welter of good-byes, feeling sad and relieved at the same time. She took the path along the golf course for the last time. Elegant white egrets pecked at the velvety green lawn with long yellow beaks. Orchids dripped from a spreading banyan. The sun sparkled on a fountain, turning it into a spray of diamonds.

This was paradise. Now Helen was barred from it forever.

"Hey, you, look where you're going," an unlovely voice honked. Helen recognized it immediately: Blythe St. Ives.

She turned around for a good look at her telephone tormentor. A tall gray-haired woman with a large wart on her chin was bullying her way down the path in a striped golf cart. Pink-covered clubs bristled in the golf bag. A ridiculous ruby bumblebee was perched on the woman's golf visor.

Blythe St. Ives was golfing alone. Now that Brenda was dead, she had no one to play with.

Blythe whipped around Helen so fast, her cart nearly tipped. Helen giggled as she watched the woman sail past. Then she started laughing. "Good-bye," Helen said, waving at the disappearing cart. "Good-bye for good."

She'd never have to deal with the snakes in this paradise again. She was free.

She sang her three-word anthem to freedom all the way back to the Coronado. The Toad bucked and lurched, but made the final trip.

Helen expected to find a disapproving Margery waiting for her. Instead, there was Phil, sitting out by the pool. He stood up, and once again, Helen was startled by his broad shoulders and deep blue eyes. He was wearing jeans and her favorite blue shirt. His silver-white hair was pulled back into a ponytail. Ah, those eye crinkles. He should smile more often, Helen thought.

"Let's go for a walk along the beach," Phil said.

A midmorning walk along the ocean. That was true luxury. They rode to the beach in Phil's battered black Jeep. It was a sunny day, but a blustery wind stirred the sand into stinging needles and kept the beachgoers away.

Helen and Phil covered their eyes with sunglasses and turned up their collars, like spies in a movie. They watched a single windsurfer ride the turbulent water. A gust knocked his brightly colored sail over and he fell into the water, then got up and started skimming over the waves again. He'd go for a good distance, then another gust would send him flying and he'd fall again. And get up. He always got up and tried again. Helen liked that.

As she walked along the wild water, Helen talked about her final visit to the club. "There's a happy ending for everyone, Phil. Xaviera will marry Steven at last. Jessica has a serious part in a TV show. Kitty is back with her husband. Jackie will be taken care of for the rest of her life. Marcella sailed off into the sunset with her club concierge. Rob walked away with a million bucks. I can't believe that con man got away with his crooked schemes."

"Are you sure he got away?" Phil said. "How do you know he's alive? No one's seen him since we delivered him to Marcella's yacht. Marcella says he left town, but we only have her word for it."

"What are you saying?" Helen asked.

"Just giving you something to think about," Phil said. "He's gone, but do you really think Rob got away?"

"Yes," Helen said. "If South Florida were nuked tomorrow, Rob and the cockroaches would crawl out of the steaming ashes. He'll be back to torment me. I know it."

"We could go back to St. Louis and face your problems together."

"No," Helen said. "This episode taught me one thing: Rob will always win. I have to stay ready to run. He could drag me back to my old life anytime."

"So there's no happy ending for you?" Phil said.

"I don't have that kind of luck," Helen said. "I was a fool twice with that man."

"No, Rob is the fool," Phil said. "For throwing away a treasure like you."

Helen watched the wind whip his silver hair and thought again how handsome he looked.

"Rob wasn't the right man for you," Phil said. "But he's gone. You're a different woman now. And I'm not Rob. We could have a happy ending."

He fumbled in his shirt pocket and pulled out a blue velvet box. Inside was a sparkling blue-white diamond ring—two diamonds side by side, equal in size, set in platinum.

"Marry me, Helen," Phil said.

Helen couldn't find the right words. She was too surprised. But she was soaringly happy. "It's beautiful," she said, finally. "Is it an antique?"

"This is a new ring," Phil said. "For a new life."

Suddenly, Helen knew exactly what to say. "Yes," she said. "Yes, yes, yes."